THE CRYSTAL THRONE

PRAISE FOR THE CRYSTAL THRONE

WINNER OF THE EPPIE AWARD, 2002—BEST FANTASY!

"…The action is practically non stop throughout the story. Each incident takes you to the next until, before you realize it, you've reached the end. The plot moves smoothly, while it grabs and holds on to your imagination. Young adults aren't the only ones who will enjoy this tale. Anyone who holds a fascination for the world of magical creatures will undoubtedly enjoy the fantasy as well."

—Brenda Gayle
The Write Lifestyle

"4 1/2 stars…Sullivan has created a magical kingdom guaranteed to hold the reader spellbound by the superb imagery and characterization…The story glides along like a swan on a lake, flowing freely from chapter to chapter, with all questions answered and conflicts resolved by the end. I will certainly be looking out for more of Kathryn's writing in the future. I could read *The Crystal Throne* many times over…I would love to see this story on the big screen, sharing the limelight with *Willow* and *The Dark Crystal*. If you feel like losing yourself in a fantasy adventure, I would highly recommend this book."

—Rhiannon West
Timeless Tales

"4 stars…An exciting young adult fantasy tale that will remind readers of early Norton and *The Lion, The Witch, and The Wardrobe*. The story line is enjoyable as the two intrepid heroes battle impossible odds to try to save a realm while seeking a passage through the haunted tree to their home. Sullivan demonstrates her abilities as a first-rate storyteller with this fabulous teen fantasy adventure."

—Harriet Klausner
Sime~Gen

"...Excellent story! Filled with goblins, trolls, dwarfs, ghosts (life-drainers), windborne hounds, a wizard, elves, shadow creatures...you get the idea. Jeanne and Peter seem to be in their mid-teens, but no exact age is given. All-in-all, in my opinion, this is one of the best fantasy e-books I have read! Highly recommended!"

—Detra Fitch
Huntress Book Reviews

ALSO BY KATHRYN SULLIVAN

Agents & Adepts

THE CRYSTAL THRONE

BY

KATHRYN SULLIVAN

*To Janis
a great golfer
Hope you enjoy*

AMBER QUILL PRESS, LLC
http://www.amberquill.com

THE CRYSTAL THRONE
AN AMBER QUILL PRESS BOOK

This book is a work of fiction. All names, characters, locations, and incidents are products of the author's imagination, or have been used fictitiously. Any resemblance to actual persons living or dead, locales, or events is entirely coincidental.

Amber Quill Press, LLC
http://www.amberquill.com

All rights reserved.
No portion of this book may be transmitted or reproduced in any form, or by any means, without permission in writing from the publisher, with the exception of brief excerpts used for the purposes of review.

Copyright © 2003 by Kathryn Sullivan
ISBN 1-59279-942-6
Cover Art © 2003 Trace Edward Zaber

Rating: G

Layout and Formatting provided by: ElementalAlchemy.com

PUBLISHED IN THE UNITED STATES OF AMERICA

*For Joseph Terrence Sullivan,
who always believed in his writerchild.
Thank you to Larry & Lori Juliano,
Marty Siegrist, and Sheri Frey
for comments and encouragement
over the years.*

CHAPTER 1

THE DOOR

"Down, girl! Steady!" Jeanne Tucker clutched the reins and tried to keep her seat as the frightened Appaloosa reared wildly. The skittish mare came down on all fours and backed up a step, her eyes showing white and rolling at the leaves swirling on a gust of wind. Jeanne clung to the horse with knees and hands, using all the tricks her brother had taught her to bring the Appaloosa under control.

The horse reared again. "Down, Robin!" Jeanne jerked the reins and managed to turn the big head as the mare tried to bolt off the trail into the dark tangle of trees. Robin tossed her head, fighting the bit, whinnying with fear.

Finally, the mare quieted. Jeanne carefully released one hand from the reins to stroke the night-black neck. "Easy, girl. Easy now." The horse stood quietly, calming under the continuous flow of talk and patting. Jeanne could feel the taut coil of fear loosen, the mare's body slowly relaxing beneath her.

"Silly. A bunch of dried-up old leaves and you act as if a ghost is after you. Maybe you ought to write that essay on the haunted tree for me. You certainly get scared often enough."

Robin swung her head back, nickering softly, and Jeanne suddenly felt tears of frustration springing to her eyes. "Oh, why can't you behave, Robin? You know Mike's going to sell you if you keep this up! He almost sold you last time, when I ended up in the hospital, but I promised you would behave. You've got to, girl!"

She wiped her eyes on the rough sleeve of her brother's red wool jacket and shook her long brown hair back over one shoulder. "We'd better get home, girl, before anything else happens."

Despite her words, the girl sat still a moment longer. The wood rustled softly about them, leaves painted the color of flames by the setting sun. *Now why did I feel that I had to come to Wilson's Forest today?* she wondered. *Especially at this time of the afternoon.* She shook her head and nudged the mare into a walk. *I certainly wasn't thinking straight, or else I wouldn't have brought Robin here. Starbolt or Firebird would have ignored the shadows and leaves, but not my poor Robin.*

The Appaloosa shivered, nickering uneasily. Jeanne patted the smooth neck. "I know, honey. It's dark and spooky out here." *That does it*, she decided. *Feelings or no feelings, I'm getting Robin home.*

She eyed the deepening shadows of the forest preserve, breathed in the dusky scent of autumn. The soft clops of Robin's hooves on the dirt trail and the creak of the saddle echoed in the stillness.

She tensed and pulled the mare to a halt, hearing voices raised in anger above the rustling leaves. Jeanne glanced about nervously, recognizing the thick stand of trees. *Oh gosh, I'm practically right by the haunted tree!* She shook herself. *You're more of a chicken than Robin. Ghosts out in daylight? Angry ghosts?*

Listening to the irate mutter of the voices, she dismounted and pulled Robin onto a tiny path almost hidden by thick bushes. The path was seldom used. People usually stayed away from the haunted tree.

Jeanne shivered as she came within sight of the tree. *Almost thirteen and you still believe in Grandpa's stories?* she scolded herself. *Trees don't move.* She shivered again.

The tree did look haunted. The huge trunk of the ancient oak was bent and twisted with age and the heavy snows of past winters. The branches were bare of leaves even in the summer and the lower ones resembled twisted claws waiting to grab anyone who came too close.

She saw the Burns twins arguing in the clearing before the tree and paused a moment in surprise. Peter and Jody were new to town—their parents had moved in just before school started—but even newcomers would have been warned about the tree. Peter reached up and pulled one of the dangling, claw-like branches down. Jeanne caught her breath and almost called out a warning, but Peter had released the branch after a curious glance.

It figures, she thought. *Miss Long says to write something about the haunted tree, so Peter comes and studies it as if it was a specimen in biology class.* She glanced at her watch. *He skipped gymnastics practice to be here at this time. Why? Wonder what Jody's doing here.*

Jody appeared to be arguing with her twin. Peter ignored her, brushing his dusty hands on his jacket and jeans. The fraternal twins were so different that the term "twin" didn't seem to apply to them. Peter was a little shorter than his sister and his hair was sandy where hers was pale blonde. Their personalities differed also. Peter was more independent and often seemed older than his twelve years. Jody, on the other hand...

Jeanne cut off that line of thought. Now that she was closer, she could feel the hot flames of anger within the two. *Now how do I do that?* she wondered, asking the same tired question. *How is it that I always know what people are feeling?*

She turned away and began to lead Robin back to the main trail. Robin tossed her head and suddenly whinnied.

"I told you it was haunted!" Jody screamed.

"Oh, bother," Jeanne muttered. She pulled Robin into the clearing and almost bumped into Peter. "Hi. Sorry to frighten you. You scared me, too. Didn't expect to see anyone out here."

Jody glared at her with unfriendly blue eyes and Jeanne felt the dark chill of the taller girl's hostility. Jody's gaze flicked to Jeanne's oversized jacket and heavy jeans, and Jeanne suddenly felt very sloppy in comparison to Jody's fashionably bright colors and expensive jacket. *But you can't ride a horse in that*, she cheered herself. "Hi, Jody. Do you have to write an essay on the tree, too?"

Jody sniffed.

Peter glanced over at his twin. "Jody..."

"I don't have to speak to farmers," Jody drawled arrogantly. "And especially to her. Amy Evans says she's weird. Amy says that—"

"Oh, shut up, Jody," Peter interrupted. "You sound like you're stuck in a loop."

Jody glared at him.

"Go ahead," Peter said slowly, tightly controlled anger in his voice. "Go ahead, add one more of Amy's comments. I dare you."

Jody sniffed again. She strode haughtily past Jeanne back to the trail. "I'm telling Dad on you!" she yelled and ran.

"I'm sorry, Jean," Peter sighed, drawing a hand through his rumpled sandy hair. "Jody's been hanging around that Evans crowd too long."

Jeanne shrugged. "I've heard worse names from Amy."

Peter suddenly looked past her and his blue eyes widened. "Hey, Jean, is that an Appaloosa?"

"The name is Jeanne," she said, adding the "ie" sound to the name, "like the genie of the Lamp." At his blank expression she mentally sighed and continued, "Yes, she's an Appaloosa." The mare nudged Jeanne, and she automatically started stroking the silky neck. "Do you ride?"

"Don't I wish! We've always lived in cities or suburbs before now."

Jeanne suddenly heard her voice saying, "I could teach you if you want." Her hand froze on Robin's neck. What had she said? She couldn't teach him; couldn't afford to be around him. What if she made some dumb slip that showed him exactly how different she was from others? No, safer not to teach him. And yet...

Peter's smile grew even wider. "Could you? That would be—naw," he interrupted himself. "I couldn't pay, and it would take up your time—I know you probably have chores."

He sounded so dejected that she couldn't let him down. *Maybe I could trust him. It would be nice to have a friend my own age, not just the stable gang. Sure*, she corrected herself cynically. *As long as he thinks you're normal. But if he notices that you're a mite too perceptive, then watch him draw away, just like all the rest.*

But somehow, the words slipped out without any thought. "I never said anything about money. What do you think I am? We're friends, aren't we? And one of my 'chores' is exercising some of my brother Mike's horses, so you'd be helping me."

Robin nickered uneasily and Jeanne led the mare over to the cleared area in front of the haunted tree, away from rustling leaves. Peter followed. "Your brother has horses?"

"My oldest brother raises horses. He bought Robin here in the spring."

"She's beautiful." Peter moved towards them, and Robin tried to hide behind Jeanne. He stopped and waited for the horse to quiet. "Did I do something wrong?"

Jeanne held the bridle firmly. "No, Robin just frightens very easily. Move slowly. I won't teach you on her. She's bad enough for me."

Peter patted the sleek hide. "Why do you ride her then?"

"Mike told me that if I could cure her, she's mine."

"He must not have much confidence in you. Aren't horses expensive?"

Jeanne smiled. "Oh, he does. He just thinks I've met my match in Robin. You see, Robin's previous owners were very cruel to her. She still doesn't trust people."

Peter eyed her curiously. "You know, you're a lot like your horse. I don't know why Amy's been picking on you but with her around I can see why you're always on your guard."

Jeanne felt a slight shock at the unexpected remark. "I'm not—"

"You are. I've watched you in class. You're awfully edgy around people. You hiding some deep dark secret? Why do you let Amy push you around?"

"I don't." She glanced down at the ground, confused and unaccustomed to the kindness behind his remarks. "Don't mess with Amy's crowd, Peter. I can handle her better than you can. We've been enemies for a long time. You're a newcomer. Amy could—"

"Amy couldn't do anything to bother me."

"Amy's already bothering you through Jody. And you don't know what one rumor in this town can do."

"Like the one she told Jody?" Peter asked. "That you have magical powers?"

Jeanne flushed in anger. That rumor was too close to the truth for comfort. "I don't—"

"Of course not. There's no such thing as magic—or haunted trees, for that matter. Hey, I was meaning to ask you. How come when Miss Long mentioned this old tree, practically every kid in class looked scared? What's the big deal about it? It's just a tree."

Jeanne glanced nervously at it and found herself wondering if it had heard. "Miss Long is new to town—she doesn't understand yet," she said swiftly. She turned back to Peter. "There—there're stories."

"Such as?"

"Such as people vanishing."

Peter frowned. "Oh, come on! What does that prove?"

"Not much, I guess. It did happen almost a hundred years ago. But sometimes you can hear voices here, only they don't sound human." Jeanne warmed to her subject, feeling as if she was reciting from one of the fantasies she loved to read. "And there've been lights—dancing, bobbing lights, like a will-o'-the-wisp, only there's no swamp near here. The tree has been known to walk, too."

"Walk?"

"Sure. Raccoon Creek is about a hundred feet through there," she said, pointing into the thickly tangled underbrush. "And the tree used to be on its banks."

"Huh?"

"Yep. Stood right on the bank of a creek a hundred feet from here, though the bank was undercut so badly by the water that the tree was just about ready to fall in. This was back when Wilson's Forest was private property, before the Wilsons donated it to the town as a forest preserve. Anyhow, the Wilsons decided to cut the tree down." She paused for effect.

"And?"

"And when they got out to the creek, the tree was gone. They finally found it right here."

Peter silently studied the gnarled old tree. "You're kidding," he said finally. "You actually believe that stuff?"

"Some. My grandfather remembers when the tree was on Raccoon Creek. He was my age then."

"Trees don't move," Peter said flatly. "Your grandfather was only kidding you."

"No, I can tell when someone is lying. And I also believe him because every time I come here, near the tree like this, I get the feeling that there's someone watching me." She shivered. "Like right now."

"It's probably just Jody sneaking around." Peter glared into the shadows, looking for his twin.

"She's just as confused and hurt as you are, Peter. Give her time."

He glanced at her sharply and she realized her slip. "I—I mean," she faltered, cursing her stupidity, "it's always rough when my brothers and I fight. Must be worse for twins."

Peter frowned at the surrounding trees. "Yeah, it is. She won't even listen to me now."

Jeanne forced herself to remain silent, although she wished she could say something to comfort him. She felt fear rising strongly in the mare's trembling body. "Gosh, it's late. I've got to get Robin back."

She swung up into the saddle and looked down at Peter, remembering her promise. "Could you come out to the farm tomorrow? It's Saturday; I'd have time to start you then."

"That soon? Gee, that would be—"

The Appaloosa suddenly squealed with fear and reared. Jeanne, caught off guard, lost her balance and tumbled off Robin's back. Time seemed to slow as she fell. She heard Jody's laugh; saw the swing of dark cloth. *Where's the tree? Omigosh, I'm going to hit—*

Suddenly she felt herself caught and cradled in two great arms, then dumped into a pile of leaves.

A bell chimed in the distance as the two huge branches moved away from Jeanne to hang from the haunted tree again. She stared at the haunted tree now in front of her, knowing it had been *behind* her only seconds ago. *No. No, I'm dreaming. Trees don't move. They don't, they don't!*

The trunk of the tree seemed to ripple like water and Peter fell out of the brownness, catching his balance with a gymnast's reflexes. He turned and stared down at her, his eyes glassy, as a chime sounded in the stillness.

"P-peter?"

"You...you fell through the tree!" he stammered. "I tried to catch you but you hit it and fell through! Then this...tree grabbed me and..."

Jeanne heard her voice saying calmly, "And now we're here."

Peter gulped, his face regaining some of its tan. "But where's here? Look, the forest is gone."

Jeanne looked about her. Peter was right; the forest was gone. They were in a great meadow, empty except for the haunted tree. Jeanne tried to orient herself, but there were no familiar landmarks. Green and golden hills rose in the distance where the town should be, and the stretches of farmland outside of Wilson's Forest had become a dark and forbidding woods.

"Even the town's gone," Peter said in a strange voice. "And this dead tree has green leaves now! What happened to us?" He glanced at his watch. "We haven't lost any time, but if someone knocked us out and drugged us, they'd probably reset the watches as well."

Jeanne climbed to her feet and walked over to the tree. "We fell through here," she said slowly, remembering books she had read. "We should be able to go back." She gathered her courage and pushed against the trunk. Nothing happened.

"It's solid," she sighed. "Whatever...door...that let us through is closed now." She pushed her hair back out of her face and studied the tree. "Well, what do we do now?" she asked the tree.

"I don't know," Peter replied, studying the ground. He was growing more and more convinced that he had imagined stepping through the tree. This couldn't be the same tree from the forest; the forest was gone. But how had they arrived in this meadow? "The only footprints around are ours. No tire marks...no hoof marks... Why would someone go to so much trouble to kidnap us?" He spied a glint of metal rolling through the fallen leaves towards them. Under his gaze the rolling metal suddenly stopped and fell over. He fished it out of the leaves and found that he held a gold ring. He placed it on the palm of his hand and watched, startled, as it started to roll again. He tried again and noticed that, no matter in which direction he held his hand, the ring always rolled toward Jeanne.

Jeanne walked away from the tree, her eyes studying the sky. Peter joined her, absently pocketing the ring. "What are you looking for?"

Jeanne shrugged, her eyes on something that had suddenly appeared on the horizon. "Don't know. I just suddenly got this feeling that someone's watching us."

"I don't see anyone," Peter commented, looking about the empty meadow.

A shrill scream trembled through the air. "What was that?" Peter exclaimed.

"Peter!" Jeanne pointed into the sky.

Gliding swiftly towards them across the windless sky was something that resembled a red-violet dragon. The cruel beak opened in a horrid grin as it shrieked again.

"Wow! Great special effects!" Peter said. "You can't see any wires or blue matte outlines. Wonder how they're projecting that pteranodon?"

The thing was not far from them now. "Two legs, so that's a drake, not a dragon," Jeanne muttered.

"No, definitely a pteranodon," Peter said.

Jeanne could see the huge eyes on either side of the ugly, wedge-shaped head. A chill wind suddenly rose, cutting through her jacket as the massive wings angled toward the ground. The long body swung forward, the giant talons opening.

"This is too large to be radio controlled," Peter observed.

Jeanne, sensing the greed and hunger in the creature's mind, stared in amazement at Peter and suddenly realized why he was being so calm. She shoved him to the ground and followed.

Moving too fast to stop, the thing swooped through the space they had been, the talons snapping shut just over their heads. It started to curve back into the sky when suddenly the tree rustled. Long branches whipped out like tentacles and wrapped about the creature. The thing struggled wildly, shrieking its horrible cry, but the branches relentlessly drew it against the tree trunk. As they watched in amazement, the creature suddenly vanished in a puff of green particles. Jeanne could see Peter rubbing his eyes as the green smoke slowly drifted to the ground. The branches shook more of the dust off, then returned to their original position. "Where are we?" she breathed.

"What are you doing here?" a strange voice suddenly demanded from above them.

They looked back over their shoulders. A tall, gray-haired man frowned down at them. He was dressed in a loosely fitting shirt and trousers that glittered with a dull metallic gleam. The folds of a cloak of the same dull silver rippled about him, then stilled, though no breeze had blown. The man's face was smooth and unlined, despite his long gray hair, but something about him, in his bearing, in the way he stood waiting for their answer, reassured Jeanne, although she couldn't explain why.

"Who are you?" Peter asked.

The man stared at them, and Jeanne could feel his bewilderment. "You are not elves," he said slowly. "You are humans!"

"Of course we're humans," Peter replied, equally puzzled. "There aren't any such things as elves."

Jeanne felt her mouth go dry. Elves? Where had they come to?

The man shook his head. "Children!" he said to something unseen. "Now you would bring children into this?"

Peter climbed to his feet and held his hand out to her. "C'mon, we're leaving," he whispered. "This guy's a nut case."

Jeanne sat up but ignored his hand. She hugged herself, trying to shut out all the strange feelings crowding in upon her. "Where do we go, Peter?"

"Anywhere. C'mon!"

"And two of them," the man said slowly, folding his arms. "The Watcher has never brought two through before." He rubbed his thumb along the smooth edge of his jaw. His gray eyes studied them.

"Who are you?" Peter demanded.

The man nodded. "The question is typically human, but the attitude is wise in the Lands today." He bowed slightly with an elegant sweep of his cloak. "I am called Graylod."

He folded his arms again and stared at them thoughtfully. "I...cannot read you. What magicks do you two possess?"

"What?" Peter began.

"Wait, Peter." Jeanne climbed to her feet and faced the silver-garbed man. "Let's start at the beginning. I'm Jeanne Tucker and he's Peter Burns. We fell through that tree. It was all an accident, and we would be very glad to go back if you would tell us how." She hesitated, caught by the absent look in his eyes. "Mr. Graylod?"

Graylod blinked, and his gaze softened. "Are you the healer?"

"Am I the..." Jeanne repeated in amazement.

THE CRYSTAL THRONE

"Neither of us are doctors," Peter said. "How do we get back?" Jeanne noticed that he didn't add "through the tree."

Graylod was rubbing his jaw again. "But the prophecy specifically mentioned a—eh?" He turned his attention to Peter. "Back? Through the Watcher? You cannot."

"Can't?"

"Never?" Jeanne added faintly. Graylod was telling the truth; she could not sense the double echo of a lie. She shivered. *Elves*, she thought. *My biggest dream come true. Then why am I so frightened?*

Graylod watched her. He said gently, "You cannot go back. The Watcher has picked you, the both of you, to save our land and until that is done it will not allow you to leave."

"What do you mean, 'will not allow'?" Peter demanded. "Who is this Watcher, anyway?"

"It stands behind you," Graylod said. They both turned.

"The tree?" Peter said scornfully.

"The Watcher is the door to all human lands and our guardian of last hope. When the Free Lands are threatened and a human can save us, it brings him here. Thus it was promised and thus it is done. Your coming was no accident. You two can help us, though I cannot see how, and so the Watcher brought you here. Then it summoned me and protected you until I could arrive."

"The tree?" Peter said scornfully.

"That's why that thing vanished!" Jeanne exclaimed. "Magic!"

Graylod nodded.

"Don't believe him, Jeanne," Peter said angrily. "There's no such thing as magic."

Graylod drew himself up to his full height. "For one who knows so little," he said, his voice full of authority, "you should not claim to know so much. Watch!" He lifted his right hand. A swirl of color appeared at his fingertips, a dancing rainbow of dazzling colors. Slowly out of the dazzling swirl a solid object grew—first a short, slender rod of gray, then it lengthened into a long staff. Graylod hefted it, sending a wave of colors moving up and down its length.

"Magic," Jeanne breathed. "You're a wizard!"

Graylod nodded. "Hear me out, Peter Burns," he ordered, as Peter was about to speak. "The Watcher has picked the both of you to help us and by right you must know what you are to face.

"This land was once a fair land, from Beginning Time the refuge of all magic you humans denied in your world. Ages past, the Evil Ones had been defeated in this land and thrust out into the realm of the Shadow Land. Its borders watched against trouble, our land settled into contentment and forgot the dangers that once threatened it.

"But we forgot too soon. Witches united forces in the Shadow Land and broke through our protective safeguards. Our most powerful guardians were killed in a great battle of magic. Three witches survived. They now control our land and have placed our people under a curse until they can gather enough strength to move against your own land."

"A curse?" Jeanne asked. "Can't the witches be stopped?"

"The curse is one of forgetfulness," Graylod said slowly. "Very fitting, since it is what led us to our downfall. Many of us, including myself, have forgotten our ways of magic. We remember only a little of what we once had. Important spells, cures—these are gone from our memories.

"The curse rids our land of any potential threat to the witches, for we cannot remember how to rid ourselves of them. A legend says that the witches' power will be broken by a human Sensitive. I had hoped one of you would be that Sensitive."

"Didn't that, er, Watcher find anyone else to help you?" Peter asked, frowning. "Jeanne and I don't know any magic."

"The Watcher has found others who tried to help," Graylod said slowly. "All of them failed, although they were skilled in magic. Perhaps the Watcher knows you possess other talents that may help." He watched Peter's face as he added, "I cannot send you back to your land. The Watcher has picked you, and only it controls the doors to your land."

"Well, tell your Watcher to send us back," Peter said angrily. "I'm not volunteering for this."

"It is not 'my' Watcher," Graylod said patiently, "but the Land's."

As Peter argued, Jeanne irritably rubbed at her right eye. The "anger ache" behind her eyes throbbed as if her brothers were quarreling. *What's wrong with me? Peter's not family. I've shut strangers out better than this*!

The icy touch of wrongness crept once again up her spine, and she worriedly glanced at the sky. "Watcher!" she yelled.

Shrill screams echoed from the sky. Graylod turned as two drakes raced from the horizon, heading unerringly toward them. "The hounds!" he exclaimed. "Stand close to me!" He swung his staff in a wide, blazing circle...and the drakes were gone. So was the haunted tree.

Peter blinked. One second they had been in an open meadow and now they stood on a flower-lined pathway of brightly shining stones deep inside a forest. The time had changed as well. There had been three hours before sunset and now, from what he could see of the sky, they had closer to four hours left of daylight. They must have been transported west, but how?

"The witch hounds know you are in this land," Graylod said briskly. "Soon one of the witches will know also. You will stay here until we can organize an expedition against them."

"Where is here?" Peter asked.

"A day's travel west of the Watcher. This is an elf-village." Graylod frowned. "Though I do not know where its people are. They should not be hiding from me."

Peter looked at the tall trees like living walls about the path, glanced at Jeanne and shrugged. There had to be some way for them to escape from this madman.

Graylod's staff shimmered into liquid light, then solidified. "I do not sense any traps. Follow me." He strode down the path, Jeanne and Peter on his heels.

Jeanne shivered, feeling as if eyes were watching their every move. The silence was oppressing; no birds sang, no insects cricked in the shadows. She saw burn scars and axe marks on some of the trees, noticed that patches of the beautiful flowers had been uprooted and carelessly tossed aside or trampled under booted feet. She shivered at the deliberate vandalism and glanced aside at Peter. What had they gotten into?

Graylod stopped abruptly. "The Open Door has been closed!"

Jeanne heard the shock in his voice and wondered briefly at it. Before them two living trees formed a tall arch above the path. The path ran through the arch and continued on until it wound out of sight. There was no visible door anywhere.

Graylod moved his staff before the two intertwined trees. He stamped the end of his staff on the ground. "*Rwit!*" he demanded.

Jeanne caught her breath as green and silver symbols appeared on the tree trunks, some shining where burn scars had been but seconds before. Green light shimmered in the archway.

"Begone, creatures of the night," a thready voice hissed at them. Peter turned, trying to locate the speaker as the voice murmured musical syllables that yet seemed full of menace.

Graylod raised his blazing staff, and the voice stopped short. "Graylod! Forgive me! Enter the Open Door!"

CHAPTER 2

DECISION

"Walk through the archway," Graylod directed them.

Peter glanced from the wizard to Jeanne, shrugged and started forward. The delicate scent of the flowers competed with the tang of wood smoke. Red, green, and blue stones glinted under their feet as they stepped under the arch...and into sudden blackness.

Peter bumped into Jeanne and dazedly realized that a solid floor, not the pebbled path, was under his sneakers. Graylod chuckled behind them in the darkness. There came a click from his staff striking the floor.

A white fire leaped into being in a large fireplace to their left, casting its soft light on a long block of cloudy crystal not far from them. Seated behind the crystal were two men and two women dressed in silvery gray, their hair ranging from pure silver to solid black although their ages were not apparent from their faces.

Peter frowned thoughtfully. There was something strange about these people, something about their faces that didn't look normal. It wasn't, he decided, that their noses and mouths were small, but in comparison with the enormous, faintly slanting eyes, they seemed almost tiny. He had never seen such big eyes on any human before.

"Elves," Jeanne breathed softly in amazement. Peter looked at her and then back at the "elves."

"Welcome, Graylod," a voice said. Peter blinked. He had the strange impression that none of the elves' lips had moved.

Graylod rested one end of his staff on the floor and leaned on it. "Council of Elders," he said solemnly, "why do your people hide from me? I came to ask help of you, to give sanctuary to these two humans until I can return."

The voice sighed. "We cannot, Graylod."

Graylod straightened. "Cannot? That is a harsh word, Elders."

"But truth, Graylod. The Dark One attacked us not long ago, taking with her captives to be Changed." Jeanne shivered. That word had an ominous ring to it.

The word also affected Graylod. "Changed? She had learned that dread art, then?"

"And learned it well. You can understand now, Graylod, why we cannot give these two sanctuary."

"Yes," Graylod mused. "But you can ready them for travel, giving them reliable guardians—the Windkin would be best—and send them on to Gimstan Mountain."

"It will be done," the voice said. "The call will go out."

"And tell them of their path, so that they will be wary," Graylod added. He turned to Peter and Jeanne. "I am sorry, but I have so little time, too little to warn you of this land's ways. I will meet you at Gimstan Mountain, Green willing." He smiled sadly at them, then suddenly vanished. A soft breeze touched them; the white fire flickered, then steadied.

"Peter Burns," the voice said. Peter looked warily at the Council. "Our power of seeing the future is slight now, and we can see only patches of what is to come. For you, we see only that your journey will be hard. Do not be deceived by outward appearances.

"But you, Jeanne Tucker," the voice continued, "we see great evil in this for you, daughter. But we cannot see beyond it, for another power blocks our sight. Peter is too different from us. We cannot hide him from the witch, but we could hide you. Do you still wish to continue?"

"I—" Jeanne felt the faint touch of the Council's concern and her own fear rose. What was she to say? Everything was happening so fast.

"Stay here, Jeanne," Peter whispered. "You'll be safer here."

Jeanne looked at him. "But you—"

"I'll be all right. You're a girl. This isn't for you."

Jeanne mentally sighed as she caught the same "protectiveness" radiating from Peter that she had often sensed from Mike. "Yeah, right," she replied, remembering his reaction to the witch hound. *He's the one who needs protecting*. She turned and faced the Council. "The Watcher picked us both. I'm going with Peter," she said firmly.

The voice sighed. "Very well. We shall help as much as we can. You will be given clothing and weapons. We see you will meet one on the trail who will later help you in times of danger, but, as a further protection, we will give you a powerful gift. Peter, step forward."

Peter took a deep breath and did as he was told. "You are the skeptical one and thus will not waste this gift," the voice said. "We will give you three spells, each of which can be used only once." The four elves stared at him, and Peter suddenly felt dizzy. The feeling was gone as fast as it appeared, and the voice continued, "Use these spells wisely."

"Wait a minute," Peter said, feeling slightly dazed. "What spells? How am I supposed to cast spells?"

"You will know when the time comes." As one, the Elders turned their attention to a section of the block before them.

"Hi, Peter! Awake again?"

Peter turned as Jeanne emerged from the shadows. "What do you mean, 'awake again?'" What happened? And where did you get those clothes?"

Jeanne looked down at herself with a faint smile. "Not bad, huh?" She was dressed in a loose brown shirt and a gray vest and trousers. Small pouches dangled from a belt about her waist, and a bundle of gray material was draped over her arm. "Wish I was taller," she sighed. "I'm going to be tripping over this cloak. The elves gave me these while you were out."

"Out? Out where?"

"The Elders hypnotized you to imprint the spells so you couldn't forget them. You've been standing there about an hour, I'd say."

Peter looked at her. "Hypnotized me? Just like that? Without even a 'pardon me' or 'do you mind'? There's such a thing as asking permission—" Peter started, turning towards the Elders, who were still studying a section of the block of crystal. He looked closer at the block. Was there something wrong with his eyesight or were the cloudy swirls in the crystal moving?

"The customs here are different, Peter," Jeanne said. "I wasn't too happy with that, either. They wouldn't even let me stay with you. But they didn't mean to hurt you, just to protect us in their way."

"Come," a dark-haired elf said, stepping forward out of the shadows behind her. "The *Fleogende* will soon be arriving to take you to the mountains."

"Who are Fleogende?" Jeanne asked as they joined the elf.

"Graylod said something about Windkin, too. What are they?"

"'Windkin' is the wizard word for those we elves call Fleogende, the Fleet Ones. They are the fastest runners in the Free Lands." She opened a side door and ushered them into a long corridor lined with doors. "We do not have much time—the witch will send out more hounds to search for you."

"Only one witch?" Jeanne asked.

"Yeah," Peter agreed. "Why don't they just come all at once and overwhelm us with power?"

"The witches are very jealous of each other," the elf explained. "The one witch whose hound was destroyed has not informed the other two as yet. They will usually not ask the help of each other unless they have no other choice. It is a wonder they have ruled together this long."

"How do you know what the witches are doing?" Peter demanded.

"Our Council members are seers. Some can see into the future, others can only see the present."

"So that was the purpose of the crystal," Jeanne said thoughtfully. "But they told Graylod that the Dark One had attacked here. Didn't they foresee it?"

"Their power is greatly diminished under the curse. We had no warning." She opened a door to a torch-lit room lined with books. "In here, Peter."

"See you outside, Peter." Jeanne waved and continued down the corridor.

"What's wrong with our own clothes?" Peter asked as the elf held up a warm green shirt. She glanced from it to him, as if checking the size, and replaced it atop the dark gray trousers draped over the back of a chair. Short gray boots stood before the chair.

"Your clothes will not protect you against the elements and other hazards, as these will. The witch will be expecting strange garments. You will be harder to find when dressed like our people." She shook out the folds of a gray cloak lined with a silvery fluff, glanced at him as if checking his height, then replaced it atop the nearby table and headed for the door. "When you are dressed, the door at the far end of the corridor will lead outside."

Peter fingered the strange fabric of the shirt as the door closed behind the elf. It felt unlike anything he knew, not cotton nor synthetic nor leather. "This isn't a dream—it's a nightmare!" he muttered, glancing about the small library. "What can two kids do against three witches except get themselves killed?"

He dressed hurriedly and went through the pockets of his discarded clothing, moving the bulk of the items to a pouch on his new belt. He wasn't about to leave behind his Scout knife, and duct tape might come in handy. He had re-rolled the tape on a small spool to make it pocket-sized, and it slipped easily into the pouch. He found the gold ring and left it with his clothing, then unconsciously retrieved it and stuffed it into the pouch as well. Still struggling with the unfamiliar cloak, he headed towards the door at the far end of the corridor.

The door opened on a greenish shimmer. Peter took a deep breath and stepped through to find himself on the far side of the archway. He turned and looked at the intertwined trees. "Magic," he said in disgust.

Behind him, a snort echoed his disgust. Peter turned, to find himself facing a sleek blue-black stallion, bigger and taller than Earthly horses. It looked Peter over with an icy stare, then snorted as if in contempt. "Well, I don't think much of you, either," Peter told it, finally tying the cloak properly about his neck. The horse looked startled.

"I see you two are getting along nicely," Jeanne said from behind him. Peter turned with a sigh. Why was she constantly popping up behind him? A gray and white spotted stallion followed so closely behind the girl that his breath ruffled her hair.

"Don't look now, but you've got a shadow," Peter chuckled.

Jeanne smiled as she looked over her shoulder. Her shadow murmured softly and crowded up against her, nudging her with his soft muzzle. "I'd like you to meet two of the Windkin. This is Elin," she said, drawing out the initial "e" sound. "And you've already met Hahle." The black snorted a "hah" sound in reply.

The gray and white horse seemed to speak in a strange, slurred manner to her, then trotted amiably up to Peter. He looked Peter over with a friendly glance, blew the boy's hair into his eyes, then moved over and seemed to talk to the black horse.

"Where's our guide?" Peter asked, watching the horses suspiciously while he pushed his hair back out of his eyes.

Jeanne smothered a laugh. "But they're...oh, you mean the elf? She's been loading supplies in the Fleet Ones' packs. I guess she went to get something."

"What's so funny?" Peter asked curiously.

"Nothing. Nothing at all." Jeanne grinned. "Just something Elin said."

Girls, Peter thought in disgust. He looked at the horses. "The saddles are different here," he commented, eyeing the light pads with stirrups and remembering what he had seen of the saddle on Jeanne's horse. "No bridles?" he added, noticing that the reins were attached to simple halters. The stallions both turned to face him, their ears up.

Jeanne looked closely at him. "The reins are only needed when the witch hounds are around."

Peter hoped his face didn't look as blank as his mind felt. He kept trying to add up his observations, but the end result was confusion. Horses that didn't need reins unless witch hounds were around? What did the witch hounds have to do with horses? Just how intelligent were these horses?

The blue-black stallion murmured what seemed to be a question. "Ready for Peter, Hahle?" Jeanne asked. The horse nodded his head. Jeanne checked the saddle girth, then nodded at Peter. "Okay, Peter, mount up."

"Me? Mount him? I'd need a stepladder!" Peter protested.

"Yeah, they're both kinda tall. But you can use the saddle to pull yourself up. Just put your left foot in the left stirrup and then swing your right foot up and over."

Peter looked at the distance. "You're worse than the coach." He stuck his left foot in the stirrup, grabbed a handful of mane and tried to pull himself up into the saddle. The horse beneath him snorted and danced forward a few steps. "Hey!" Peter protested from the ground. "That's not fair! He's supposed to stand still!"

Musical laughter answered him. Peter could see the bright eyes of children watching him from among the trees across the flower-lined path. Hahle swung his big head back and met Peter's eyes. The boy hesitated, oddly caught by that calm gaze. The horse looked amused as well.

Jeanne looked thoughtful. "That's odd. Pulling on the mane never bothered horses back..." She shook her head. "Try grabbing hold of the saddle, Peter, not his mane."

"Oh. Sorry, Hahle." Peter repeated the entire performance, this time remaining in the saddle. "You know, it's really not so bad after all." He looked down at the distant ground. "Uh, how do you get down?" Hahle shook his head, tossing his mane in an odd manner. Peter had the distinct impression that the horse was laughing at him.

Jeanne swung up into her saddle. "I hope that elf hurries. We have to leave soon. The Elders said that hounds are patrolling the area by the Watcher. Sooner or later one might circle this way."

Peter turned in the saddle and looked through the supplies in the pack. "We have food and blankets, but what's going to stop a hound from coming after us?"

"These," the elf said, suddenly appearing beside them. She held up two long, sheathed objects.

"Swords?" Jeanne queried.

"And daggers, too," Peter added, spying the two additional weapons in the elf's belt.

"Not all the dangers of this land are magical," the elf said, answering Jeanne's inquiring look. Indicating her own sword, the elf showed them how the scabbard and belt buckled about the waist and demonstrated how to draw the deadly weapons. "We have not the time to test its fit to you," she said as she strapped one sword to the saddle of Peter's mount, "but we could not let you go completely weaponless." She handed him a dagger and moved to Jeanne.

Peter looked at the dagger, hefting it thoughtfully as he glanced from it to the sword. He had had to plead for years to get his Scout knife and now he was given both a dagger and a sword? He didn't notice the argument beside him until he heard Jeanne say, "I'll take the dagger, then, but not that!"

He looked up to see Jeanne push the sword away. "You might need that," he commented.

She shook her head. "I can't use it," she said firmly.

"I don't know how to use a sword, either."

"I won't take that with me! I won't kill people!"

"And if they try to kill you?"

She returned his gaze. "I won't kill, Peter. I...can't!"

"I don't think I can, either, Jeanne. But if anyone tries to kill me, I'm going to fight back." Jeanne did not answer, but her face looked stubborn. Peter sighed. His favorite television hero also refused to use weapons. "Your choice."

The elf looked back and forth between them. "You should bring it along, even so."

"No, we won't," Jeanne insisted. Beneath her, Elin muttered, and the elf nodded and put down the sword. The blue-black stallion pawed the ground with one hoof.

"Whose is that third horse?" Peter asked, suddenly noticing a roan with reins but no saddle watching them.

"The one who you will meet on the trail will need him," the elf explained. The roan shook his mane and nudged one of the shy elf children out of hiding while another slyly crept up and tweaked his tail.

"How do we get where we're going?" Peter asked. "Is there a map?"

"The Fleet Ones will be your guides as well as transport," the elf said. Hahle pawed the ground again, seeming impatient.

"The horses? Guides?"

"We're not in our world, Peter," Jeanne said in an exasperated tone of voice. "Elin and Hahle are not horses, not dumb animals, but as intelligent as you and I."

"Huh?" He turned to her. "How do you know?"

She looked startled. "Can't you hear them?"

"No."

She flushed. "And here I thought you were being rude to them. I'm sorry, Peter. I should have realized that you couldn't hear them yet."

"Yet? They *do* talk? But how—"

Hahle murmured swiftly and started forward. Peter clutched the saddle and looked wide-eyed back at Jeanne. She waved and thanked the elf as Elin and the roan moved to keep up with Hahle. The Fleet Ones moved swiftly down the glittering path.

"Hahle's the leader at the moment," Jeanne explained as Elin caught up with the black stallion at the end of the flower patches. "He thought we had wasted too much time back there."

The sparkling path ended as they entered the deep woods. The dirt trail winding among the tall trees was wide enough for two Fleet Ones and Elin kept pace alongside Hahle, the roan bringing up the rear.

The gray and white stallion murmured swiftly and Hahle and the roan snorted. Peter looked back and forth between the Fleet Ones. "What was that about?"

Jeanne reached across and grabbed Hahle's reins. "Oh no, you two. No gallops yet. Peter has never even been on a horse before. You two clowns can play all the games you like after he gets accustomed to riding." She dropped Hahle's reins and turned to Peter. "Elin said—"

"Let me guess. A bigger waste of time to walk instead of gallop, right?"

She smiled. "Close. You're starting to understand them?"

Peter shook his head. "Just a guess. But how can you understand them? And how did we understand the elves? That couldn't have been English that they were speaking!"

Jeanne grinned mischievously. "You aren't speaking English, either," she said, switching to another, oddly familiar language.

Peter stared at her. "You're...that's English!" He listened to the words he spoke. "What am I speaking, then?"

"The Common Tongue of this land. According to the elves, the Watcher gave us the spoken languages of this land when we entered."

"Huh? *Gave* us?"

"Magic, remember? The Watcher is half in this land and half in ours, so the curse didn't affect it. But we only understand the common, everyday languages used here. The Old Tongue, the one most spells are in, sounds like gibberish. I couldn't understand a word of the spells they were putting in your memory. And that was before they shooed me out."

She straightened Elin's tangled mane. "I guess the Windkin's language just takes longer to pick up. I didn't understand it at first, either. One moment I was listening to these two murmuring as they came up the path and the next I realized they were wondering what kind of nuisances they would have to nursemaid this time."

Peter had to chuckle as a protesting murmur came from Elin. Hahle's comments sounded amused, also, but Jeanne frowned uneasily.

"I caught the drift of Elin's protest, Jeanne, but what did Hahle say to make you look so thoughtful?"

Jeanne started. "Oh, sorry, Peter. Hahle just added that, besides, most humans don't understand them anyway. Why is that, Hahle?"

Elin answered instead, and Jeanne, her voice sounding puzzled, quickly translated. "'Belief is a good part of magic, and, since most humans don't believe that 'animals' can speak, the Watcher's spell doesn't work.' Elin, it can't take only disbelief to affect a spell!" She hesitated. "Or can it?"

From behind them, the roan murmured exasperatedly, then rudely brushed past Hahle and galloped ahead down the trail. Jeanne translated almost absently. "Renw said that if he knew we were going to have a discussion on magic, he would have gone ahead to scout sooner."

She watched the distant figure of the roan. "Elin, what's wrong with him? He sounded angry, but there was such sorrow in his voice."

Hahle answered, and Jeanne kept pace. "'Renw and an elf, Leereho, were the two best scouts among all the Folk. They were the ones who entered the depths of the Mist Lands, the witches' own land, and returned with valuable information on that land's defenses.'"

"Were?" Peter asked softly.

"'Leereho was captured by trolls'—what is that word, Elin? Not long ago?—'while checking on reports on the Dark One's recent raids into northern lands. Renw was in the east on a mission for the

Windrunner'—that's the Windkins' Elder, Peter—'but he still blames himself for his partner's capture.'"

Jeanne sighed, her eyes turned toward the empty trail before them. "I hope the Watcher is right and we can break the curse."

"You're not the only one. I can imagine very clearly what the witches will do to us if they catch us now."

"And I thought you didn't believe in witches."

"I don't. It's just that...everyone else seems to." Jeanne laughed, and Peter smiled at how that comment sounded. "So, I'm willing to accept that there's a problem and somehow we can help. But what can we do against whatever is supposed to be a witch?"

Jeanne shrugged. "I don't have the faintest idea. But these people are just as powerless and I'd say they're holding their own against the witches."

Suddenly the shrill shriek of a witch hound tore through the air. The blue-black stallion reared, dancing about in fright as Peter clung to the saddle. Jeanne, fighting the equally terrified Elin, shouted, "Lean forward and grab the reins, but don't pull them!" The gray and white Fleet One murmured nervously, but Jeanne had him under control.

The blood-curdling scream came again, and Peter's weak control evaporated. Hahle reared, whinnying in fear, and galloped away at a bone-rattling speed. Peter clung to the saddle; all memory of how to stop an Earthly horse fled as he tried not to fall off at that dangerous speed. The reins, utterly forgotten before, now dragged on the ground, and Peter kept his fingers crossed that the stallion would not step on them and fall. He could do nothing else but cling to the saddle as the Fleet One pounded along the winding trail.

The trail suddenly straightened, and out of the corner of his eye, Peter saw the gray and white stallion streaking up beside him, Jeanne leaning low over the Fleet One's neck. Peter tried to warn her away, but she wasn't watching him. She kept her eyes on the dragging reins as she leaned farther away from her mount, keeping one hand on her saddle and her own reins. While Peter closed his eyes, dreading to watch her miss and fall, Jeanne reached out and grabbed one of the dragging reins. She pulled Elin slowly to a halt, leaving the black stallion nothing else to do but stop as well.

Jeanne swung out of the saddle, firmly maintaining her grip on both sets of reins, and went to the Fleet Ones' heads. She grabbed their halters, forcing the struggling beings to look at her. "Quiet down," she said angrily, "that thing never spotted us with all those trees." She spared a furious glance at the sky. "And it's already flown on."

She turned back to her audience, still restrained by her grip on the halters. "Now listen closely, you two. I know, this fear of witch hounds is just part of the curse for you Windkin, but you better start trying to fight it! You almost killed Peter, Hahle! Some 'guardian' *you* turned out to be!"

The black stallion protested, but Jeanne wasn't about to listen. "Don't tell me you can't help it. 'Belief is a good part of magic,' remember? You wouldn't be afraid of that big bully in a fair fight, would you?"

In the midst of the commotion, Peter released his shaky hold on the saddle and slid to the ground. His knees suddenly rubbery, he found a comfortable spot on the dusty trail and sat there, relieved to feel solid ground again.

"Peter, are you all right?"

"Yeah," he sighed. "I'm all right. I think." He looked up and tried to see if the hound had returned, but the overhanging trees blocked out any sight of the sky. *That's odd, I wonder how Jeanne knew that the hound was gone.* The next second he scolded himself. *Don't be stupid, it would have shrieked again by now. Good thing the trees are so close together. The hound won't be able to bother the elves or us if it can't land.*

He glanced over at his fellow travelers. The Fleet Ones had regained enough control of themselves for Jeanne to release their reins, but they still shivered at sudden sounds. Jeanne was trembling as well, he noticed, in spite of her anger a moment ago. *And why should I blame her for that? If she hadn't kept her head, I could have been very badly hurt.* He thought ruefully of his twin. *Jody would have been in hysterics. Guess I shouldn't compare them. Didn't realize girls could be so different. I always had to protect Jody from everything, and now look who's being rescued!*

"How far away is Gimstan Mountain, Hahle?" Peter asked, climbing to his feet as pounding hooves announced the return of Renw. "Will we be in the forest the whole way?"

Hahle looked up at the protecting trees and shuddered, then murmured swiftly. Jeanne frowned thoughtfully. "Sorry, Peter, but it sounds like your first riding lesson is going to be a long one. Hahle says it's about three or four days as elves measure distance."

Peter shook his head at the translation. The Watcher's spell wasn't perfect. "Then we better keep moving, right?"

Jeanne nodded. "Right. We'll take it in easy stages and alternate walking and riding so you won't get too stiff and Hahle and Elin won't get so tired."

Peter took a deep breath and adjusted his dagger. "Fine by me. Why don't we start walking now? Hate to say it, Hahle, but I'd much rather walk than ride at the moment."

Hahle shook his mane, and Peter knew the Fleet One was amused again. Renw wheeled about and vanished down the trail, Hahle following more sedately. Elin bowed his head, then bobbed it with a short murmur. Jeanne nodded her head in return and started after Hahle. "I take it he said, 'after you?'" Peter asked, following.

CHAPTER 3

NIGHT EYES

Late at night, the Fleet Ones stopped in a small clearing. Stiff and bone-weary, Peter gingerly slid out of the saddle. Hahle swung his head back and studied his rider. Peter returned the gaze with a yawn.

"'That's all the riding for you tonight,'" Jeanne translated as she pulled Elin's saddle off. She studied him worriedly. "Sorry, Peter. I should have stopped them. That was too long a ride for you." She chuckled. "Your knees look permanently bent."

"I'm all right." He yawned and stretched casually, but stole a quick glance at his knees and decided she was joking. "Just tired."

He watched over her shoulder as she unsaddled Hahle, showing him how two tightly clinging straps of cloth made up the saddle girth and how pulling one particular way could separate the straps. Peter fingered the straps, feeling the roughness of one and the smooth texture of the other. "The elves designed the girth straps so that the Fleet Ones can take the saddles off by themselves," Jeanne explained, lifting the saddle off the impatiently fidgeting Hahle. "Easier than buckles."

She caught up a handful of grass and started to rub the stallion down, but with a shake of his head and a soft murmur, Hahle went to join the other Fleet Ones. Jeanne shrugged and began gathering wood for a fire. "See if you can find a clear packet of small sticks in one of the packs," she called.

Peter rummaged through the packs. "Is this it?"

Jeanne glanced at Elin and Peter realized where she had learned some of her newfound knowledge. The stallion snorted, nodding, and Jeanne finished arranging the campfire. "Right. Elin says not to open it completely. Just ease one out. Those sticks light up when they come in contact with air."

"Really?" He watched and counted the short space of seconds before the yellow tip of the exposed stick sprang into flames. "Elfin matches, yet."

Together they coaxed the small campfire into life. With light available, Peter unstrapped his sword from the saddle and tried to remember how to fasten the belt. Succeeding at that, he drew and hefted the long sword, surprised at its lightness. It fit his hand as if it had been made especially for him.

Jeanne went back to the packs. "You very hungry?"

Peter's abused stomach winced at the thought, and he said as much.

"You have to eat something. We missed dinner." She surfaced with a small packet and peeled off a little of its leaf like covering. "Elin, is this journeybread? It feels softer than I thought it would. Looks like bread." She peered closely at it. "Stuffed with nuts and dried fruit." She tossed one packet to Peter. "Here, try some."

Peter looked at it suspiciously, then peeled off its protective covering and bit into it. "Hey, this is still warm!" He took another bite. "Delicious!" He finished the bread quickly and Renw snorted.

"I guess the elves make two meals from one packet," Jeanne laughed. A whisper of sound came to her ears and she looked worriedly into the shadows. "Peter, did you hear something?"

"No." He fell silent and listened. "No, nothing." He yawned. "Do you want to get some sleep? I'll stand watch."

Jeanne smiled and tossed him a blanket. "Elin says they'll stand guard tonight. Tomorrow it will be our turn." She turned and watched the dark forest as if listening. Peter found himself straining to catch what had so bothered her, but he could hear only the same nighttime sounds he remembered from camping trips with the Scouts. He shrugged and, after trying to figure out what to do with his sword, curled up in the blanket, his aches disappearing in sleep.

Sometime later that night, Jeanne awoke with a start. The fire crackled cheerily before her; the blanket-wrapped bundle that was Peter breathed softly nearby. She sat up and added more branches to the fire, sensing something wrong.

Elin murmured in welcome as she began to explore the clearing. She smiled absently, her eyes on the shadows. "Elin, Hahle, any of you hear anything out there?" she asked softly. Elin snorted, shaking his head. "I hope you're right," she replied worriedly. A shriek echoed from a nearby tree, and Hahle murmured nervously. "That tree's too small for a witch hound, silly," Jeanne scolded him. She found herself shaking with mixed relief and fear. *Silly*, she told herself, *it's nothing but a little owl. Look, you can see its eyes shining above that branch.* "Awfully *big* eyes," she muttered aloud.

She returned to her blanket and sat beside the fire, watching the night suspiciously. A shadow moved, and she froze, but it was only the roan moving among the trees. *What's the matter with me?* she thought, half-afraid. *I've camped out in a forest before. Now calm down before you start imagining monsters hiding in the trees.*

She glanced again at the big yellow eyes of the owl and suddenly noticed that all three stallions were watching them also. She climbed to her feet and hurried back to Elin.

"What is it, Elin?" she whispered. The stallion didn't move, not even when she pushed him. All three stared at the yellow eyes, barely breathing.

She turned at a sudden movement behind her. The fire was out! "Peter," she called urgently. "Peter!"

Branches rustled in the owl's tree. The big eyes were gone, but *something* was climbing down out of that tree.

She made no further sound. Her eyes watching the tree before her, she moved back to where Peter was still curled up in his blanket. Only someone else was there before her. She felt something sharp prick her side. "Do not move," a voice said. She obeyed and felt her dagger taken from her belt. The figure stepped away. "Wake him," the voice commanded.

Jeanne moved to Peter's side and shook his shoulder. Peter woke slowly. "What?" he mumbled in a voice filled with sleep.

"Trouble," Jeanne said dully. Her attention was on the squat figure bending over the embers of their fire. She remembered stories she had read and realized that she was looking at a troll. His large yellow eyes did not seem to belong to the thick body squeezed into a uniform of deep violet. A heavy, curved sword hung at his side.

The troll tossed a powder into the embers and dark, dreary red flames leaped up. The large eyes swung to regard Jeanne. "Too much light is bad for the eyes," he chuckled hoarsely. Jeanne shuddered.

"What's going on?" Peter demanded. Their other captor was quickly taking his weapons. The red light shone full on him, and it was not without some surprise that Jeanne realized that their second captor was a tall, blond elf.

The troll rubbed his hands briskly together. "The Dark One will enjoy entertaining these two." He pointed at Jeanne. *"This* one is no escaped elf. I thought my eyes were failing when she walked away without freezing." He grinned evilly. "Just human."

The elf turned to study her, and Jeanne had to restrain a shudder. Although he wore the violet uniform of the witches, it was clear to her that he didn't do so willingly. The eyes looked trapped, and his face was gray with pain. The dull gaze shifted to the troll. "The Fleet Ones?" he snapped.

The troll leered again. "Frozen. They'll keep until the hounds arrive."

"See that they do." The elf's voice was cold, without emotion, and Jeanne shivered. The voice was too lifeless. Peter tried to get to his feet, and the elf's sword swung instantly toward him. "Can you paralyze these two until the hounds return from the Last Door?"

"Some humans are resistant. *She* is."

"Try him."

The troll fastened his gaze on Peter, widening the yellowness, and with a stab of fear, the boy felt a hypnotic numbness steal over him. Try as he would, Peter couldn't avoid looking into those yellow eyes. He felt himself falling into them. He couldn't move, forgot even to think.

Jeanne caught her breath in fear at the blank expression on Peter's face. She touched his shoulder. "Peter!"

Peter blinked and shook himself. The troll turned to the elf. "Resistant, too."

The elf looked up at the sky. "The sun will soon be rising. The hounds should have come by now, but we can wait no longer for them. We best find a cave or deep shadow for you."

The troll nodded. "I have no desire for the Sun to turn me into a stone statue. But what about the Four-Footed Ones? They'll have the entire countryside looking for us."

"Not if we keep them with us until the hounds come. Turn them loose."

The troll barked hoarsely. "And how do we stop them from trampling us? No, the Four-Footed Ones have to die." He drew his blade. "The Dark One warned me that you might not be able to kill. I'll do it."

The elf shook his head. "They will break free. Your power will not hold them against their will to live."

"I said I'll do it," the troll snapped. He moved toward the stallions, his long, curved blade in his hand. His eyes were focused on those of the Fleet Ones, the yellowness widening.

"No!" Jeanne gasped.

The troll turned toward her. "Keep her quiet," he told Peter. "I don't need distractions right now." He gestured with his sword.

He turned back to the Fleet Ones, but before he reached them, Elin suddenly stirred. The stallion screamed with anger, shaking his head, and thundered toward the troll. The troll dropped his sword and scurried up a tree. "He won't freeze!" he wailed from among the branches.

The elf pulled Jeanne away from Peter. "Hold, Fleet One, or she dies," he said coldly. Elin stopped, his gaze on the sword now so close to Jeanne.

The glistening blade wavered in and out of Jeanne's vision. The elf's emotions flooded her mind: a bewildering confusion of pain, resistance, and a numbing coldness that chilled her heart more than the sword's threat. She tried to push the ice out of her thoughts, to concentrate on her surroundings.

The elf watched Elin. "You will let him down from that tree and let him freeze you again. After we have gone, you will not sound the alarm—"

Peter moved abruptly, and the elf stepped out of reach, dragging Jeanne with him. "Move back with the Fleet One," the elf ordered, shifting the sword closer. Peter moved back.

The troll scrambled down from the tree. "The Sun!" he wailed. "It'll be rising soon!"

The elf suddenly shivered. "Freeze the Fleet One," he ordered. His voice sounded weaker, but still he held Jeanne hostage.

The small troll edged away from Elin. "I can't!" he wailed. "My power weakens! The Sun is rising!" He turned to run, but Hahle suddenly came to life and moved to block the troll. "Let me go, let me find a cave!"

The elf shivered again. He dropped his sword and fell to his knees, trembling violently. Jeanne, freed, suddenly did not have the strength to run from him. Dizzy, she felt Peter beside her, supporting her. "Don't faint now," he said.

The elf pressed trembling hands to his forehead. "The Change," he said in a wondering voice. "It...it is gone."

The troll dodged Hahle and ran away through the trees. The sun's rays streaked the sky, and Hahle nodded wisely to Elin. The blue-black stallion trotted off on the troll's trail.

"I'm...okay, Peter." She slipped free of his grasp and moved to the elf's side. "What's wrong?" she asked, sharing his confusion. "Can we help?"

"The Change is gone. I...I am free. And alive!"

"So?" Peter asked, retrieving his sword and sheathing it. He picked up the elf's blade also, but held it ready, watching the elf suspiciously.

"I was dying before," the elf explained. His voice grew stronger. "Only then can a witch Change a resistant will. But now I am myself again and alive!" He climbed to his feet. Peter kept his borrowed sword pointing toward the elf, but the elf ignored it. "This is bewildering. A Changed slave can never be freed—and live."

A happy murmur came out of the shadows, and Renw rushed toward the elf.

The elf smiled at the excited Fleet One. "Battle kin!" he greeted him. "How came you here?"

"Peter!" Jeanne gasped. "That's Renw's partner, Leereho!"

"So I guessed," Peter said thoughtfully, watching the reunion. "I wonder how the elves knew that we would meet him?"

Hahle trotted back into sight, murmuring swiftly. Renw turned from the elf to reply and Jeanne groaned. "Oh, Hahle, do we have to leave now?"

"He is right," the elf said. Renw murmured at him, but the elf began to smother the small campfire. "He is right, Renw, we must leave. The hounds will be here and we must be gone."

Peter and Jeanne exchanged glances. "Hounds," Peter repeated. Jeanne nodded and they began gathering up blankets and packs.

With the elf's help, they were soon ready to leave. "Hahle," Peter said as he swung up into the saddle, hampered somewhat by his sword, "what about that troll? He's going to tell the hounds that we've gone."

The stallion shook his large head. Peter listened closely, but still could not make out any words. "Jeanne—"

"Can you not understand their speech?"

Hahle murmured swiftly as Renw and the elf stopped beside them. Elin replied, starting forward onto the trail, and Hahle and Renw followed.

Peter glanced at the elf. "No, I still can't understand them. Jeanne can, though." The elf glanced at Elin's rider. "About that troll," Peter persisted.

"The sun caught him," the elf said. "He is now stone."

Peter shook his head. "Just from being in the sun? But—" He flung up his hands as the elf looked at him curiously. "Okay, okay, different world, different rules. Maybe you can tell me instead how everyone can still use magic if the curse erased all memory of spells? Graylod's vanishing act, those Elders in the village we came from knew you were going to be around—"

The elf looked surprised. "They knew?"

"Yeah, and I want to know how!"

The elf shook his head. "I am only a scout, not a student of lore."

Jeanne interrupted. "Elin says that not all memory of spells was erased. Books were left unaffected, and so were those who studied magic but never used it. Many spells were regained that way."

The elf rubbed his forehead. "We have been fighting for years and all of the knowledge we regained was not easily won. The witches have...hunted down and destroyed places of power..."

Jeanne turned in her saddle. "Are you all right?"

The roan stallion murmured and slowed his pace, falling behind Hahle. "Renw thinks you're tiring Leereho," Jeanne explained, as Elin slowed to move alongside Hahle.

"I need answers and he's got them." Peter glanced back at the elf. "He owes us."

The gray and white stallion murmured swiftly. "Elin says he and Hahle can try to answer some of your questions." She frowned. "But later, sounds like they want to get far away from here fast."

Peter sighed as the Fleet Ones began to gallop. *Now I know how Todd at school feels. Only I'm lousy at lip-reading.*

Although they traveled quickly that day in an attempt to avoid the hounds that would have carried them to the witches, Peter made use of any available time to query the elf. He was not aided by Renw, who seemed to think that his questions were bothering his partner and came between whenever the elf seemed in pain or weary. Peter persisted, however, finding it faster to question the elf than wait for translations from the Fleet Ones.

"So, what else do you remember of the witch, other than shadows?"

"Renw, I think I told of the Glen!" The elf lunged to his feet. "I must warn them!"

"'Leereho, you've been gone for—months? Elin, what did that word mean?"

"Jeanne, never mind!"

"'Any warning would come too late.' Renw's probably right, Leereho."

The elf took a deep, shuddering breath. "I must try. I must report at least what I have remembered of my capture, thanks to Peter's questions." He turned toward the Fleet Ones. "Please."

Hahle and Elin looked steadily back at him, while Renw fidgeted. Hahle murmured and Jeanne translated, "We will discuss it. Your path would not need to depart from ours for a time yet, so rest.'"

"But the speed you travel at for these humans—" the elf began.

Elin stamped, and Renw hung his head, murmuring. "'You won't travel any faster with only me, partner. In case you haven't noticed, you still aren't too well.'" Jeanne took a deep breath and added, "He's right, Leereho. And the Elders said you would be traveling with us for a time."

The elf sighed. He turned and walked to the edge of the light from their small campfire to stand staring up at the stars.

Peter edged closer to Jeanne. "I don't remember them saying that, Jeanne."

"They didn't," Jeanne whispered back. "But Elin and Renw want him to rest and you can see yourself that he's not fully recovered from the Change." She glanced aside at him. "You still don't trust him, do you, Peter?"

Still watching the elf, Peter shrugged. "I don't know, Jeanne." He sat down on the grass beside her. "What freed him from that... Change spell? Is it normal for spells to break on their own like that? The Fleet Ones trust him, but...what if it's a trick of the witches?"

Jeanne was silent. She had puzzled over the same questions and one more without an answer. What had caused her sudden weakness right before Leereho had been freed?

* * *

Soon they had left the woods behind them and ventured out onto the plains. In the mid-afternoon they rested above a wide stream while the Fleet Ones drank the cool water or grazed on the long grass lining the banks. The elf was silent all through their meal, watching the sky and the horizon. Renw trotted up to him, murmuring softly.

"What, is it time to leave so soon, Le?" Peter asked, standing up and stretching.

The elf pulled himself up onto Renw's back and looked down at them. "It is only time for myself and Renw to leave. You must continue on without us."

Peter glanced over at Elin and Hahle. "You two finally decided, then?" Hahle snorted.

"Peter, I would not be much help to you now," Leereho said slowly. "The dwarfs do not care for elves, and I doubt their welcome so long as I wear a violet uniform. I would only be a hindrance to you. Graylod will bring you to the Glen of Voices. I will meet you again there." Renw swung about and crossed the stream. Then he began to gallop.

"Jeanne? Did they say how much longer it is to Gimstan Mountain?"

She shrugged. "We'll probably reach it by tonight. Le put torches in our packs. He said that ever since the Dark One ordered the dwarfs to mine gold and gems for her, the dwarfs have darkened all their tunnels and hidden deep under the mountain."

"That doesn't make sense. You'd think they'd have the tunnels brightly lit to bother the trolls."

Hahle and Elin trotted up to them. Elin bumped his head playfully against Jeanne's shoulder and murmured gently. "Elin wants to know if we've rested enough. They're ready to move on."

The humans re-saddled the Fleet Ones. Peter tightened the saddle girth. "Shall we walk and let you two rest longer, Hahle?" he asked, patting the sleek hide.

The black stallion shook his head, then reached back and indicated the saddle, murmuring slowly. Peter still wished that he could understand their murmurs as Jeanne did, but all he had been able to do so far was catch tones of voice. The horse was becoming impatient, so Peter gave up his attempts at translating and swung into the saddle. He'd ask Jeanne later.

* * *

Twilight was settling when they came within view of the mountains. None of them felt like stopping, especially with Gimstan Mountain so near. They rode on.

"No stars tonight," Jeanne commented, watching the night sky. "Somehow it seems ominous." She shivered and fidgeted with her cloak.

"Cold?" Peter asked.

"No. No, it's not that. I don't know, I've got a funny sensation, as if something's going to happen."

Peter glanced worriedly at the dim outline of the mountains ahead. They were so near; they had to reach there safely! Yet Jeanne had been right more times than he cared to remember. *Why hasn't this land affected me the way it has Jeanne? I can't even understand Hahle!*

"Elin," Jeanne said suddenly, "you and Hahle did promise to try and fight your fear of witch hounds, didn't you?"

Elin gave a surprised snort.

"Good. You two better prepare yourselves, then. I can't help but feel that one is coming."

Hahle murmured quickly to Elin and the two Fleet Ones surged forward into canters. The mountains drew nearer and nearer.

"It's not much further, Peter," Jeanne called.

Peter crossed his fingers and kept his hands close to the reins.

Suddenly a screech echoed through the night. The canters broke smoothly into gallops, and the plains pounded away under the Windkin's hooves. The screech came again, and they could feel a wind moving high up in the sky, the faint *swish* as the hound circled in the air above them.

"Can it see us?" Peter yelled.

The shriek echoed again, and the shape seemed closer to the ground.

"I'm willing to bet on it," Jeanne called back.

The Fleet Ones' hooves clattered across a stone bridge, then thundered onto a stone road and off again, on up to the mountain itself. The hound shrieked again and swooped lower, but was brought up short by the mountain peaks. Peter ducked reflexively as the hound flew overhead, then straightened worriedly as it circled higher, leaving the travelers temporarily alone on the mountain slope.

"Now that we're here, how do we get in?" Peter muttered as Hahle murmured worriedly to Elin.

Elin lowered his head and studied the ground carefully. He snorted and moved cautiously among the rocks. Hahle followed as the terrifying shriek echoed again. Peter could feel the stallion trembling, but the horse was fighting the spell-induced fear.

The Windkin followed a faint trail winding among the fallen boulders. With Elin in the lead, they came upon a higher portion of the stone road and galloped along it to a steep cliff-face. The solid rock rose in an unbroken wall up hundreds of feet to the top of the cliff. "Where do we go now?" Peter muttered. "Up?"

The stallions paused before the rock barrier. Elin snorted and followed the rock wall, Hahle behind him. The hound shrieked and swooped closer, and Elin suddenly broke into a gallop, heading straight for the cliff-face. Peter almost flung his arms in front of his face as the solid rock wall loomed closer. He pulled the reins uselessly.

The Fleet Ones thundered through the wall of stone, stopping when they were completely through the illusion. Hahle murmured in an amused manner as Peter released the reins to look about in relief.

They stood within a gigantic cavern. Phosphorescent stones glowed in the otherwise dark shadows. The luminous stones varied in color, some seeming a rose red, others a bright green or a deep violet. Jeanne dismounted, her eyes searching for something other than the beauty shining in the darkness. Peter followed her lead, and his right hand strayed to the hilt of his sword when he stood on the floor of the cavern.

"Back for more, trolls?" a voice boomed from the shadows. Peter whirled, but it was difficult to tell where the voice had come from; the echoes distorted it and bounced it from wall to wall. "We killed the last group of you skulkers she sent in. We won't mind killing more."

Hahle whinnied loudly, and Jeanne shouted Elin's comments. "Do trolls ride Fleet Ones now? A fine welcome you give to friends!"

"Elves," the voice said in deep disgust.

Peter's dark-adapted eyes caught a sudden movement and he turned to face it, his hand on the hilt of his sword. He blinked in surprise as two dwarfs stepped into the brighter light of the cavern.

Both of the dwarfs stood well under five feet tall and were dressed in brown and gray garb—earth tones, he reminded himself. What surprised him was not the axes—as long as the dwarfs were tall—that they carried, but the impression of sheer strength and endurance about their stocky frames. *Guess I must have been expecting those ridiculous tiny people from fairy tales*, he thought ruefully. *And they certainly aren't those*.

"What do you Firstborn want now?" the smaller, black-bearded dwarf asked. "Our Elder has had word of your gathering."

"We're humans, not elves," Peter said heatedly. Hahle suddenly whacked him with his tail and Elin sighed deeply. "I wasn't supposed to say that?" he whispered to Jeanne.

"I guess not," she whispered back. "You two could have warned us," she added, turning to the stallions.

The dwarfs' eyes glittered dangerously. "Humans!" the black-bearded dwarf said with an even deeper loathing than he had expressed for elves. He lifted his double-bladed axe.

The taller, gray-bearded dwarf caught him. "We of the dwarfs and mortal men have long warred, all for the glitter of our gold," he explained quickly. "If it is our gold you seek, it is best that you leave now, before the others renew our long feud."

"And give you the same welcome we give to the Dark One!" the blackbeard snarled. "And her shadow-lurking, sticky-fingered trolls!"

"We're only looking for Graylod, not your gold," Peter said, feeling exasperated at their suspicions. "And we'd leave right now, except for the fact that a hound chased us here."

"Hounds!" blackbeard growled. "That's right, lead the hounds to one of our hidden entrances. Soon there won't be any secrets left around here at all." The graybeard bent over and whispered to him hurriedly.

Jeanne tensed and tilted her head. She edged back and nudged Peter. "Listen," she whispered.

Blotting out the taller dwarf's whispers, Peter could hear a tiny thread of sound running below it. It was so faint as to be almost unnoticed—the slight pad of boots against stone. Peter could almost imagine an army of dwarfs moving through the inky blackness. He fumbled for the hilt of his sword, but Jeanne placed her hand over his, keeping the sword in its sheath. "Not yet," she whispered. "Let them make the first move."

Suddenly they heard the angry shriek of the witch hound coming from outside the entrance. "We can't stay here," Jeanne yelled over the shrieks.

The taller dwarf bowed. "Graylod has not been here, but we will take you to a safe place to await him. Follow us."

A tunnel lined with luminous stones led from the cavern. The hound's cry was soon lost in the distance.

The dwarfs led them deep into the mountain. The luminous stones dwindled to only a few scattered patches, and then only the soft pad of the dwarfs' boots on the stone guided the humans.

Peter peered through the dark in an attempt to catch sight of the dwarfs. After what seemed hours in the absolute blackness, he felt totally bewildered. He rested his arm on Hahle's back and let the Fleet One, who seemed to be able to see in the darkness, guide him. *If I'm ever asked to find my way out now*, he thought, *forget it. The place is a complete maze.*

Hahle stopped, and Peter walked into him in the dark. The Fleet One murmured anxiously. Elin answered the murmur with a nervous snort. Peter pushed at the large body, but the black stallion refused to budge. "Move over," he said, pushing harder. Hahle snorted. Peter squeezed past him and tried to peer through the blackness.

"Peter?" Jeanne's voice seemed to come from further ahead, but Peter couldn't see her. "Elin says that he's not going to move another step for those dwarfs."

"Can't say as how I blame him." Peter listened for the dwarf's footsteps, but it was as if they were completely alone. "Hey!" he called.

"HEY... Hey...hey..." the echoes answered him.

"Can Elin see them?" he asked Jeanne.

"No. He can't hear them, either."

"Wait a second." Peter rummaged for a pouch on his belt. "I'd almost be willing to believe that the dwarfs just renewed the feud and this is a trap," he muttered as he felt through the pouch. He couldn't erase the memory of the army of dwarfs they might have heard. "Why didn't these two put in a good word for us? Ah, here it is." He dug out the slender sticks the elves had given them and fumbled one out of its airtight container. The stick sprang into flames, lighting up the darkness.

"Some of the Folk can't understand Fleet Ones, either. Here's a torch." Jeanne pulled hers out of Elin's pack.

"Good. Let's have a look at this place."

The torch produced a steadily burning flame, much brighter than the slender stick, and its glow was a relief after the oppressing darkness. Peter no longer felt that eyes were peering at them from the shadows. Hahle murmured and rested his heavy head on Peter's shoulder for a moment, craning towards the torchlight.

Peter lifted the torch. Ahead he could see where the tunnel branched into two openings. From one branch billowed small clouds of steam and the brimstone smell of sulfur. The other...

He started forward to investigate it when Elin suddenly went wild. The gray and white mount screamed and reared, dancing forward on his hind legs and swinging his hooves dangerously.

Trying to avoid him, Jeanne slipped and fell against the tunnel wall, and Peter hurried back to help her. Hahle murmured questioningly.

Before he had reached them, however, Elin suddenly quieted. The stallion moved over to Jeanne and nudged her gently. "I'll forgive you if you'll explain why you did that," Jeanne muttered, rubbing her sore shoulder.

"You all right, Jeanne?" Peter helped her to her feet.

"I'm fine." Jeanne brushed her trousers. "Just fine. Elin, what do you mean, something hit you? Do you see anything?"

"I don't." Peter looked again for their missing guides. "I don't even see the dwarfs." Jeanne shivered and looked behind them. "Jeanne, what's wrong?"

Jeanne shivered again. "Something's going to happen," she said in a frightened voice. "Peter, let's get out of here! Now!"

"What?"

A wild shriek from behind them woke the sleeping echoes. The Fleet Ones, taken off guard, squealed and ran for the two tunnels. But when they reached the fork, they avoided the two tunnels and instead disappeared into the solid wall separating them.

The shriek came again, echoing horribly. "Follow the Fleet Ones!" Jeanne yelled over the echoes. "That wall is another illusion!" Peter grabbed her hand, and together they ran through the hidden doorway, the hound's wild cries spurring them on.

CHAPTER 4

CAVERN LIGHT

They ran until they could run no further, until the sounds of pursuit behind them had died away. They had absolutely no idea where they were. They had dodged down so many different passageways and taken so many twisting turns that Peter couldn't even be sure if they had not gone in a complete circle. Time had no meaning in the dark. They rested only to continue onward through the silent tunnels and caverns.

The walls of the cavern glistened in the torchlight, turning brilliant and beautiful shades of green, red, and yellow as the torch moved. Dripping stalactites glistened like wet crystals from the ceiling, forming tall pillars where they met stalagmites growing up from the floor.

"It's beautiful," Jeanne sighed.

"And dangerous," Peter added, peering into the yawning mouth of a sinkhole. The sloping sides of the hole seemed tō go down forever, and he hastily backed away from the crumbling rim of the opening. "It certainly is big," he commented as they walked, looking up toward the faraway ceiling. His voice echoed eerily in the cavern.

In the torchlight Peter could see where a doorway had been carved in the cavern wall. "Let's try that opening," he suggested. "Maybe this one will lead to the dwarfs. It seems odd that we haven't seen *anything* of them, just carvings."

"Leereho did say that they were hiding from the witch."

"Yeah, but from us, too?"

"The witch hound did follow us in." Jeanne shivered and drew her cloak tighter about her as they neared the doorway.

Peter ducked under the low arch and straightened, raising the torch.

Behind him Jeanne sighed in wonder as the flames revealed that the sparkling colors of the rock walls were mirrored in a calm body of water. "Look, Peter!" she exclaimed. "An underground lake. Isn't it lovely?"

Peter looked at the cavern walls hemming the lake on all sides. On their side was a wide beach that ended at an enormous tunnel from which a stream emptied into the lake. "It's going to be hard getting around," he commented, looking across the lake to the only other exit. He caught sight of a wide lip of the cavern wall jutting out over the surface of the water. In some places the rim of the ledge seemed to slope into the water, but the lip was very wide and seemed to run all the way around the lake. "Let's try that ledge over there," he decided.

"No eye for beauty," Jeanne muttered. She held the torch while Peter scrambled up the closest edge of the lip.

"Okay, toss it up," Peter called. He caught the flying torch and stepped back to allow Jeanne room to climb up. Suddenly his boot slipped on a patch of slime. The torch flew out of his hand as he stumbled backward. Before Jeanne could catch it, it had toppled over the ledge and into the lake, dying in a rise of steam.

Peter leaned over and fished the bobbing wood out of the lake. "One wet torch," he sighed. "Just great."

"There's light enough from the rocks," Jeanne said quietly. She found herself growing cold again, the knowledge that *something* was going to happen again stealing over her. *What's the matter with me?* she worried.

Peter looked along the ledge, knowing that where the luminous glow ended the water was. He heard a squashy sound from the darkness before him, as if something wet moved there. He peered through the darkness, dimly seeing a white bulk somewhat like a seal drag itself out of the water. He was so intent on the creature that when something behind him brushed his shoulder, he nearly fell into the lake.

"What is it?" Jeanne whispered.

"A white seal, I guess," he said, catching his balance. "And stop sneaking up behind me like that, will ya?" He pulled out his sword and handed Jeanne the extinguished torch. "We'll have to get around it," he explained. "So we may as well see how friendly it is."

He strode forward determinedly. The seal-like creature grunted and crawled away from his approach. It slid against the cavern wall and huddled there, staring at Peter with blind eyes. "It's safe enough," Peter called back after he had passed the small creature. "C'mon!"

Jeanne started forward, then froze as she heard someone laugh in the darkness behind her. She hesitated, peering into the shadows hiding the beach.

The shrill shriek of the witch hound tattered the echoes. "You are trapped," a shrill voice—almost as terrifying as the hound's shriek—called. "The garb of elves you wear, and the friends of elves you rode. But no elf would enter the domain of dwarfs. Humans you must be, and Watcher-picked humans at that. Come willingly now to me or be destroyed as you stand!"

Jeanne felt terror root her in place. The very thing they had been trying to avoid had tracked and found them! Waves of panic washed through her and receded. *She's nervous, she's afraid of us, that's why she warned us*, Jeanne told herself. *She's trying to frighten us, and doing a pretty good job of it, too.* She took a firmer grip on the torch, watching the ledge behind her. She knew she was the closest to the witch.

Peter knew that also, and worried. Being the closest meant Jeanne would be the first one harmed. He tried frantically to think of something. Where was a sulfur spring when they needed one!

"Stubborn, hey?" the witch mumbled uneasily. "Very well. The fate you have chosen shall be yours!"

Jeanne edged along the cavern wall. Mentally she crossed her fingers as she neared the spot where she had last seen the seal. An angry growl came from the blackness before her. *I found it all right*, she thought. *Now to get around it.* She could see the seal in the glow of the walls. Its blind eyes were fastened on her, and sharp teeth were bared in a snarl. "That's not very friendly," she whispered. "You don't want to get mixed up in this when there's a lovely lake to swim in." Confusion and terror warred in the creature.

Peter, meanwhile, was vaguely starting to remember something to produce light. Not the slender sticks, their light was far too weak. Something that produced a big flame, a circle of light. While Jeanne was cautiously edging around the seal, Peter began to mumble to himself. Words grew out of the mumble, words of power and light. "...*verd rwit*!" he finished loudly. A sudden rush of sound answered him, and he came out of his daze.

Peter suddenly discovered that his eyes were tightly closed. He opened them, not at all prepared for the sight that greeted him.

Jeanne was running up to him, brandishing the burnt-out torch. Waves washed over the ledge behind her, while on the beach a hunched-over hound was encircled in flames. A heavily cloaked figure seated on the back of the huge hound hid its face with one protecting arm while with the other it gestured at the flames, seemingly trying to extinguish them. The air was filled with the screams and shrieks of the two prisoners. Peter stared. "I did *that*?"

A sobering thought hit him, and he grabbed Jeanne's elbow, pulling her away from the prison of flames. "C'mon, the spell only lasts a few minutes," he yelled over the shrieks.

They stumbled off the ledge and into the tunnel leading away from the lake. Behind them, the flames were dying down, and a wild scream followed them. "I shall get you! You will never escape me! *Never!*"

They ran until, finally, out of breath, they had to stop. Luminous rocks glowed all around them, and behind them, they could hear the sounds of pursuit. Peter was too tired to run any further, but so far he had not found a place for them to hide.

"Peter," Jeanne gasped, pulling at his arm, "we can't stop now. She'll be on us in a moment. Please, Peter."

He shrugged off her hand. *We can't outrun them*, he told himself. *We've got to hide. Hide...hide...hide...* The words echoed in his brain, bringing a sense of power in their wake. The words of the second spell rose easily to his lips.

To Jeanne, who was anxiously watching the tunnel behind them, Peter's mumbles seemed oddly familiar. She turned to drag him on when she stopped short. Peter was slowly fading right before her eyes! She looked at her hands in amazement. They were becoming as transparent as glass! She could see the walls of the tunnel through them!

Totally bewildered at first, she sat down on a boulder as it slowly occurred to her what was happening. She took a shaky control over her jangling nerves and watched Peter fade. When he was completely invisible, the mumbling broke off short, and a startled voice came from out of the air, right about where Peter had stood. "What happened? Jeanne? Jeanne, where are you?"

"Right here," she answered, resisting a hysterical impulse to giggle. "You've just turned us invisible."

"Oh." Peter digested that piece of news, then started, "But..."

"Shhh!" Jeanne hissed. "Listen."

The echoes threw ahead the sounds of their pursuers. The invisible pair could hear the witch shrieking angrily. The huge hound lumbered along the trail and stopped right in front of the silent watchers. The witch on its back mumbled angrily to herself, then suddenly noticed that the hound had stopped and whipped it on. Peter held his breath as the hound's huge head swung toward him, suspiciously staring into the shadows.

"Onward, you blundering fool!" the witch ordered. "There's nothing here! Nothing at all! Hurry, they mustn't get away!" The hound obediently lumbered on and soon the strange rider and mount disappeared in the maze of tunnels.

"Just in time," Jeanne commented. "You're becoming visible, Peter."

"So are you." He sat down on the boulder beside her. "Well, if we weren't lost before, we certainly are now. And I for one don't want to follow the witch through this maze. She might decide to backtrack, and then we're trapped again."

"I'm so tired," Jeanne sighed, "and hungry. I wonder how long we've been in here?"

"Years, according to my stomach. Did you have to mention food? Good thing that there's so much water around. At least we won't go thirsty."

Jeanne suddenly straightened. "Peter, do you hear something?"

Peter jumped to his feet. "Is the witch coming back?"

The girl frowned and slid off the boulder. "No, the sound is coming from behind this old rock fall," she said, crossing the tunnel. She peered at the ground. "Peter, give me one of the fire-sticks."

In the sudden blaze of light, Peter saw the birdlike tracks of the hound in the dust. Jeanne moved the light over before the rock fall and there, before the tumbled rocks, were the prints of unshod hooves. "The horses!" Peter exclaimed. "But the trail leads right into the rocks!"

"And so do a few boot prints," Jeanne observed. "The dwarfs have been this way." She touched the tumbled rocks. "It's no illusion. Look for a hinge or some kind of door release on that side, Peter."

Peter ran his hands over the chilly wall, feeling the damp slickness of the living rock. He found a pebble embedded in the otherwise smooth surface that clung to the wall despite his efforts. In exasperation, he hit it with his fist. He heard a sharp *snik* as the pebble vanished into the wall.

With a faint grinding sound, the rock fall swung inward, and yellow torchlight flowed into the tunnel, dazzling their dark-adapted eyes.

"All right!" Peter quickly lowered his voice. Light might mean dwarfs and maybe even food, but there was no telling what else was nearby. "Good hearing, Jeanne! Amy Evans was right, you do have magical powers."

Jeanne looked frightened. "No, no magic," she said in a small voice. She tensed suddenly. "Follow me." She stepped cautiously through the rocky clutter and darted into the lighted tunnel.

"Jeanne, wait!" Peter hurried after her. The door was so well balanced that he could close it with a slight push. Jeanne was already halfway down the tunnel, following the trail of hoof prints.

He finally caught up with her as she entered the small cavern at the end of the tunnel. "Jeanne, it was just a joke..." A sparkling gleam caught his eye. "Look!"

Gold and silver objects were scattered haphazardly over the floor of the cavern, and jewels glittered in the light. "This must be their vault." Peter could not tear his eyes away from the sparkling sight.

Jeanne shivered. "It feels like a trap. Let's get out of here, Peter."

Peter shook himself. "Yeah. It would make good bait for trolls."

"Correct," a voice said behind them. "And a good test for humans."

They turned. A gray-bearded dwarf stood in the doorway. He swept his hat from his head and bowed deeply. "A test that you have passed."

Peter felt hot anger rise in him. "You abandoned us in the tunnel for a stupid test? The witch almost got us because of you!"

"You met the witch? And survived?" The dwarf looked frightened. "Mighty Ones, forgive us! We will delay your journey no longer!"

Armed dwarfs suddenly appeared in the entrance, and the humans found themselves hustled through the tunnels behind a highly nervous escort. "Did you have to brag?" Jeanne whispered, seeming highly amused at his discomfiture. She turned to the graybeard beside them. "No word of us should pass beyond this mountain," she said firmly.

"Of course, Mighty One," the dwarf agreed. He added confidingly, "We were to have guarded your passage through the tunnels, but after you vanished into the Hidden Ways, the witch came and in the confusion we lost your trail. The Fleet Ones found us, but even together we could find no sign of you."

"Has Graylod come yet?" Peter asked.

The dwarf looked puzzled. "Graylod? No, we have had no word of him."

"If he does come," Jeanne said, "tell him we have gone to the Glen of Ancient Voices."

Peter raised an eyebrow at her.

"Well, that's where Le said we should go next."

"Yeah, but I'm not sure if they needed to know that."

"You don't trust anybody, do you, Peter?"

Soon the tunnel ended in a star-lit darkness. Peter took a deep breath of the cool, fresh air. "How long have we been in there?"

"Elin!" Jeanne called, spotting the Windkin being saddled by their former escort. The Fleet One whinnied as the girl flung herself at his mane.

The Fleet Ones waited only long enough for their riders to mount before they hurried off into the night. "Good luck!" the graybeard called after them. "Henceforth you shall be welcome in all of the mountains of dwarfs."

"We may be welcome there," Peter muttered softly, "but he sure pushed us out fast. Without even offering us any food! I'm starving!"

Jeanne took a deep breath and sighed happily. "Unless my nose deceives me, these sacks the dwarfs hung on our saddles contain food!"

Peter uttered a small cheer and decided to see if he could eat and ride at the same time.

The Fleet Ones trotted briskly across the open plain, anxious to put miles between themselves and the witch. The mountains slid swiftly into the distance as they hurried on under the starry sky. To keep awake, Peter told Hahle of their adventures in the tunnels. Elin, listening, snorted in amusement when Peter told how they had tricked the witch.

Peter paused after explaining about the hidden door. "Hey, Jeanne, you never did say how you knew that that door was there." Jeanne stiffened, but he couldn't see her face in the dark. "And why did you act so strangely? I was only kidding about the magic."

"Peter, do you believe in E.S.P.?"

Peter felt a slight shock hit him. He hadn't expected that question. "What?"

"E.S.P. Extra-sensory perception. Like telepathy, psycho-kinetics, clairvoyance."

"I know what it is. But what does it have to do—" He stopped. "Clairvoyance! That's how you knew the tunnel was there!"

Jeanne shook her head. "Not quite. Uh, you know how telepathy is reading another's thoughts?"

The shock spread over him, chilling him. What was she saying? Remoteness crept into his voice. "Yeah, sure."

"Well, I've...got something similar. Mike calls it empathy."

"Empathy? I thought only aliens had that. You mean you..." He suddenly couldn't continue.

"Feel what others feel. Their emotions." She saw Elin's ears perk up in interest, but her attention was on Peter. Although he made no movement, she could feel him draw away from her, his mind close against her. *Him, too?* she wondered in despair, feeling an old wound re-open. *Am I really so frightening?* She plunged on. "I guess I felt the dwarfs waiting in the tunnel, although I could never sense that far before." *Is he listening?* She sighed. *Oh, forget it. Forget everything. I don't need any friends, especially him.* A tear slid down her cheek.

Peter abruptly shook himself. "Don't know what I was expecting," he said in his old voice, "but it certainly wasn't that." Laughter was in his voice as he added, "I'll have to remember not to tell any more lies."

She stared at his darkened figure, unable to believe her senses. "You...you don't mind? You don't hate me for being able to..."

"Hate you?" Hahle's ears laid back at the outburst. "Why should I hate you? Hey, keep the twins straight. I'm not Jody." He paused. "Now, that explains a lot. But, Jeanne, what made you think I hated you? I'll admit I felt a little confused, but hate? You of all people should know better. Couldn't you tell?"

She shook her head. "No. I couldn't pick up anything. It was as if you had put up a wall, shutting me out."

She felt Peter's puzzlement. "Really? Sorry, Jeanne, I didn't mean to." He shrugged. "I did have trouble believing you at first—I'm not too accustomed to all this magic, and then to have E.S.P. thrown at me, well..." He hesitated. "Don't let people like Amy try to convince you that you're weird, Jeanne, 'cause you're not. Anybody with any brains can guess a person's emotions just by looking. You're just more perceptive than others, that's all. Wish I had some of that, might help me get along with Jody."

She looked at him, sensing the feelings behind the words. *He really means it!*

Elin murmured softly and she laughed, grateful for the interruption. "Elin says you're doing well enough with the spells. He hasn't heard of such a perfect trick played on a witch since—who?"

"I didn't have anything to do with it," Peter denied. "All post-hypnotic suggestion."

She listened to the stallion. "Peter, I wish you could hear this. It seems that there was a leprechaun who—"

Hahle snorted in exasperation.

"Two spells," Jeanne said, answering the black stallion. "He used two. One for the circle of fire and another for the invisibility. Only one spell left now."

"I feel like a time bomb," Peter grumbled. "I have no control over these."

"I'm glad the elves gave them to us," Jeanne said softly. "Without those spells, we'd…never see home again. Our parents are probably really worried about us by now. I wish…"

"Hey, don't start crying," Peter interrupted, trying to forget his own homesickness. "We'll get back. Just worry about all the homework we'll have to catch up on."

"I'm not—*snif*—going to cry."

Elin murmured softly and Jeanne tossed her hair back. "Race you to that stream up ahead!" she called as Elin surged forward.

"Hey! No fair!"

Hahle shook his mane and darted after Elin, heading into the growing dawn.

CHAPTER 5

THE WARNING

The setting sun found them camped on the open plain. The Fleet Ones grazed on the long, sweet grass while Peter and Jeanne had some of the dwarfs' nut bread along with dried fruit from the elves.

"No wonder the elves call them Fleet Ones!" Jeanne marveled. "Do you realize that they've brought us more than twice as far as an Earthly horse could in a day and they're just starting to look tired?"

"How much farther do we have to go?" Peter asked, brushing off crumbs.

"Not too much—maybe another day's ride, I guess." She eyed his cautious movements. "Getting a few sore muscles?"

"I can handle it." Peter stretched carefully. "Hahle, Jeanne and I can walk if we're going any farther tonight."

The black stallion shook his head. "'No cover in this grassland,'" Jeanne translated. "'Speed is our only defense while we're in the open.'"

"But you can't run all night," Peter argued, "and it doesn't take any time to get in the saddle."

Elin suddenly lifted his head and sniffed the wind. He stared at the southern horizon and snorted nervously. Hahle stopped arguing to listen.

Jeanne rose to her feet. "I hear it, too. Elin, you promised!"

"I don't hear..." Peter started, when the faint shriek of a witch hound came to his ears. Suddenly there came another, and another, until the air was filled with their cries. "Sounds like millions of them," Peter said grimly. "We'd better saddle up."

"No time." Jeanne glanced worriedly at the sun sinking toward the horizon. "They'll be on us in a few moments. Leave anything you can't carry behind and mount up, fast!" She scooped up a pack and, slinging its straps over her left shoulder, struggled onto Elin's broad back. Peter tried pulling himself up onto the tall Fleet One and Hahle swung his head back and boosted him up with his nose.

Jeanne gripped the stallion tightly with her knees as the Windkin wheeled and galloped away. She heard Hahle whinny reassurance, but Elin remained silent, knowing as well as she did that they were too weary to easily escape from the wind-dependent hounds this time. His despair frightened her.

The Fleet Ones' hooves tossed up clods of dirt as they pounded on across the long grass. Peter looked over his shoulder at the sky. A solid line of hounds followed them. The volume of shrieks increased as the hounds spotted their quarry.

Peter's jaw thudded against his chest as the Windkin clambered into, then out of, a deep gully. A fiery red glow filled the sky from the sun setting on the horizon. Peter looked back again.

The hounds began to circle lower. Their weak feet extended to brake the landing, they descended to the long grass. One hound landed and waddled awkwardly through the grass. Suddenly it began to shrink as it ran, losing its wings and bending over, the stubby remnants of its wings dragging on the ground as it scurried after the Fleet Ones. The wings developed into legs within seconds; the back legs straightened and grew fur, as did the rest of the hunched-over body. The long beak shrank to a furry muzzle. More hounds had landed and were going through the transformation.

Peter heard a gasp from Jeanne. "Wolves!" she cried in a voice filled with despair. "They're changing into wolves!"

The sun sank with a rush as the Fleet Ones pounded away, faster and faster. Behind them the wild howl of wolves on the hunt rose on the wind.

Jeanne choked down a sob of terror. The plain stretched on endlessly ahead of them. *How long*? she asked herself. *How much longer can we out-distance them*? She could feel Elin's heart pounding madly beneath her, his lungs heaving as he tired. She saw Peter glance back, then draw his sword as the two Windkin raced on, side-by-side. She looked back.

The wolves' eyes gleamed in the night as they gained on the exhausted stallions. The two had slowed so much already that hounds were landing ahead of them. Soon a wolf pack ran to meet them and they knew they could run no further.

The wolves raced toward them, the packs dividing to form a circle about the Fleet Ones, from which individual wolves ran up to leap and snap at the riders. Peter swung his sword, knocking the wolves down. The Windkin, experienced fighters, lashed with teeth and hooves at the steady stream of attackers. The circle closed in.

Jeanne snapped the ends of the reins like small whips in the faces of the snarling wolves, her terror growing. *I can't shut out this much pain...too many emotions*! Elin's hooves smashed a too-eager wolf, and Jeanne doubled over, sharing the wolf's hurt.

"Elin! Don't let them separate us!" Peter shouted.

Jeanne lifted her head and saw that the wolves were slowly forcing the two Fleet Ones apart. "Elin!" She tugged weakly at his mane.

Wild with anger, Elin heard only his enemies. He reared, dancing on his hind legs, wolves backing away from his menacing hooves. Jeanne kicked his side as he chased the decoying wolves. "Elin!"

A hot flame ran down Jeanne's leg. Suddenly weak and dizzy, she lost her grip on Elin's mane and fell into spinning blackness.

Elin screamed and whirled, searching for his fallen rider.

"Jeanne!"

Hahle turned at Peter's cry, and together they tried to force their way through to where Jeanne had fallen, only to find that the wolves stood firm against them. Elin was slowly being backed toward Hahle. Peter could see nothing but the dark backs of wolves.

"Jeanne!"

Jeanne tried to focus on the dim shapes moving about her. She had landed on her feet, but one leg had crumbled beneath her with a sharp stab of pain. She looked up at the fiery eyes hemming her in. The wolves did not attack; instead, they formed a circle about her and waited. Jeanne waited also. Her fingers brushed the hilt of her dagger, then she remembered her cloak. She hurried to unfasten it.

Suddenly a wolf howled and was answered by the shriek of a winged hound waiting in the sky. The circling wolves left the girl to push Elin and Hahle farther away.

Cut off from any help, Jeanne tried to climb to her feet and failed. She waited for the hound, her cloak ready.

The violet hound swooped down at the girl. Jeanne flung the cloak in the air above the reaching talons and ducked, rolling out of reach. Moving too fast to avoid the intruder in its space, the hound became momentarily entangled with the cloak. It started to fall, then finally shook itself free, the cloak falling to the ground some distance beyond Jeanne. The hound shrieked angrily.

Elin screamed an answer. As the hound circled to try again, the Fleet One suddenly broke through the wall of wolves and stood protectively over Jeanne. A few wolves snarled and slunk towards the stallion.

Blocked from reaching the girl, the hound shrieked angrily and glided away. The wolves dropped the attack as the hound left and scattered over the plain, leaving the four alone.

Peter slid off Hahle and caught Jeanne as she tried again to climb to her feet. "I'm okay," she insisted weakly.

"Sure you are." Peter draped her right arm over his shoulder and caught her waist. "Just don't faint until we get clear." Elin kept trying to nudge them as Peter guided her around the huddled bodies. "Elin, get out of the way, huh?" He half-expected the fallen wolves to suddenly resume the attack.

"It's on fire," Jeanne murmured strangely.

Peter glanced down and noticed the torn cloth flapping about her leg. He felt a stab of fear. Jeanne didn't seem to see where she was going, and most of her weight was on his shoulder.

With a sense of relief, he noticed that they had reached the end of the battlefield. He gently eased her to the ground, and her eyes suddenly seemed to focus on him. She touched a cut on his arm. "You're bleeding," she said dazedly.

He pulled away and rummaged for a pouch on his belt. "It's just a scratch."

Jeanne seemed to call on a hidden reserve of strength. "That's a bite! Where's the pack?"

"On your shoulder," he said gruffly, starting a small fire with several of the fire wands, "but I don't know how you managed to hang on to it."

Jeanne reached for his arm and dabbed a clear liquid from a small vial on the bite. He caught a whiff of a pungent, but pleasant, fragrance, and the slight ache faded.

He glanced down at the wound in surprise. "Thank you! Now let me look at your leg." He gently pulled the ripped cloth away and felt his heart sink. There was a small, blue-tinged scratch on the outside of her knee, but the slash widened as it ran down to the top of her boot. The long slash bled very little, looking more like a blue line drawn down the outside of her leg. The torn cloth around it was stained a dark blue. He moved her leg gently and Jeanne winced. "Jeanne, I think it's poisoned," he said slowly, watching her face.

Jeanne's eyes lost their focus. "The elves warned me," she said, as if in a dream. She caught her breath. "First it burned, now it's so cold!" Her blue-gray eyes suddenly saw him again. "What...did I say?"

Peter felt a chill touch his heart. He also remembered the elves' warning. *"We see great evil in this for you, daughter. But we cannot see beyond it."* He felt warm breath on the back of his neck as Elin studied the slash. The Fleet One flung up his head and called to Hahle, and the two Windkin went back among the bodies of the dead wolves.

"What was that about?" Peter asked as he moistened a cloth with liquid from the vial.

Jeanne looked after the Fleet Ones. "I'm not sure. He just told me not to worry, that a *bataog* must have scratched me, and that I would be all right. But why did he sound so frightened?"

Peter dabbed the blue line with the moist cloth. The blue tinge vanished as the cloth went over it and the slash started bleeding freely. "Now I've done it!" Peter exclaimed, trying to stop the flow of blood.

"No, Peter, it's helping. Maybe it will draw out the poison."

"Hope so," he muttered, tying a bandage about her leg. "Looks like Hahle's found something. Think you can manage?" He helped her to her feet and noticed that she still could not put her full weight on her right leg. "Here, put your arm around my shoulder again and let's go see what they're so excited about."

It was such a little thing. Jeanne couldn't see why Elin was making such a fuss over a tiny creature that looked like a black toad with hand-like paws. Then Elin carefully turned the crushed body over with a hoof, and Jeanne tried not to shudder at the long curved thumb claws.

"That rode on a wolf?" Peter asked in amazement.

Elin nodded and murmured.

Jeanne shivered. "Elin says that they're quite rare, normally only found in the Fens, far north of here."

"One of the witches seems to be keeping track of our whereabouts," Peter said grimly as he studied the sky. Hahle and Elin exchanged glances. Hahle started pawing the ground and indicating his back. "Just a minute, Hahle," Peter grinned. "We have to collect our luggage before moving on."

Hahle whuffled worriedly and turned to Jeanne. "He means the pack, Hahle," she explained.

Peter looked again at the bataog. "Are humans immune to the poison, Elin? Is that why Jeanne shouldn't worry?"

The Fleet One nodded, but Peter thought he looked guilty about something. "It didn't scratch you, did it, Elin?" he added. At the Fleet One's negative shake, Peter took a tighter grip on Jeanne's waist and arm and started back to their small fire. "If you two Fleet Ones will come back to the light," he said over his shoulder, "we'll treat your cuts, too, before moving on."

* * *

They stopped in the early dawn to rest. All around them stretched the wide plain, but far in the distance ahead Peter could see a forest, one which would, he hoped, contain the glen they sought. He flexed his sore arm and glanced at shrinking scabs. His cuts were healing fast.

He glanced at Jeanne, feeling the faint fear touch him again. Though she tried hard to conceal it as she limped about, the slash on her right leg was giving her trouble. Peter's eyes narrowed as she winced and leaned against Elin.

"C'mon, Jeanne, I'm not blind. That leg hurts, and you shouldn't even be on it. Sit down and let's see how bad it is."

Jeanne started to argue, then frowned and sank onto the grass. "All right, but it doesn't feel any different than it did before. I don't think it's even started to heal."

Peter gently unwound the bandage. "You're right," he said softly, changing the stained dressings, "it hasn't healed. It's still bleeding. Elin, I thought you said humans were immune."

Elin murmured swiftly, too swiftly, Peter thought. "Elin says that sometimes there's a slight reaction to the poison, but I'll be all right." She shook her head thoughtfully. "Why do I get the impression that you're holding back something, Elin?"

The Windkin looked startled. He snorted something, then trotted away.

Jeanne looked after him. "I didn't mean to hurt his feelings."

Peter tied the fresh bandage. "How much farther is it to the Glen, Hahle? Is there someone closer who can help us?"

"Peter! It's not that serious!" She listened to Hahle's directions. "The Glen is about a day's fast ride from here. No one else is any closer, so I guess that settles that, Peter Burns."

"Just stop reacting to the poison and start healing, hmm?"

* * *

By mid-afternoon Peter stopped believing in humans' immunity to the poison. Jeanne had become feverish, and Peter's worries turned into fear for her. He turned for the thousandth time that day and watched her try to keep conscious and hang on as the Fleet Ones followed a narrow path between the trees. Elin was concerned also; the stallion kept turning to watch his rider and his walk now had a gentle, swaying motion that somehow kept the weakened Jeanne on his back. Peter hoped they would reach the Glen soon.

* * *

Dusk had deepened the shadows when Peter had Hahle stop and wait for the other two to catch up. Elin stopped beside the black stallion, waking Jeanne from her feverish half-daze. "How do you feel?" he asked.

Jeanne smiled weakly. "Awfully warm. But my leg is numb now," she lied, concealing a sharp stab of pain.

"Do you think you can hang on a while longer?"

"Sure. Lead on, Peter." Jeanne mentally crossed her fingers. Everything kept blurring before her eyes lately, and she was sure she had blacked out a few times. She felt so dizzy and weak that she marveled at how she had stayed on Elin's back this long. Peter had put together a harness with the Fleet Ones' halters, reins, and some tape he had had in his pouch to keep her on Elin's back, but she hadn't had to depend on it yet.

She lifted her head and tried to focus on Hahle and Peter as they scouted ahead down the trail. She wasn't sure if it had been a dream or not, but she vaguely remembered a one-sided argument between Peter and the Windkin earlier in the day. Peter had thought it safer for her to ride with him on Hahle. Jeanne took a tighter grip on Elin's mane and silently agreed with that idea.

But Elin hadn't. "Ride ahead with him," Elin had told Hahle, "and keep him away from her. His disbelief might disturb her powers."

Jeanne mentally shook her head. She *had* to have been dreaming.

* * *

As they rode slowly through the woods, Peter seemed to suddenly hear voices in the wind. A lilting peal of laughter rang above him and a wind rustled down to swirl about the Fleet Ones.

"Look, look! Humans!" a voice said lightly. Hahle snorted, and another light peal of laughter swirled about them.

"Who are you?" Peter asked, looking about for the source of the voices. "Where are you?"

A small bubble of light floated down from the leaves and hovered lazily before the Fleet Ones as they walked on. "Elin, Hahle," a merry voice greeted them. "Windlords, you have come seldom to the Great Woods. And now humans travel with you! The Three would be greatly interested in such news."

The bubble drifted up to land between Hahle's ears. Peter found himself staring at a tiny man dressed in a brown tunic of overlapping scales. Long transparent wings, like those of a dragonfly, lifted over his head, then folded against his back. The tiny face was all sharp angles, with its prominent cheekbones and pointed chin. The large golden eyes studied Peter from under a cloud of golden feathery hair. "Well met, Human!"

Hahle murmured swiftly and the tiny creature laughed. "No, Hahle, we will not spread tales on the winds. What care we for the doings of the Big Folk? The Elves have spoken to us of the witches' threats, but threats cannot harm those of the Old Magic."

Elin snorted exasperatedly and the tiny man sprang into the air and darted over to hover above the stallion. "Ah, Windlord! Almost you convince me to join the Free Folk in their struggle. Almost!"

Jeanne stirred. She slowly lifted her head and caught sight of the golden bubble. "A fairy!" she breathed in awe. The tiny creature laughed merrily and swung closer.

"So we are still known among the humans! Well met indeed, Human! For that, I will warn you, Windlords. You should not have brought them this way. Trolls and goblins have been roaming the Great Woods, cutting and burning, and the old trees are awakening in anger. They may try to do your humans a mischief, for there have been tree-murdering humans in the past and centuries-old wounds are but a day ago to the trees." He looked upward as laughter echoed among the leaves, then waved and sprang upwards.

Time passed slowly as the Fleet Ones walked on into the night. Peter suddenly began to feel uneasy. The trail ran now among dark, gnarled trees that creaked ominously as they passed. The branches hanging over the trail seemed to move, reaching down toward their heads. Even the shadows seemed alive with creakings and rustlings. Peter almost wished the fairy would return. He looked back, but saw no sparkling lights, just the shadows closing about them.

Jeanne lifted an unsteady hand to her head. "Something...is wrong. Deep anger...all around us."

Peter glanced at the trail, only to find that it suddenly disappeared into a closely-knit wall of tree trunks before them. The Windkin stopped and murmured uneasily. "I don't mean to insult you, Hahle, but are we lost?"

Leaves rustled dryly behind them. Elin snorted and tried to turn on the narrow path. Peter looked back and saw that the trail behind them had vanished as if it had never been. The trees creaked about them.

A golden bubble darted at the wall of trees. "Back, Old Ones! Let the Windlords pass!"

A branch brushed Peter's cheek when the stallions surged forward, following the bubble as it opened a path between the angry trees. A large branch swung slowly down at Jeanne. Elin was able to dodge underneath, but Hahle had to shy aside as the branch smashed into the ground. The black stallion reared and leaped into the opening left by the attacking tree.

Elin had vanished in the shifting shadows, but Hahle did not falter. The black stallion twisted among the reaching trees. Peter hunched low and felt branches scrape across his back. Roots humped under the stallion's hooves, snaking across the ground to trip him as he weaved among the swaying trees. A thick bough clubbed Peter's shoulder, almost knocking the boy off Hahle's back, and he flung his arms around the great neck, hanging on through sheer stubbornness.

Finally they had passed the last of the dark trees, but still Hahle raced through the quiet forest. The clear whinny of a Fleet One called through the night. Hahle answered as he ran.

In a short while the two entered a clearing deep in the woods. The stars shone coldly through the opening in the treetops, and in the starlight a gray and white stallion stood in the center of the clearing, nuzzling something on the ground. "Jeanne!" Peter cried. He slid off Hahle and knelt beside the silent girl. He turned her over, studying her white face with a growing fear. "Jeanne!" he called, trying to bring her back to consciousness. "Jeanne, don't give up now! Not now! Please!" The girl moaned softly. Her forehead was so hot that Peter panicked. "Jeanne!"

A gentle breeze ruffled his hair. "Why are you here?" a voice asked.

Peter looked up. A tall, dark-haired man muffled in a dark cloak stood behind him. "She needs help, badly," Peter explained anxiously. "A bataog scratched her and—"

"A bataog! And she still lives?" The man knelt beside Peter and lightly touched her forehead. "Thank the Green! Her life-power holds!"

"Where's the Glen?" Peter asked.

The man stood up, cradling the unconscious girl in his arms. "Near here," he replied and walked into the nearest tree.

CHAPTER 6

THE SENSITIVE

After one startled moment, Peter followed the man and Jeanne through the tree. He found himself in a space filled with white light—the floor as far as he could see radiating pure white. He could see no walls beyond its illuminated glow, only blackness where walls and a ceiling would be. He started walking, looking for some sign of the man he had followed. Near the center of the space he stopped.

At his feet were two small circles, each wide enough for a man to stand within. One was radiating a mild yellow light. The other could be a light green in color, but the light was dull on that circle. Peter wondered what the circles were. *Beacons, perhaps*? he asked himself. He looked up above the circles, but the blackness stopped his gaze, hiding what lay beyond it.

On a sudden impulse, he unslung the pack and laid it on the yellow circle. He waited a few seconds and was about to turn away when suddenly the pack rose. It shot straight up into the air, rising beyond the confining blackness.

"You are interested?" a voice asked behind him.

Peter whirled, his sword out before he had even completed the turn. He found himself facing a tall blond, seemingly teen-aged human dressed in yellow and gray, but with the unmistakable look of the elves in his large gray eyes. "Le!" Peter stared at the elf as he sheathed his sword. "You look younger."

"The result of many days healing. The Change is not kind to those under it. Your travels have made you older, Peter."

Peter shook his head. "Where is Jeanne?"

"In our place of healing," the elf replied. "She will be well cared for." He pointed to the circles at their feet. "I see that you are interested in our lift of air."

"Very." Peter grinned. "I can't decide if you people actually rely on magic or just a more advanced science than my world."

"Magic. Science." Leereho shrugged. "Is there a difference? You stand within the Watch Tower, built many ages ago when our Ancients were at the height of their strength and wisdom. You decide, Peter."

Peter looked at the expanse of white floor and the blackness surrounding it. "Watch *Tower*?"

The dim circle suddenly flashed a light green and the pack descended upon it with a faint sigh of air. Peter stared at the pack a moment, then slowly lifted his head to retrace the pack's descent. The yellow circle was now dim. "An up and a down shaft?" he asked, scooping up the pack.

"Exactly," Leereho nodded. "Would you like to try it?"

Peter grinned and stepped onto the yellow circle. "Step out at the first level, Peter," Leereho said.

The yellow circle flashed, and Peter could feel himself rising. He reached out cautiously and felt a circular wall, invisible but solid, all about him and rising with him. *It's no more than an invisible elevator*, he thought, somehow disappointed. He looked down past his feet and saw the distant floor. The elf was rising far below him. *Well, maybe more. Wish Jeanne could see this.*

The lift's speed seemed to slow. Peter shot through an opening in the once-distant ceiling and hovered, his feet a few inches above and in front of the floor in a darkened room.

Peter stepped down from the lift. Three small rectangular lights sprang on in the darkness, the faint light glowing from three screens standing atop a long counter set in the center of the tiny room. "Television, here?" Peter muttered as he strode over to investigate.

It wasn't television. A "screen" consisted of a rectangular crystal set in an open framework stand without any wires or contact with the table except the stand. He puzzled over the geometric patterns set in the counter before and between each blankly glowing screen.

"This is our public viewing room," Leereho explained as he stepped off the lift. "All of our people are allowed here. None but guardians and trained observers may enter the other rooms of this level or the eight levels above."

"Viewing room? What do you view?"

"This is the Watch Tower. We can survey many parts of this land on these screens." He moved his hand over several of the patterns as he spoke. "Or, for several people..." He waved his hand over a circle at the end of the counter. A swirl of light hovered in the air beyond the counter. "Behold," Leereho gestured.

"Nice special effects," Peter began, then stopped. The swirl expanded and solidified, and a forest clearing could be seen. In spite of the night's darkness, a magical glow seemed to hover over the clearing.

"That glow..." Peter said uneasily.

"The Glen produces its own light," Leereho said reverently. "Look closer."

Peter suddenly saw that the clearing was filled with blackened stumps and fallen trees and ashes. He could almost smell the burned wood. "A forest fire?"

Leereho nodded. "The witches do not like forests, least of all this one. Their soldiers come and kill our trees with their axes and their fires. And the witches kill our lives through the destruction of our trees. Many of us would gladly go with you on Graylod's expedition, but we would forget more the closer we go to their castle."

"Castle?"

Leereho moved his hand over the patterns again, and the swirl changed. Out of the spinning light rose a lonely crag surrounded by a sea of gray. On the top of that crag—silhouetted against the night sky by the glowing grayness below it and the glow of violet within it—was a huge castle. It seemed like a monstrous beast perched atop that crag, watching and waiting...

Peter felt his heart sink as he watched it. He suddenly remembered something Le had said. "You said 'Glen' before," he started, turning to look at Le instead of the menacing castle, "you mean, you were too late? The witches..."

Leereho nodded sadly and the swirl changed back to the original fire-blackened clearing. "That is the Glen of Ancient Voices, out beyond our lodge."

"That?" Peter looked about at the ashes. "I'm sorry you didn't arrive there in time." He paused. "Wait a minute, you said 'Graylod's expedition.' Has Graylod been here recently? He never came to Gimstan Mountain. The dwarfs never saw him."

"I heard he was here." Leereho gestured at the image. "And there, in the Glen, at the exact time the fire began, he vanished. The witches must have him."

"And you aren't going to do anything about it?" Peter asked. "They burn your woods, capture Graylod, turn you into a walking zombie, and you still do nothing?"

"We cannot *do* anything!" Leereho exploded. He visibly controlled himself and erased the image. "Our powers are sapped by the witches," he said slowly. "Our magic is leaving us, and with that, our lives. You and the girl can help us, or so the Elder says. Myself, I believe Graylod's legend of a Sensitive."

"What is a Sensitive? And how could he help you?"

"A Sensitive...it is hard to define." Leereho mused. "He is a healer—at a single touch he can heal. He is sensitive to the emotions of others and therefore he could not physically harm anyone, not even a witch, when in full possession of his powers. He can also harness another's emotions to his will, making him do whatever wished. I am not sure how these and the other powers of a Sensitive could destroy a witch, but that is the one clear memory that Graylod possessed, and he was a great wizard before the witches came."

"What good are wizards, anyhow?" Peter blurted. He could have bitten his tongue after he asked, but Leereho didn't seem to take offense.

"The wizards are the guardians of our lands," Leereho said slowly. "I know that you believe they failed in this case, but we did have victory with our defeat. Nine witches and warlocks banded together to attack our land. Only seven of our guardians woke to the danger soon enough."

Leereho stared at the blank screens. "They had planned their attack well. We would have been lost except for their overconfidence. Through that we were able to attack them and defend our land. Of our seven guardians, six died—taking six with them. The only survivor was Graylod."

"Six and six—I wouldn't call that a victory," Peter disagreed.

"You do not know the ways of magic. Witches and warlocks, users of the Evil Ones' strength, have almost limitless powers. A wizard's magic is the green of life and the use of that power drains the user. The loss of our six was overbalanced by the loss of their six and the weakening of the remaining three."

"The three witches are weak?" Peter shook his head. "If they can cause all this trouble when they're weak, I'm glad we're not facing them at their full strength."

"They are still very dangerous," Leereho agreed. "But even witches have their vulnerable point. You discovered for yourself in the caverns that the Dark One, the shadow witch, hates light."

"That was the Dark One?" Peter gulped. "The one that turned you into a zombie? Wait, how did you know we met her? Were you watching us?"

Leereho nodded. "Even with Elin and Hahle to protect you, I was worried as to your safety. I only found you that one time on the viewer and even that was by accident. The viewers focus only on places—they do not locate people."

"I guess that makes sense," Peter yawned. "I'm too tired to even try to figure out how these viewers work without cameras." He yawned again. The effects of riding all day and worrying about Jeanne had finally caught up with him. He felt exhausted.

Leereho noticed the yawns. "I am sorry. I had forgotten that humans need sleep. We need it only when we are badly wounded. Follow me, Peter."

When they returned to the clearing outside the Watch Tower, the dark-cloaked man was waiting by the Fleet Ones. "So you have returned, Leereho. I have been waiting to speak with Peter." He dismissed the Fleet Ones and strode up to them. "The Fleogende speak highly of you, human."

"As do I, also, Elder," Leereho added.

"Elin tells me that somehow you or your friend have broken the curse of the witch hounds."

Peter wondered at the cloaked one's words but felt too tired to try following the conversation. "How is Jeanne?" he asked.

"She has not regained consciousness yet, and I see trouble for her unless..." He glanced sharply at Peter. "But I see Hahle was correct to warn me of your fatigue. You will sleep first, and later I will tell you more."

"No, tell me now," Peter insisted. "What's wrong with Jeanne?"

"Sleep first," the Elder replied. "You will need your wits about you."

"I'm not that...tired," Peter protested. He yawned. The Elder seemed amused, and a sudden thought hit Peter. "You're not...going to put..." he yawned, "...me...to sleep." He could no longer keep his eyes open. He suddenly seemed to be drifting down a long shaft, cushioned by the surrounding darkness. He toppled forward and was fast asleep when the Elder caught him.

*   *   *

Peter slowly opened his eyes. He blinked sleepily at a wall-sized panel of stained glass. Bright colors rippled across the floor and ceiling, patterned the neighboring walls. He burrowed under the blankets heaped over him, trying to get back to sleep, when he suddenly remembered what had happened the night before.

He climbed out of bed and, after discovering that he wore only a long shirt that reached to his knees, began searching for his clothes.

The door slowly creaked open. "Who's there?" Peter called, diving back into bed.

Leereho appeared around the half-open door. "It is only I," he said cheerily. "Are you going to sleep the day away?"

"Some chance with you around. How's Jeanne?"

Leereho's cheeriness dissolved. "Not good. The Elder wishes to see you."

"Where're my clothes?"

* * *

Peter's expression was grim as he followed Leereho down numerous corridors. Before, this journey and its dangers had seemed but an unreal adventure. He had never thought that either of them could be badly hurt or killed. *Not Jeanne, please*, he pleaded silently. *Don't let her die.*

He stared blindly at the door before him, not hearing Leereho's calm assurances. Then the elf left him, and he stood alone before the door, still staring at the rich grain of the wood and seeing instead his last sight of Jeanne. He slowly opened the door.

The room was filled with light and color. Peter briefly saw panels of stained glass in the ceiling and walls, and pillars and beams of silver-hued wood, before his attention focused on the tall elf at the other side of the large room. The Elder sat at the center of a curved table, his dark eyes staring fixedly into a small white crystal sphere before him on the table top. Peter hesitated as he neared the table, reluctant to disturb the stillness.

The Elder looked up, his eyes welcoming. "I sent for you, Peter," he started gently, "because I know that we cannot help your friend."

"Can't? But—"

"I have examined the past," the Elder continued, ignoring Peter's interruption. "You found a ring when you entered our land—a plain band of gold. Do you still have it with you?"

"Why, yes, I think so," Peter replied after some thought. He dug into the pouch on his belt. "Yes, here it is. But what does it have to do with Jeanne?"

The Elder rose. "Come with me," he said. "Bring the ring also."

Silvery curtains, delicate as spider web, divided the healing place into large and small sections, seemingly at random. Sleeping elves occupied most of the beds they passed, but Peter did spy a bandaged dwarf, whose snores stirred the gauzy hangings.

Someone robed and hooded in dark green stepped from the section ahead. The Elder fingered the thick layers of web. "So much shielding, Healer."

The cowl was lifted from long white hair, but the woman's face was unlined and ageless. "She is too weak to shield herself from the pain of others, Elder."

"Jeanne?" Peter asked. "Is Jeanne in there? How is she?"

Tears glistened in the healer's blue eyes. "The poison is stronger than any of my remedies."

Peter fumbled for the opening in the curtains. The Elder joined him at Jeanne's bedside. "Her fever's gone, but her hand's so cold! Can't you do anything?" he pleaded, glancing up at the tall elf beside him.

"There is only one thing that can be done," the Elder said solemnly. "Give her the ring."

"The ring?" Peter queried, looking from the plain band of gold in his hand to the pale face of the girl before him.

"Yes," the Elder said. "Put it into her hand."

Peter, greatly mystified, did as he was directed, and was startled at the sudden change in the girl. Jeanne shivered, then her breathing quieted and her face grew peaceful.

Peter looked up at the Elder. "Is she…" He left the word unsaid.

The Elder smiled. "She sleeps now."

"But the ring," Peter persisted. "How did that…"

"The only person a Sensitive cannot heal by herself," the Elder said, "is herself."

CHAPTER 7

THE TAKEN

Peter stared at the Elder in bewildered surprise. "You mean, *she*'s a Sensitive?"

The Elder nodded, seeming both surprised and amused at Peter's disbelief. "Yes, she is. You did not know that anyone but a Sensitive would have died moments after a scratch from a bataog?"

"Died?" Peter choked.

"Leereho was released from the Change at her touch," the Elder continued. "No one but a Sensitive can free a Changed slave against a witch's will."

"A Sensitive," Peter said dazedly.

"You did not suspect? Even the Fleet Ones did, but," he corrected himself, "Elin was once a student of a wizard and would know the signs of Talent."

"I thought she was only an empath. She didn't mention anything about healing people."

"Apparently the healing Talent was not awakened until she entered this land. Had she remained in your world, she would have remained 'only' an empath, in the same way as you would have remained 'only' a human." He studied the boy closely. "She is still the same person she was, Peter."

"I know that," Peter said, rumpling his sandy hair in exasperation. "I've been around her long enough to know that it's just the name that suddenly makes her different. I mean, it makes her sound powerful when everything that makes her Jeanne also labels her a Sensitive."

One of the Elder's eyebrows lifted. "I see now why the Watcher chose the way it did."

"Well, I wish you'd explain it to me. All your Watcher has done for us is trap us in a land that we both want to leave—alive, if possible." Peter knew he was being insolent, but he was too upset at the moment to worry about the consequences.

She could have died, he thought. *Would have died, even here, if it hadn't been for that ring.* He turned back to her and caught his breath.

A shimmering light hovered about the gold ring on the palm of the girl's opened hand. The plain band of gold now sparkled faintly with soft lights, almost as though it was acquiring a life of its own from the touch of the girl's hand.

Her free hand stirred slightly over the coverlet, and Jeanne's eyes slowly opened. The roaming blue-gray eyes fastened on him as if he was the one solid figure in a dream-like world.

"Hi, Peter," she said faintly.

"Hi, Jeanne." Peter swallowed. "How do you feel?"

"Awfully tired," the girl sighed. She stirred restlessly. "Where is Elin? He lied about the bataog."

Peter heard a faint chuckle from behind him. "I know, Jeanne. We'll tell him off later. You feel better now, don't you?"

"Much better. And…different." She struggled to keep her eyes open. "Peter?"

He put his hand over hers, closing it about the ring. "I'm here, Jeanne. There's nothing to be afraid of. Just rest and get well."

He felt her hand relax and knew that she had fallen asleep. He closed her hand tighter about the ring and turned back to the Elder. "And to think I've been carrying that ring in my pocket all along. What is it?"

The Elder also watched the light shimmering about the girl's hand. "The Ring of Calada. The Name-thief's Bane. I had forgotten it."

"Why did you call it that? I thought a bane was deadly."

"When the mad king Etrom decreed that all wizards in his land give him their names to be controlled by him or face the curse of the Menstui, the life-drinker, the wizard Calada gave her name and her powers to a ring she wore and left her small cottage. The Menstui twice found a ragged peasant with a glittering ring, but never the wizard it sought. The mad king later lost control of the Menstui and was killed by it, after the visit of a strange peasant woman to his hall."

"And Calada?" Peter whispered.

"There are many more tales of Calada. But we were speaking of her ring. It appears and disappears again and again in our history, choosing now a wizard, then a ruler, and once a peasant child to belong to and work with. All of its powers have never been listed, but we do know that it amplifies the powers of its owner."

"And now it's chosen Jeanne," Peter marveled.

The Elder nodded. "Until it was dampened by your disbelief. Your powers are strong, but contrary to magic."

Peter shook his head. "I don't have any powers. But I do wish I could sense things as Jeanne does."

"It is not difficult to learn," the Elder said. "You have learned from Jeanne already. All you need is belief that it is possible."

Peter opened his mouth to disagree and the tall elf firmly ushered him out of the place of healing. "Jeanne will need rest to fully recover from the poison. You can argue as we walk."

Peter frowned as he was hurried down the many corridors. "I still don't fully believe in magic," he said slowly.

"And that is your strength. That is why the Watcher picked you, along with Jeanne." At Peter's startled look, the Elder continued, "I will explain more, later, Peter. We are in the midst of preparing for a gathering of people from all across this land. And I fear that even in this sheltered place you and Jeanne will need guards against the witches' spies."

Outside the door to the Council Chambers stood the patient Leereho. "Did you wish to see me, Elder?"

"Yes, Leereho. Peter, Jeanne should be stronger by tonight, and I will try to explain your powers to you both then. Until that time, Leereho will be your guard and guide to Drwseren."

* * *

Leereho's task was not as easy as it sounded. The elves' "village," Peter discovered, was a sprawling building that would have rivaled an Earthly mansion. From the inside. From the outside, however, the building was as invisible as those in the village of the Open Door. "Why should we disturb the beauty of the forest?" Leereho asked after Peter's muttered complaints.

"Yes, but how do you ever find the door?" He walked around the entrance, touching trees and bushes, and found that no solid building blocked his way.

Leereho tested his bow. "Our friends know the entrances. Others who come for the gathering will have trouble finding our home, and I must help give directions, as well as guard against intruders. I am glad that you are patient enough to accompany me."

"Beats sitting in my room. What is this gathering?" Peter asked as he watched the elf pick his way soundlessly through the fallen leaves. Leaves rustled at Peter's every step.

"People from all over the Free Lands will come to meet here and discuss the woes of the witches' rule. Some would say that this is useless talk, for we cannot plan against the witches, but in this way we learn what the witches are doing throughout the lands and can make some guess as to what they will do next.

"All will come—dwarfs from the Healic Ranges and Gimstan Mountain, my cousin and kin from all the scattered forests and glens, Renw's people, the wizards that are left, and others of the Free Folk."

"But the witch just burned your Glen! Is it safe to hold a gathering here?"

"No place is safe from the witches. Our more powerful people patrol the borders of the Mist Lands—the Glen will be close enough for them. The Glen is also centrally located to the two dwarf strongholds."

"I thought dwarfs didn't like elves."

"Only in their mountains. The dwarfs prefer to keep the secrets of their strongholds safely hidden. They are good people, and valuable allies. The Folk would not have lasted so long without their strength."

A twig snapped under Peter's foot, and a startled rabbit looked up and scurried away. Peter sighed as the rabbit disappeared into the underbrush. "I'm about as quiet as an elephant. I wish you could teach me to walk the way you do, Le." He picked up the broken twig and threw it after the rabbit. There was a startled sound as the twig landed, and bushes waved wildly.

Peter looked curiously into the deep shadows. An eerie chill crept up his spine when he suddenly noticed a pair of angry red eyes staring back at him. "Le!" he whispered warningly, backing a step as he fumbled for his sword.

He barely had the blade clear of its sheath when a huge wolf crashed through the concealing bushes. Its red eyes still fastened on the human with an evil malice, the wolf gathered itself, and sprang.

Its weight knocked Peter to the ground, and he struggled frantically, trying to use his sword, which was pinned under the wolf. Suddenly he realized that the wolf was not moving.

"Are you hurt, my friend?" Leereho asked anxiously. With one hand, the elf pulled the heavy body off the boy, and Peter suddenly saw the bright feathers of an arrow buried deeply in the dark fur.

"You...shot..." Peter forced himself to take a deep, shuddering breath and release it. "Th-thanks, Le." The elf nodded as he drew another arrow from his quiver.

"T'which I add me thanks, also, Leereho," a cheery voice suddenly said. "That one had pursued me long."

"Who's there?" Peter called, watching the silent forest.

Leereho dismissed the voice. "It is only Bryan. Are you quite sure you are unhurt, Peter?"

The voice sputtered with anger. "Only Bryan? Tis that the welcome I be getting? Be not surprised t'find yerself ensnared by the nearest tree. Only Bryan! An' who be that odd young elf with ye?"

"I would introduce you if you would stop hiding," Leereho said calmly. Peter tried to hide his smile as he sheathed his sword.

"Hidin'!" the voice snorted. A short, red-haired man jumped from the branches of a nearby tree. Peter watched wordlessly as the tiny man, who only came up to the boy's waist, straightened his green jacket and fluffed his fringe of reddish beard. "Bryan of the Emerald Wood at yer service," he said with an elaborate bow.

"Peter Burns," the boy responded, quickly copying the bow. He studied the small man. Somehow Bryan looked familiar. "You're not an elf, are you?"

"An elf?" Bryan snorted. "Did ye never see a leprechaun before?"

Peter's jaw almost dropped. "You're a leprechaun?"

The small sprite watched him warily. "Sure an' I am. An' ye are of humankind." His eyes narrowed. "I carry not a pot of gold about with me, human."

"I don't want anybody's gold," Peter sighed. "Dwarf's, leprechaun's, or even witch's."

Bryan stared in surprise. "Not want... Well, did ye ever see the like?" He shrugged and turned to Leereho.

The leprechaun straightened his jacket again, brushed at his trousers, and cleared his throat. "I was sent t' this gatherin', Leereho, t'complain of a serious problem an' t'ask yer elfin Elder for the Wise's help in the solvin' of it."

"The gathering is not in session yet, Bryan."

"Aye, but I wish t'know now from ye what yer Elder plans t'do about those accursed hounds."

"Do?" Peter inserted. "What can he do?"

"That I do not know," Bryan dismissed the question. "But t'was bad enough that we must endure the presence of witches in our fair land.

Now the Dark One demands more—me very folk!"

"You mean the witches are taking your people?" Peter asked.

"Aye, that they are. Those hounds of the shadow witch come right int' our woods, bold as ye please, an' fly off with many of me folk an' kin." The leprechaun's eyes darkened. "We be not as quick with our arrows and slings as ye elves. We are craftsmen, Green blast the creatures, not soldiers!"

"Bryan," Leereho started sadly.

The leprechaun glowered at him. "Have ye ever known me t'lightly ask the help of the Wise? Me people live not in one place as ye folk do. Our wee cottages are scattered far an' 'twixt our woods an' the nearest neighbor too far t'help. Glad we would be t'fight, but who can stop a fleeing shadow?"

"But why are the hounds taking people?" Peter asked.

"Ye might well ask why, but we have had no answer. Tis the shadow witch's winged beasties that take me folk an' few return from her clutches."

Leereho shivered, and Peter saw the effort it took for him to fit the arrow to his bowstring. The elf studied the silent forest. "Has this been happening often?"

"The takin' of me folk? Often? Hardly a day goes by that the beasties are not traipsin' through our land." He glanced at his callused palms and snorted. "Meself, the greatest warrior of the Sidhe, forced t'hide in trees like a wee squirrel. An' those beasties travel in pairs. The second one should still be about."

Leereho nodded, his quick eyes watching the forest.

"Where do your people live?" Peter asked.

"In an emerald wood in the western shadow of Gimstan Mountain."

Leereho suddenly blinked and met Peter's eyes, and Peter knew they shared the same thought. The witch was probably still searching for Jeanne and himself around Gimstan Mountain, and the leprechauns suffered as a result. He shivered at a sudden thought. If that was the case, then whose hounds had ambushed them on the plains?

"We shall speak with the Elder about this," Leereho said. He nodded to Peter, indicating that he meant their idea also.

"Aye, that we shall." The leprechaun sighed as he gazed on the blackened ruins a few feet before them. "Has ashes become the fate of yer fair Glen?"

"Yes." Leereho frowned. "The witches do not favor green."

Bryan scowled and kicked at the rubble. "The Ancients were so powerful once. An' now they cannot even protect their own." His eyes suddenly widened, and he dived into the ashes. "Some green remains!" he shouted gleefully.

The leprechaun thrust aside a charred log and uncovered a young sprout. "Look, Leereho!" The elf hurried to help the excited Bryan. Peter stared in amazement as the trees they freed stirred and began growing before his eyes. Green beckoned from further down the blackened hollow and, shaking his head in bewilderment, the boy joined the two digging in the ashes.

Peter lifted a heavy branch away from a sheltered patch of green and hesitated, feeling a chill wind suddenly rise behind him. A prickling alarm stirred.

Something slammed into his left shoulder and, with a sickening jerk that nearly wrenched his arm from its socket, pulled him up into the sky. Peter looked up—and straight into a black beady eye set in a wedge-shaped head. A hound had him!

"Le!" he shouted in despair.

An arrow whistled past Peter's head. The hound shrieked, and its grasp loosened.

Peter pulled the dagger from his belt and stabbed the talons wrapped about his left arm and shoulder. The hound shrieked again, but did not release him. Hissing angrily, the sharp beak twisted toward him.

An arrow struck the exposed neck. The hound straightened, rising higher with a jerk that sent its claws deeper into his shoulder.

Peter glanced at the treetops brushing by his feet and shuddered. It would be a long fall if the hound released him now. Steeling himself, he slashed again at the talons. He had no desire to meet the hound's owner.

The cold wind closed about them. Peter glanced downward and could no longer see the tiny figures of Le and Bryan, only the dark green of the forest far below.

CHAPTER 8

THE FLEET ONE

"Come. There is little time."

Jeanne opened her eyes and found herself standing in a yellow glow. Shimmering panels of multicolored light divided the yellow space, but she could see nothing else around her.

"Hurry." The voice was feminine and seemed to come from behind the rainbow-colored panel directly before her.

Jeanne slowly touched the panel and the shimmering light parted before her hand. She stepped through and found herself in a larger area of yellow, with more panels seemingly hung at random. "Where are you?" she asked. She had no memory of how she had come to this place; the last she remembered was Peter's voice telling her to rest.

"This is what you were meant to do." Jeanne turned towards the source of the voice. She couldn't see anyone, but this had to be a dream. She might as well go along with it. She began walking in the direction of the voice and soon found herself facing another panel.

"I will help you until you learn to do this yourself. Hurry, there is little time."

Jeanne stepped through the panel and blinked as the yellow glow vanished. She was standing at someone's bedside but she saw no more than that when her awareness of others suddenly returned. She caught the gray webbing beside her for support. The pain she sensed should have overwhelmed her, but something blocked it. "I am with you," the voice whispered. "You must do this."

"What? What must I do?" Jeanne tried not to cry at the pain. There wasn't anything she could do. Why was she here?

A glow beside her caught her attention. It seemed to be coming from her hand. She looked deep into the rainbow-colored glow, then slowly lifted her hand and reached out to touch the being on the bed.

A gasp came from behind her. "No, human! Do not touch—"

Her hand made contact, and a multicolored flash of light blinded her.

* * *

Peter stopped struggling when he tired. Nothing he had done seemed to have weakened the hound, which still glided swiftly on the cold magical winds. The forest vanished into the distance. Below him the waving greens and browns of a plain diminished into a growing stretch of white.

Peter closed his eyes in despair. He had never felt so helpless. *I'm trapped in a nightmare*, he thought. *This can't be real*!

The hound suddenly shuddered, and the cold wind bearing them vanished. Peter looked up and saw the mighty wings beating with an effort, the ugly head straining to lift the massive body. Peter renewed his struggles, slashing the gripping talons with his dagger. The hound tried to regain lost altitude, but Peter's struggles dragged it down. Thirty, fifteen, then ten feet...the ground came closer. Suddenly the talons released their cruel grasp, and Peter fell the short distance to the ground. He rolled and sat up, spitting sand, to watch as the hound fought to regain the skies.

The ugly creature abruptly crumbled in midair and plunged to the ground a short distance from Peter. He watched the huddled heap suspiciously, but it did not move again.

Peter looked about to see which direction was west. He had been carried far from the forest, but he remembered the aerial view. Using the remainder of his sleeve to bandage his torn and bleeding shoulder, he set out across the desert.

* * *

"I told you not to touch him. You are much too weak to try healing people yet."

"What..." Jeanne blinked up at the face above her. Blue eyes, long white hair, but the features weren't quite human or elf. She suddenly realized that she was sitting on the floor beside a bed.

"How could you be out of bed already? The healing trance should have kept you asleep until nightfall at the very least."

"Healing trance?" Jeanne felt very confused. What was she doing here? The pride and gratitude radiating from this woman—directed at her!—mixed with concern was also troubling. What had happened?

The woman glanced at the person in the bed and then crouched beside her. "Thank the Green, you did come, despite your own injury. It was not his time and he did not want to leave us, but there was nothing more I could have done."

Jeanne blinked owlishly at the woman. It was getting very hard to keep her eyes open. She felt so tired. The woman smiled and nodded as if she had spoken. "Now it is time for you to heal yourself. Come, I will help you back to your own bed. And there you will stay until I give you leave."

* * *

The sun glared down at him. Heat waves danced across the sands. Peter felt parched. He stared sightlessly at a mirage lake as he plodded, then abruptly shook his head and realized that he was staring at a dried lakebed. He looked closer at the land about him.

The desert, which stretched as far as he could see, oddly resembled a mixture of both forest and plains that had been struck by a sudden drought and covered with sand. He remembered the scattered patches of fallen trees he had found buried in the sand and recalled also that the trunks of several had been burned. *Wonder if the witches attacked this place like they did the Glen. But why? What's out here?*

The day wore on. Peter found ravines that could once have been streambeds and tried digging, hoping to hit water, with little success. The heat grew so intense by afternoon that Peter had no choice but to hide from the sun's relentless rays. By then he had entered an area cluttered with sand dunes of every size. He dug into one of them, making a small, cool, if sandy refuge, and tried to forget his thirst in sleep.

* * *

Jeanne perched on the edge of the bed, staring fixedly at the gray webbing before her. She found herself rubbing her right leg again, and frowned thoughtfully. The slash was gone, healed as if it had never been, and she must have been here for a long time for that to have happened. But no one was giving her any straight answers. The white-haired healer had insisted that she had to wait for their Elder for explanations, and had brought her some clean clothes only when Jeanne had promised to stay where she was. Jeanne already regretted the promise. She was obviously in a type of hospital, and she hated hospitals, mainly because of the mixed feelings of pain and fear that usually filled them. But somehow the gray webbing seemed to be shielding her. From where she sat she could still sense the emotions radiating from the patients, but the sensations were not as strong as when she had opened the webbing to look beyond. *Why do I sense things like this?* she thought tiredly. *It wouldn't be so bad if I could do something about it, but I can't!*

She looked carefully down at her left hand, remembering the strange dream about the ring she had found on her finger when she had awakened. It was still there, still only a plain band of gold, with no glow about it at all.

She looked up expectantly, recognizing the white-haired healer's emotions approaching the webbing. There was someone else with her, and Jeanne thought there was something vaguely familiar about the elf. *Elf, huh? Now I can tell if someone is an elf from their emotions?*

She tried not to wince as the webbing opened to admit her visitors, but the healer noticed and quickly sealed the opening. The tall elf with her shook his head. "I must apologize, this is not the best place for someone who can sense emotions as you can. But your condition when you arrived—"

Jeanne stood up. "You know I can sense—who told you?" *Calm down*, she told herself. *This isn't Amy Evans.*

The concern she sensed from him also relieved her fears. "Elin warned me that you were afraid to let others know of your gift. Please believe me when I tell you that we do not fear you or mistrust you because of it. Such a gift is highly valued in our Lands. Those who possess it are known as Sensitives and are much respected."

Jeanne sat down, not trusting her legs enough to stand. At the same time, she wondered why she was so surprised. In a land where magic existed, surely her ability was commonplace. *I don't have to hide anymore.* A weight seemed to fall away from her. "You know about this type of...gift? You can help me with it?"

The elf smiled at her. "I can try. But we have not been introduced. I am the Elder of Drwseren. What would you like to know first?"

"I'm Jeanne Tucker. What would I like to know?" She suddenly did not know where to begin. "Everything." She smiled. "I probably sound like Peter. Where is Peter? And how long have I been here?"

"You and Peter arrived here last night. It is now past the middle of the day."

"Last night?! But the slash is completely healed..." Jeanne suddenly remembered one story she had read. "Oh, I understand. You healed me."

"No," the healer started, then halted what she was about to say and turned to the Elder.

"No, we did not heal you," the Elder said carefully. "You did."

"I did?"

"You, and the ring you now wear. It once belonged to a powerful wizard named Calada."

"It's magic?" Jeanne looked down at the ring. It didn't look magical.

"Very," the Elder said, a hint of amusement in his mind. Jeanne looked at him, but his attention was on the healer. "It is probably why you have healed faster than either of us thought to expect. It amplifies the powers of its bearer and you," he turned his attention back to her, "like any Sensitive, can heal the ills you sense."

"Heal? Me?" Jeanne suddenly remembered her dream. *Was it a dream?* She turned to the white-haired woman. "I'm a healer like you?"

The healer shook her head. "Not like me. I must rely on spells and potions. You have the healing touch."

"Elder," a voice said from outside the webbing, "there is trouble. The healer is needed as well."

The Elder nodded to Jeanne. "We will return. I know you have many more questions." The two were swiftly gone, and Jeanne stared thoughtfully at the swaying webbing.

I'm a healer? She rose to her feet and stopped before the webbing. Taking a deep breath, she stepped through. She closed her eyes as the pain swirled about her. *It's not too bad*, she told herself. It was much less than she remembered from her last hospital stay on Earth. Most of the patients she sensed about her were asleep. She remembered that the healer had mentioned a trance of some type. Whatever it was, it seemed to be working for many of the patients. Except one. She opened her eyes, frowning slightly, and turned towards where the pain was the "noisiest". *If I'm supposed to be a healer, then I can do something about that.*

Checking to make certain the healer was not about, she let go of the webbing and started walking. She glanced down at her hand and was startled to see a faint glow about the ring. *Magic ring, remember? Wait until Peter sees this.* She wondered where he was. The Elder had seemed vaguely uneasy when she had asked about him. The glow brightened but Jeanne was suddenly only aware of one pattern in the emotions about her. *Oh, they're letting him sleep in.* The impression was faint, but that could be due to the webbing around her. *Or because*

I still don't know what I'm doing.

She stopped before a silvery curtain, then took a deep breath and entered. Inside was a small patch of green: grass that came almost up to her knees and a bush with oddly silver branches. The patient stood up, and Jeanne found herself looking into the yellow eyes of a large black wolf.

Jeanne remained still and tried to think. The pain she had sensed was coming from the wolf. And she doubted very much that the elves would be caring for a witch hound.

The wolf looked at her. "Sorry to intrude," she said, deciding not to risk rudeness. "I'm here to help, if I can." She forced herself to step closer. Almost hidden against the blackness of the fur were burns wrapping about the muzzle and the back. She blinked back tears of pain and realized that there was an odd tingle in her mind associated with the pain. "Those were caused by magic!"

The wolf yawned. "Okay, so you knew that already. I've never...sensed that before." She looked at her hands, noticing that the glow from the ring was much brighter than before, then back at the wolf. "Uh, I have to touch you. Will you allow it?"

The wolf opened its mouth in what Jeanne sensed was a laugh, then walked up and sat down at her feet. Jeanne put her hands on its head, and the ring flared with rainbow-colored light.

* * *

The shrieks of hounds woke Peter. He peeked out of his refuge to see the sun setting and thousands of hounds streaming across the red-streaked sky, shrieking to each other as they flew. He shivered as he watched the dark line—not from fear, but from the cold. He had abandoned his cloak long ago on the desert sands and now Peter belatedly remembered that nights in a desert, unlike the days, were cold. He tried to warm himself as he waited for the hounds to leave and suddenly discovered that his torn shoulder was hot and swelling.

Moving the throbbing shoulder carefully, he muttered, "The one time I can't wash out a cut so naturally it gets infected. What next?"

The last of the hounds left the darkening sky, and Peter cautiously crept out of his refuge. Cramped muscles complained and the back of his neck felt as if it had been burned red by the sun. Orienting himself with the setting sun, Peter started toward the far-distant forest, setting a fast pace for himself so as to keep warm.

* * *

Jeanne could smell grass, but the side of her face seemed to be resting on a floor rather than dirt. *Not again*, she mentally sighed. She opened her eyes and found herself looking into yellow eyes surrounded by black fur. "Hi. Feeling better?" A moist tongue caught her right in the face. She smiled. "Couldn't resist, could you?"

She slowly sat up, surprised at how tired she felt. The ground still felt like a floor, rather than the dirt her eyes said was beneath her. All this, the grass and the bush, must be an illusion. *Her idea of a healing place*. The wolf waited until she was settled, then sat, black-furred back towards Jeanne, and looked over her shoulder at the human.

Despite herself, Jeanne was shocked. The burn was completely gone. *I really am a healer*!

* * *

Something nudged his shoulder. Peter could hear voices whispering, but he somehow couldn't find the strength to open his eyes. *Probably only a dream anyhow*, he thought, wishing the chill of the cold sands would help against the fever from his infected shoulder.

"Far gone," the voices whispered. "Should we try to save him?"

"It would be the least we could do," a bass rumble answered.

"But can we? We need help from him and if he cannot provide it…"

"He will. Humans are supposedly strong."

"It's a human?!"

"Too strong. We have vengeance to settle with humans," a shrill voice chimed.

"But not with him or at this time. Haven't you heard? Old scores are to be settled."

"But where can we take him? He looks as if he cannot stand a long journey."

"The gathering will have to do for him," the rumble decided. "His own kind may be there to save him."

"But you weren't going to go!"

"No. I thought they were only going to talk. But if a human has entered the Lands again, more than talk will take place at this gathering. Nudge him again. He must be conscious by now and I can't do anything without his help."

The gentle push came again, and Peter summoned strength enough to open his eyes. But where were his rescuers? He saw nothing but the moon in the night sky above him.

"Ah, you see? His eyes are open," the bass rumble came again. "He will need help, young one."

A gentle push came from behind him, helping him to a sitting position, and Peter blinked as he saw his rescuers. The horses regarded him with unblinking eyes. The mounting fever blurred the strange sight and, with a shiver, Peter forced his gaze to clear. The Fleet Ones watched him silently as he tried unsuccessfully to struggle to his feet. A deep sigh coming from before him made him halt to stare.

The Fleet One directly before him was a mighty stallion, deep black with a few splashes of white on his muzzle and forequarters. A deep murmur came from him, and, in his dazed condition, Peter could understand its bass rumble. "Help him to his feet, young ones, and guide him to my back."

Supported by two excited young pintos, Peter stumbled over to the stallion. "Now then, human," the stallion addressed him, "I suppose you can ride a horse. Mind you don't yank my mane out."

Peter nodded and proceeded to weakly scramble onto the Windkin's back, assisted by his two young helpers. The world swam red before his eyes once he was atop the Fleet One, and he almost fell off. "Whoa, there, human!" the stallion snorted. "I expected you to stay on longer than that! Hang onto my mane—not so tightly!—and we'll be off."

A chill wind suddenly rose, and Peter felt an icy touch at his heart. "The white hounds! Windrunner, the white hounds are coming!" a shrill voice bleated.

The stallion looked into the darkness. "Marlarn, Fedder, you know what to do. Lead the spirits elsewhere, the rest take cover."

As the Fleet Ones hurried to do their leader's bidding, Peter managed to mumble, "The white hounds?"

"Spirits of those of this land who died serving Evil," the stallion quickly explained. "There will never be any rest for them as they are doomed to forever wander, always the servants of Evil and the curse of any they meet. And now, hang on!" The stallion surged forward over the desert sands.

As Peter glanced back over his shoulder, he could see white shapes floating after them. A chill crept up his spine. "Ghosts!" he whispered hoarsely.

The Windkin nodded. "Hang on tight, human. You are in for a ride!" The Fleet One shot forward with a terrifying burst of speed, leaving the chill of the spirits behind them.

* * *

"And you mean you two just stood there and let the hound carry him away?" Jeanne stormed. She glared at Leereho, but her anger was diminishing. She knew that the elf felt as badly as she did about Peter's capture.

She turned to the Windkin beside her. "Please, Elin, we have to go after him."

Elin shook his head and pawed at the ashes of the Glen. "No, Jeanne, you know we cannot," he said gently. "The Elder would not permit you to leave."

"And night would be the worst time to start across the desert," Hahle cut in. He shivered. "The white hounds are out now."

Elin blew the hair out of her face. "You just recovered from the poison, Jeanne. You are not strong enough to search for him."

"He's probably facing the Dark One right now," Renw said gloomily.

"No!" Jeanne protested, horrified. She glanced between them all, Windkin and elf, for reassurance and, finding none, whirled and started running back to the Watch Tower. She knew the Elder was still there. *Him and his "tour",* she thought angrily. *All this time he knows Peter had been captured, but he leaves it up to Leereho to tell me.*

Her speed slowed as she went back over the events in her mind. *I don't think he did it on purpose. He probably meant to tell me, but first he had to calm down the healer, and Leereho and Elin showed up for a visit...* She smiled faintly at the memory, then stopped and turned as she sensed two Windkin approaching. "The Elder will just have to listen, Elin. I'm not going to leave Peter out there."

Elin nudged her gently. "Don't pay any attention to Renw, Jeanne. We don't know anything for certain. Remember, the hound *was* wounded. And Peter is a strong human. I'm sure he escaped."

Jeanne hugged the stallion. "Thanks, Elin," she whispered into the silky mane. She moved back and started walking towards the Watch Tower, the Fleet Ones keeping step with her. "I just know he escaped. I can catch his feelings now and again. There's no fear, but I keep getting feverish impressions."

"Most likely it's your own fever returning, Jeanne," Hahle said gently. "You better get some rest. We'll alert our people to be on the lookout for him."

Jeanne looked closely at each stallion. She nervously twisted the ring on her finger. "You don't believe me," she said slowly. "I know, I'm having enough trouble believing this 'Sensitive' business myself. But Peter *is* on his way back."

The two Fleet Ones exchanged glances. "Now, Jeanne," Elin said slowly, "even our most powerful Sensitive could never sense emotions over a long distance."

"I can! And he *is* coming back!" Jeanne closed her mouth before she said any more. *It's like arguing with the healer. I'm not even normal here.*

"Magic," Hahle snorted. "I hope she's right, Elin. I rather like the boy myself."

"I do, too, Hahle." Elin sighed and swung his head towards the Watch Tower. "The Elder won't let you leave, Jeanne, and he'll probably keep us here as your guardians so that word of your presence doesn't reach the gathering. So let's think about what he *will* let you do."

* * *

Morning found the two travelers still on the desert. "See, human," the stallion was saying as Peter groggily awoke. "Forests in the distance. There'll be water and help there." The Windkin was obviously tired, but his majestic head was still held high.

"I'm tiring you out," Peter mumbled. "I better walk for awhile."

"Stay on, human!" the stallion ordered. "If you would get off, getting you back on would be more trouble than a rest is worth. Stay on and rest, human. Old I may be, but weak I am not. The forest is coming closer."

* * *

Closer, he had to be coming closer, Jeanne told herself as she adjusted the controls to the viewer once again. She had been here since morning, searching and waiting, having convinced the Elder that she would leave the Glen on foot if he didn't permit her to use the upper levels of the Watch Tower. Glancing aside at the elves crowding around the other screens, she still felt like an intruder, but she had to locate Peter.

She caught herself chewing on a fingernail and frowned uneasily. Her new powers were making her nervous. It was night once again, but the vague impression of Peter had not diminished with time. She could almost close her eyes and sense him standing before her. She changed the setting on the viewer again. "I know he's coming back," she murmured fiercely to herself. "I know it!"

Suddenly a tired Windkin, a limp figure leaning over his neck, appeared on the screen. Jeanne stared at the images, surprise, disbelief, and relief washing through her.

"They're here!" she yelled. She could hear the elves' confused questions, but she did not want to wait for their help. Dashing into the

THE CRYSTAL THRONE

lift, she went down to the two Windkin waiting in front of the Watch Tower.

"He's here!" she said excitedly, her ring sparkling. "They're just entering from the southeast!" Her excitement died as she felt the disbelief in the Fleet Ones. "Are you coming along or must I go by myself?"

"They will come along," Leereho said from behind her. "Thank the Ancients that you left the screen on. We have the exact direction." He boosted her onto Elin's back. "He found an excellent rescuer," Leereho continued as Renw dashed up to him. "The Windrunner himself is bringing Peter in."

* * *

Peter peered through the trees. Was he delirious again, or did he actually see a light dancing through the trees ahead? "Over here!" he croaked, his throat parched and raw. He waved at the dancing light and fell off the stallion's broad back.

"PETER!"

Peter felt the soft grass beneath him but didn't have the strength to move. He must be delirious, he thought, listening to the voices approaching him. He could have sworn that he heard Jeanne.

"He's so still! Peter!"

"No, Jeanne, don't touch him!"

Peter felt a gentle touch on his shoulder. Suddenly there was a flash of a rainbow-colored light, and he was sent instantly into a deep, healing sleep.

Jeanne sank to her knees beside him. She was *not* going to pass out this time. She felt so drained.

Leereho helped her to her feet. "Elin warned you. You are much too weak to try healing people yet."

"I'm fine," she protested weakly.

"And so now, too, is Peter," Elin commented. He bowed his head to the ground before the bewildered black stallion. "Welcome, Windrunner. I apologize for the inadequacy of our greetings, but we have two most uncommon humans here."

"So I gathered," the stallion chuckled. "But the explanations can wait until morning. We have both come a long way today."

CHAPTER 9

THE GATHERING

Peter awoke feeling very refreshed and alert. He cautiously opened his eyes and, seeing the bright colors patterning the ceiling, sighed happily.

"Welcome back, Peter."

Peter turned his head to the left and saw Jeanne perched on the edge of a large chair. A faint sparkle of light hung about her hand.

"Hi, Jeanne. Hey, you're looking much better than the last time I saw you! That ring did work."

"Oh, so you know about this?" She held up her hand to display the ring and grinned mischievously. "You're looking better, too."

"Me?" Memory returned and Peter abruptly sat up and opened his shirt to look at his left shoulder. Right where the hound had gripped him was a tiny scab of healing skin. He looked at Jeanne. "Wow."

Jeanne smiled crookedly. "Yeah. I'm having a hard time believing it myself."

"You? But you believe in magic. Wait…you couldn't heal before?"

Jeanne glanced at the glittering ring. "I could pick up emotions, but that was all. When I started school, I had to learn to block them out."

"Too many people?" Peter asked, remembering a television show.

"Too much pain. Scrapes on the playground, a teacher's headache, colds, the day Andy broke his leg falling off the swings—I kept thinking that I should do something to help, but I couldn't, so I tried to stop sensing."

"I'm glad you could help me," Peter said. He frowned at a sudden thought. "If the ring of Calada amplifies your own powers, then you're able to sense more. Are you okay?"

Jeanne shrugged. "Everything's a lot 'noisier.' The Elder says he can help, but he's been busy lately. Do you feel up to walking? Leereho says that the kitchens are off schedule with the gathering and all, so he's going to bring some food over to the Watch Tower for us. Unless you're not hungry?" She grinned.

"You know I'm starved! Just find my clothes and we'll get over to the Tower. I've got a few questions for Le and our four-footed friends."

"Clothes are here on the chair. I'll be outside in case you don't remember the way to the Watch Tower."

Peter dressed hurriedly. He caught up two cloaks from the back of the chair on his way out the door.

Jeanne straightened from her position against the wall as he handed her one of the cloaks and draped the other over his shoulder. Peter glanced down the empty corridor. "Where is everyone?"

"Busy with the gathering," Jeanne said with a sigh. "We have to take the back ways now and stay out of sight. Humans are very rare here and the Elder doesn't want any rumors that might get back to the witches." She shook her head. "I've gotten that lecture from both the Elder and Elin. Watch, we'll probably get it from Leereho, too."

Two corridors later, the hallway ended at a massive oak door, large enough to admit two tall Fleet Ones walking side by side. Outside, they followed the faint trail through the shadows cast by the overhanging trees. Peter could hear strange, yet oddly familiar voices up ahead.

"Elin and Hahle are waiting by the Watch Tower," Jeanne said, surprised. "I thought they would be with the Windrunner."

"That's all right," Peter said as they entered the clearing. "I want to test an idea of mine."

"So Peter's up and about!" Hahle trotted up and gently touched the boy's left shoulder. "How are you, human?"

"Fine, Hahle. It's good to see you, too."

The Fleet One backed a step. "He hears!"

Elin snorted gently. "Didn't you listen to the Windrunner last night?"

Jeanne turned to him. "Peter, you can hear them?"

"What did the Windrunner say?" Peter asked Elin.

"That our people had come upon you semiconscious and obviously you heard them before you saw and could disbelieve." The Fleet One gently ruffled Peter's hair with his breath. "I am proud of you, Peter—we all are. I'm ashamed to say that only Jeanne believed you would return."

"I'm proud that you have learned to understand us," Hahle added.

Peter could feel the flush creeping into his face at the tributes. "Where's the Windrunner?" he asked, trying to change the subject. "I wanted to thank him for saving me."

"He is attending the gathering, which," Elin nudged him, "you will miss seeing if you do not join Leereho soon."

"That can wait. Elin, Hahle, has anyone ever seen any witch besides the Dark One?"

Hahle snorted nervously and glanced at the sky.

Elin looked thoughtful. "The Dark One is often seen abroad. But we Fleet Ones saw a flame witch parch our land, drying the streams and plains until now the desert stands in its place."

"A flame witch?"

"She not only uses fire as the Dark One, a shadow witch, uses darkness, but according to some sightings she is a living flame."

"She sounds like an elemental," Jeanne said slowly.

"What is that?" Peter asked.

"The Greeks—our Ancients," she explained for the Windkin, "believed that the universe was made up of four substances—air, water, fire, and earth. In books I've read, an elemental is a powerful and destructive being composed entirely of one of the four elements."

"How did one stop such a being?" Hahle asked.

"With another of the elements. Water drowned fire. Earth smothered air."

"That takes care of the flame witch, but it doesn't explain the Dark One," Peter mused. "Or the other witch—whatever *she* is."

"I haven't heard of any sightings of the third witch," Elin said thoughtfully. "But we will ask at the gathering." The two Windkin trotted down the trail towards the hidden entrance.

"What was all that about?" Jeanne demanded as they entered the darkness of the Watch Tower.

"I did some thinking while I was out on the desert," Peter explained, lowering his voice. "Had you noticed that there are three witches but everybody only talks about one?"

"The Dark One?"

"Lower your voice. Now, the other two can't be sitting back and letting the Dark One do all the ruling. Maybe they operate on a more subtle level."

"And maybe you're getting paranoid again. Why are we

whispering?"

Peter shook his head. "There's been two separate attacks now and both were intended to be fatal."

"Only two? But..."

"Two that the Dark One wasn't responsible for."

"But those were her hounds on the plains, weren't they?"

Peter shook his head. "Her hounds are still looking for us at Gimstan Mountain—Le and I met a leprechaun whose people are being carried off by them, probably to question about us. And who burned the Glen and kept hounds hovering around it?"

"The Dark One got the location from Leereho."

"Maybe. Maybe one of the other witches already knew the location. As far as I've been able to tell, the Dark One herself was in the caverns chasing us when the Glen was burned. So who captured Graylod?"

Jeanne stopped. "Graylod's been captured?!"

"In the middle of a fire, according to Le."

"You think the flame witch did that?"

Peter shrugged. "One of them suspects that we can break the curse. Why else have we been followed so closely?"

"Coincidence?"

"One attack, maybe, but two?" He shook his head. "Flame witch, Dark One—doesn't anyone know their names?"

"In the oldest forms of magic a name was a powerful weapon. If you had a person's true name, you had power over him."

"Oh, like Calada and the mad king?"

"Right. The Change is a form of name spell."

Peter looked at her with surprise and respect. "First elementals and now name spells. You learned all this from reading fantasy?"

Jeanne laughed and stepped into the lift.

She stepped off at the second level. "Leereho got us permission to use one of the smaller rooms," she whispered as Peter joined her. He glanced about the huge darkened room filled with harried elves and row upon row of viewers and nodded wordlessly.

Jeanne led him through the crowded room over to a door on the near wall. "If you think this is crowded, just wait until you see the gathering," she said, opening the door.

They stepped through into darkness and silence. Then Peter noticed the blinking screen far ahead and a familiar figure in front of it. "I thought you said this was a smaller room." He listened to the echoes. "We could play basketball here."

"This is the hallway, silly." Jeanne pulled him toward the light. "Leereho just left the door open so we'd find him. C'mon, I'm hungry."

"Don't they believe in lights around here?" Peter muttered as he stumbled in the dark.

"Sorry, I forgot." The ring's sparkle grew brighter and they stood in a circle of rainbows.

"What?" Peter looked about in amazement.

Jeanne grinned. "I've been experimenting with the ring of Calada." She pointed into the shadows beside them and a beam of light sprang out from her hand to play over shields hung on the wall. "Makes a good flashlight, doesn't it?"

"I'll say." He glanced at her worriedly. "Does the power come from you or the ring?"

The beam of light vanished. "The ring, I guess. Why?"

"Will you stop getting so paranoid? I'm not Jody. I didn't want you to tire yourself."

"Jeanne has reason to doubt," Leereho explained as they entered the room. "Even we, who are accustomed to magic, did not heed her powers. She had to resort to threats before we listened."

"Threats? Jeanne?" Peter repeated in disbelief.

Jeanne flushed. She leaned over Leereho's shoulder and stared at the viewer. "Is that a leprechaun?"

"Hey, it's Bryan!" Peter craned forward also.

Leereho sighed. "Let me adjust the viewer," he muttered, trying to get out from under them.

The images solidified around them. "Will you look at all those people!" Peter exclaimed, turning to survey the crowded room.

Jeanne studied the small figure standing before them. "He's a leprechaun," she decided. "Look, Peter, there's the Windrunner next to the Elder."

"Where?"

"Behind that big table in front of us. Right in front of the leprechaun. See?" She turned towards the back of the room. "Elin and Hahle are just entering."

Peter glanced from one image to another, still wondering how the viewer worked. The scene was fully three-dimensional and, to the eye, they were standing in the middle of the crowded Chambers. Leereho, Jeanne, and himself were seemingly on the outer fringe of the open area before the circular table of Elders. Behind them rows of long tables lined with Folk formed a huge semi-circle facing the Elders. Peter looked at the gathering in amazement. He hadn't realized that the Council Chambers were so large nor the Folk so varied. He saw fur and feathers, scales, and a small creature with hair strongly resembling Spanish moss. His eye fell on their "neighbors."

"Jeanne, who or what is that girl beside us with the green hair?"

"Who? Oh, she's a tree dryad, isn't she, Leereho? A wood nymph that lives within a tree." She hesitated and studied the dryad. "That's odd. How can she be away from her tree?"

"Perhaps a wizard gave her a spell so that she could give her report in person," Leereho said absently. He touched a pattern and the murmur of the crowd rose around them.

"An' if it be pleasin' ye," the tight, angry voice of Bryan said slowly, "can ye tell me how I can return t' me people an' say, 'Sorry, twenty-five of us taken, but the Elders can't do anythin'?'"

"Something is wrong," Jeanne said abruptly. She turned and looked through the crowd. "Something is very wrong."

"They're only images," Peter called as she wandered off into the gathering. "You can't do anything up here."

"That's what makes it worse," she muttered.

Behind her, the image of Bryan was demanding, "Fifteen of me kin alone carried away an' ye have no spell t' help us?"

"No spells can stop the hounds for long," the Elder said. "But the Glen is growing again, thanks to your help, Bryan. Perhaps the Voices will speak once again and suggest a solution."

Jeanne turned slowly, surveying the crowded room, and caught sight of the dryad making her way to the door. In the midst of drab grays and browns, the nymph's light green hair and long gown stood out like beacons. But why did she feel that something else hung about the slim figure?

Jeanne shook her head angrily. There was a taint of wrongness about the crowd, even though they were only images. She was certain that the same taint hovered about the Council Chambers. She started moving again, her mind open and reaching for the blur of emotions back in the Chambers. Uselessly, she wished she were actually at the gathering, able in some way to prevent the power she felt growing, waiting to strike.

Bryan snorted. "The Glen hasn't spoken since the witches arrived, elf. Tis false hope ye be givin' me."

"We were not able to protect even the Glen, Bryan. What would you have us do?"

The stout, grizzled dwarf seated beside the Windrunner harrumphed. "We will send a detachment from Gimstan Mountain. No magic to help you, Bryan, none but that of good steel. Our arrows and axes should stop their raids."

"Thank you, Ronink," the Elder said.

Bryan bowed deeply to the dwarf. "Yer help will be greatly appreciated."

Jeanne found Elin conversing with a hovering golden bubble. Memory of stories she had read stirred sluggishly, and she stopped by the Windkin. Images, if they were close enough to reality, were often used in magic. Perhaps she could alert Elin to the danger. She focused her mind and slowly reached out to touch the image of the dappled stallion.

"Any more reports?" the Elder asked as Bryan returned to his seat. The crowd stilled as he drew a small globe of white crystal out of the depths of his cloak. The tall elf placed it on the table before him and slowly passed his hand over it. The globe began to glow a faint green in response.

"Hey, Jeanne, look at this." Peter peered through the crowd. Where had she gone? He spotted Elin moving slowly along the less crowded wall to the table of Elders. The stallion stopped there and spoke with a woman in brown and white.

A woman with flame-colored hair rose from her seat. Draping her swirled green cloak closely about her, she strode down the long aisle between the tables until she stood before the Elder.

On the table between them the globe pulsated slowly with rhythmic flashes of green.

"You have the gift, Guardian," the Elder stated formally.

The wizard lifted the globe and turned so that the entire hall was bathed with the pulsating green light. Then she slowly lowered it and cradled it in her hands. "The room is sealed," she said in a clear voice. "None of the violet light may enter nor hear what is spoken here."

She seated herself in front of the table, still cradling the throbbing green globe. The Elder leaned forward. "The room is sealed and nothing spoken here shall pass beyond those doors. We must begin to make plans against the witches, to put a halt to their movement out of their misty realm and drive them back to the Shadow Land."

"Wait, Jonhree!" The woman at the end of the table sprang to her feet. Elin, beside her, moved back into the crowd as she consulted a pendant about her neck. "There is a Changed One among us."

"What?" Peter watched as the crowd in the Council Chambers looked around in confusion and suspicion. "Jeanne, did you hear that?"

"I told Elin to warn them," came the reply.

Peter looked for the girl, but she was still somewhere in the crowd. He studied the wizard. Her long skirt was brown, as was the furred vest over a loose white blouse. Her face was small, framed by long, light brown hair that heightened the green of her eyes. She lifted the gold chain about her neck and studied the brown stone in her pendant.

"Do not attempt to flee, spy. The room is sealed—you cannot run from us." She turned slowly, directing the pendant over all of the gathering.

"NO!"

Peter turned at Jeanne's cry and spotted her running toward the door. She leaped over a table in her path—*why jump over an image*, he wondered—and raced toward the green-haired dryad.

The dryad furtively pulled a glittering dagger from her long sleeve and eyed the brown-garbed wizard, measuring the distance between them. She drew the dagger back to throw and Jeanne flung herself at the image, catching the nymph's arm and knocking the both of them to the floor. The dryad's scream was cut short, and Peter felt fear touch him as those nearest the dryad lunged toward her and Jeanne.

"Jeanne!" Peter ran though the images. "Le, shut off the viewer! I can't see her!"

The images vanished and darkness returned. Peter still could not find her, could not even see the sparkle of her ring.

"The Change is gone!" Leereho exclaimed, watching the small screen.

"I've heard that before," Peter growled. "What did you expect?"

"A Sensitive can heal only by direct touch," Leereho said in bewilderment. "This cannot be possible!"

"Trust Jeanne to do the impossible," Peter muttered. "Jeanne, stop hiding from me!"

"I'm not...hiding!" a faint voice protested. "It took...more than I expected."

"Jeanne!" He found her huddled on the floor, her back against the wall. He knelt beside her.

"Salanoa is questioning the dryad," Leereho reported. "The Elder is trying to maintain order, but the Folk are worried. They saw only the dryad drop the dagger and collapse."

Jeanne looked up at him with haunted eyes. "Peter, I couldn't let her kill."

"I know, but couldn't you have stopped her in a less obvious way?"

"The Guardian has opened the room, and she and Salanoa are taking the dryad out," Leereho reported. "The Elder seems to be dismissing the gathering for now." He paused, then added, "He looks angry."

"Can't blame him," Peter said. "Hope he found a good explanation for the dryad's recovery."

"Jeanne, how did you release her from here?" Leereho asked.

"She believed that the images were real," Peter explained.

Jeanne looked at him in amazement. "How did you know?"

"The way you charged over that table. Why else jump over an image? And how else could you have grabbed her arm? Did you ever stop to think that, for as long as she was real to you, she could have hurt you with that knife?"

Jeanne glanced down at her dimmed ring and nodded.

Peter sighed and held out his hand to help her to her feet. Jeanne looked at it and Peter frowned. "Something wrong?"

"No. It's just that...direct contact...and I don't want to pry but I can't shut you out if—" She shook her head and climbed to her feet.

Peter stood up. "Sorry, guess I am a little mad. C'mon, eat something and get your strength back. Then we better get our explanations straight before we have to face the Elder." He thought of something. "Jeanne, is there still anyone in the healing place? Or did you heal them all already?"

*   *   *

The Elder was waiting for them at the bottom of the lift. "As if we had not troubles enough, you had to betray your presence to a roomful of loose tongues," he scolded. "How can we protect you if you keep reminding the witches of your existence?"

Jeanne took a deep breath. "I could not let her kill, Elder," she said firmly. She ignored Peter's attempts to interrupt and went on. "Salanoa was not expecting the attack—did you wish me to stand by and do nothing?"

"Thank the Green that you did not," a gentle voice said. "And thank you, Jeanne Tucker."

They turned as a woman in brown and white stepped out of the shadows. "Salanoa," Jeanne breathed.

The wizard smiled and inclined her head. "Never before had I heard that the Ancients' viewers could also transmit spells. Jonhree will have to set guards about his Watch Tower, once the other wizards hear of this."

"I didn't mean to—" Jeanne started.

"Cause trouble?" Salanoa finished. She shook her head. "Yours is a wondrous gift, Jeanne. I could not detect the dryad even after Elin's warning."

"How is she?" Jeanne asked.

"Confused, but alive and healthy and homesick for her tree." Salanoa laughed merrily. "I would not be surprised to learn that a badly damaged tree on Dewin Heights, far to the north, is whole and healthy again."

"Tree," Jeanne said absently. "I thought I felt two sources of pain when I touched her."

Salanoa watched her. "The link between a dryad and her tree is a strong one. The witch could capture her only after the tree was mortally injured."

"Which witch captured her?" Peter asked.

"Which?" Salanoa turned to him. "I do not know. But I will ask her." She lifted her pendant uneasily. "Jonhree, you did not tell me that Peter has such a strong barrier against magic."

"Barrier?" Peter repeated.

The wizard glanced at her pendant. "A very strong one. It affects the curse as well as my small powers."

"Me? Affecting the curse?" Peter looked at the Elder for an explanation.

"You didn't know?" She glanced from Peter's face to the Elder's. "Jonhree, you haven't told him?"

"The Windrunner only returned him last night," the Elder said dryly.

Salanoa laughed at the look on his face. "Poor Jonhree. Humans have been gone from this land for too long. No wonder you asked my help. Jeanne, can you control your powers yet?"

"Control? No. They...just happen."

"Which drains you more than it should." Salanoa frowned thoughtfully. "I learned my first spells from a Sensitive. It's only fitting that I teach you what I know of the ways of a Sensitive, Jeanne. And perhaps you will teach me some of your spells that Jonhree insists are impossible."

"I...that would be wonderful," Jeanne stammered.

"Good. Let us begin." Salanoa grasped her pendant and they vanished.

CHAPTER 10

THE RIDDLE OF THE GLEN

"Where did Salanoa take Jeanne?" Peter demanded.

"Watch the entrances, Leereho," the Elder ordered. "No one is to enter except the Fleet Ones." Leereho nodded and stepped into the shadows. The Elder turned back to Peter. "Jeanne and Salanoa are at the Glen," he said.

"The Glen! But what about the hounds?"

"Elin and Hahle are on guard, although no hounds have been seen since you were captured. The Glen contains the highest concentration of magic about here and Jeanne can tap its energies for training without tiring herself as she has been doing. We must train each of you to realize your own powers before you can work together as a team."

"But I don't have any powers!" Peter protested. "And what is that...barrier that Salanoa mentioned?"

The Elder looked thoughtfully at the deep shadows. "Humans are a strange people. Something deep inside their spirits will not permit them to believe in what they do not understand." His piercing gaze met Peter's. "In you this disbelief is very strong—strong enough that, if you control this force properly, it could affect the strength of magic used about you."

"But I can't control this!"

"You can learn, and there I can help you." At Peter's questioning look he continued, "This type of power was mentioned in our records from the days when humankind lived in the Lands. It was never a strong Talent, since, when one is raised with magic, it is difficult to disbelieve its existence entirely. But some humans were able to use their disbelief defensively."

"A talent for disbelief?"

"Disbelief or belief." The Elder looked self-conscious. "Some of my ancestors were human. I, too, have a little of the barrier you possess because of that, which is why I know of the records, but not as much nor as powerful as yours is. Thus I can teach only a little of what you need to know—the rest you must discover on your own."

"I can't learn something like this," Peter muttered.

"But you can! Peter, we stay here rather than anywhere else because this is the only part of Drwseren that is not dependent on magic and thus will not be affected if you disbelieve too strongly."

Peter did not answer. The Elder glanced at the shadows, then said kindly, "Peter, you seem to believe that you are unimportant here."

"But I am! Look, Jeanne's your Sensitive—I don't have any magic. And this 'disbelieving' stuff—I don't see how that could help you at all."

"By itself it will not. Jeanne by herself will not help us either."

Peter was surprised. "Huh? But Graylod's legend—"

The Elder sighed. "Graylod has forgotten much, as we all have. As for you, Peter, remember always that the Watcher chose you along with Jeanne. The two of you are a team and must work together as a team.

"As a team, you balance each other. You do not believe. Jeanne believes too much, and the witches can hurt her where they might not touch you. Magic must be believed in to work effectively, that is the only way it *can* work. If you do not believe in the witches' magic, but do in Jeanne's, together you two will help us far more than you now realize."

"Well, stop telling him that, Jonhree," a bass rumble commented. "Show him. Give him something to work on besides words."

"I was waiting for you, Windrunner," the Elder commented dryly.

"I am honored. So we meet again, human." The black stallion trotted out of the shadows.

"I believe you know the Elder of the Fleogende," the tall elf said to Peter.

"Yes, he saved my life," Peter said. "I didn't get a chance to thank you before, Elder."

"The title among my people is 'Windrunner,'" the stallion replied. "And as for thanks, let us wait and see how you help us. Jonhree, cast a spell—a small one, please."

"Small ones are all I can remember," the Elder muttered. He

suddenly turned invisible.

"Ask for a small one and he gives you one of the hardest," the Windrunner complained. "But it will do. All right, Peter, see if you can find him and damp his spell."

"Find him! How? He's invisible!" Peter protested, looking at the deep shadows surrounding him.

The stallion was patient. "Look closely. Analyze. Look for flaws in everything you see. How do the shadows merge? Smoothly, or is there a sudden sharp break as if someone is standing there? You have to question everything that you see. Is it natural or does it look wrong? Just by finding him you break the spell because you no longer believe what you first saw."

* * *

At the Glen, Salanoa was saying, "A Sensitive constantly puts herself into another's place. It's a combination of your head and your heart. With your head you begin to know the person and with your heart added you *are* that person."

"But how do you stop?" Jeanne asked. "I can't block all those feelings out completely now that I'm wearing this ring."

"Can you raise and lower your block at will, Jeanne?"

"Lower it!" Jeanne felt confused. "I...never tried. I usually try to keep it raised."

"Poor human." Jeanne felt the light touch of Salanoa's sympathy. "Have your powers brought you that much misery, that you must deny what you are?"

Jeanne frowned thoughtfully. Had she been wrong to develop her block? She cringed at the vivid memory of her first school year and quickly erased that doubt. No, she had had no other choice but to find some way of shielding herself from the ceaseless torment of emotional "noise". But why, then, did Salanoa sound as if she had firmly shut an important door? As if she had purposely crippled herself? What else could she have done?

Salanoa looked speculatively at her. "We had best start with your block rather than your powers," the wizard decided. "You must learn to block selectively, to protect yourself from emotional attack while sensing and using your opponent's weaknesses." She glanced at the guarding Windkin and touched her pendant. "Try blocking without the ring. It will protect you only against physical dangers, not magical, but I want you to become accustomed to your own limitations without drawing on the ring's energies."

Jeanne uneasily slipped off the ring. "It...doesn't seem to want me to put it down," she said slowly, staring at the ring.

Salanoa smiled. "Put it in your pouch. The ring is attuned to you alone. If placed anywhere away from you, it will try to return to you."

Jeanne slipped the ring into a pouch on her belt, firmly denying the small rainbows tugging at her. She tossed her hair back over her shoulder and waited.

Salanoa touched her pendant again. "Lower your block completely."

"I can't!" Jeanne froze as the hurtful memories jabbed once again at her, twisting her thoughts. "No!" Jeanne backed a step. "All those emotions—I can't!"

Salanoa reached swiftly for her, let her hand drop as Jeanne avoided her touch. The wizard smiled sadly, and Jeanne felt a warm calmness soothing her fears. "Shush, child. I have set a protective field about you. Only Elin, Hahle, and myself stand with you. Surely you do not fear us?" Again her mind touched the girl's, smoothing the jagged panic.

"Please try, filly," Elin said gently, and Hahle lightly nuzzled her hair.

Jeanne cautiously lowered her block and felt, not the blurring whirlpool of emotions she feared, but the calm concern broadcast by the surrounding three. She smiled shyly, feeling defenseless without her shield yet protected and safe within their circle.

"Now to begin. I will be your enemy and Hahle an injured ally whose life is maintained only by your will."

Hahle adopted the role with enthusiasm. He fell to his knees and rolled on his side, moaning loudly. Jeanne giggled while Elin looked down at his clowning companion, radiating mild disapproval.

Salanoa smiled. "Now, Jeanne, you must block against my attacks and yet hold open to Hahle." The stallion moaned again. "Begin."

* * *

The days passed in a blur of lessons and repeated practice. Jeanne learned how to withstand Salanoa's attacking bolts while simultaneously slipping within the wizard's emotional defenses. Cloaked under illusions, the two shadowed animals through the woods while Jeanne learned to control the emotions of the smaller creatures: first, to follow without being detected, and later, to call them to her.

Under the Windrunner's guidance, Peter found that he could extend a field of disbelief out from himself for a short distance. He learned how to control the focus of the field, narrowing it to a tight beam or expanding it to an enveloping sphere, within which no magic could exist.

In the evenings, when the Windrunner attended the later sessions of the gathering, Leereho instructed Peter in the art of swordplay, using a clearing far from the crowded lodge for the lessons.

"Not so violently!" Leereho scolded. "Lose your balance on such a wild swing and your opponent has an opening to strike." He lowered his practice sword and leaned on it, studying the human thoughtfully. "You were much better yesterday, Peter. What is the problem?"

Peter frowned and slammed his practice sword into its sheath. "Earlier today Salanoa and I uncovered something that had been forgotten under the curse."

"Grim news, from the look of you. What was it?"

"You should have seen Salanoa, if you think I'm upset. She remembered that—" He broke off suddenly and tilted his head as if listening.

"What is it?" Leereho scanned the forest, his sword out before him.

"No danger, Le," Peter said absently. "Oh, I asked the Windrunner yesterday how Jeanne, with her belief in magic, and myself, with my disbelief, could ever work together as a team. He told me that no one knew, since it's never been tried before, and then today he had Salanoa teach me a little mind-work." He studied the forest thoughtfully, as if he expected to find someone hidden among the shadow-dappled trees and bushes.

Leereho stared at him. "Mind-work! With your powers? How could that be?"

Peter suddenly noticed a butterfly drifting aimlessly on the fringe of the clearing. "The weather's been too cold lately for butterflies, Jeanne. Why sneak up on us?"

"Just testing what Salanoa told me." The butterfly vanished and Jeanne appeared. "You need a little practice on distance and direction sensing. I sensed you looking for me before I even arrived here."

He nodded with a certain sense of relief. Then she hadn't heard what he had started to tell Le. "Salanoa said you'd help me with that."

"Did Salanoa teach you anything else besides empathy?" Leereho asked.

"No, I couldn't believe in anything else. She could only teach me empathy because I had already picked some of that up from being around Jeanne. It's still very unreliable. She said that I'll probably only be able to sense Jeanne since Sensitives broadcast so strongly."

Leereho shook his head. "I would not have believed it possible." He retrieved his bow and quiver of arrows. "Is Salanoa with you, Jeanne?"

"Salanoa? No, she sent me off to do some tracking hours ago. Why?"

"You are alone?" Leereho looked horrified.

"Jeanne can take care of herself," Peter said before he remembered that there was no protection for her against—He suddenly realized that he was broadcasting his worry, and clamped down on it before Jeanne would notice.

Jeanne glanced sharply at him. "Thanks for the vote of confidence," she said slowly. "Too bad you didn't mean it." She sighed inwardly. *First Salanoa's acting oddly and now Peter. What's the matter with everyone today?* A familiar sensation brushed against her awareness.

"Now wait a minute, Jeanne. I didn't mean that you couldn't—"

She waved him silent. "We've got company and they're not friendly."

"Close?" Leereho asked, pulling an arrow from his quiver.

Jeanne turned slowly, scanning the forest. "Too close to make a run for the Tower. I should have been paying attention. Three of them—two in the sky and one closing from my right. Get ready, they're tensing to move."

Alerted by a faint rustle, Peter looked up at the protecting treetops and suddenly saw two pairs of eyes staring down at him. "Scatter! They're in the trees!" he yelled.

Wings lifted, thrashing the air wildly, as the three on the ground ran for the shelter of the trees. A spear hurtled down to bury its tip in the earth before Peter. He changed direction and dove into the bushes.

An arrow flew from Leereho's bow and a wolf that had leapt into the clearing staggered and fell. There was a sharp cry, quickly muffled.

Peter heard a gasp of dismay from Leereho. "Jeanne?" the elf called softly.

"Sorry," her voice said faintly. "Didn't think it would hurt so much!"

After watching Leereho melt out of sight on the edge of the clearing, Peter felt very exposed simply standing behind a tree. He drew his sword and slowly edged around the tree. He could sense Jeanne's presence across the clearing but could see only bushes there. *Illusions, again?*

A bush across the clearing flickered under his gaze, revealing a tiny sparkle of rainbows in its center. "Oh no," he muttered, glancing at the intruders. "Some partner I am. I hope they don't notice that."

The hound swooped down from the treetops. On its back was a bony purple creature wearing the violet uniform of the witches and holding a glowing purple globe. It threw the globe at the rainbow-speckled bush.

"He noticed. Jeanne, look out!"

The bush abruptly vanished, and the globe hit a nearby tree instead. The sphere exploded on contact, releasing a dense cloud of evil-smelling smoke. Peter could hear Leereho coughing somewhere beside him, but he could not see anything in the swirling smoke. "Jeanne!" he called.

The smoke slowly cleared. Across the clearing, the tree, surrounding bushes, and a neat circle of grass about them had vanished, but Jeanne had appeared in the center of the clearing. Apparently dazed by the explosion, she wavered unsteadily to her feet. The hound swooped down, claws extended.

"Jeanne!" Peter dashed across the clearing and knocked her to the ground again, out of reach of the grasping claws. He glanced up and saw the hound hovering above them. The rider laughed as he aimed his spear.

The ring of Calada blazed out from Jeanne's hand with a heatless green fire, burning the spear in the bewildered creature's hand. Peter took advantage of the creature's confusion to help the groggy Jeanne to safety.

The hound and its rider shrieked with fury when the two reached the shelter of the trees. The rider kicked the hound viciously and the thin-skinned creature soared up to the treetops.

"Now, Jonhree!" a clear voice called.

The treetops suddenly came alive. Branches reached out and ensnared the hound, knocking its rider off. Other branches caught the rider and brought him down to stand before a brown-garbed wizard. She pointed her pendant at him, and he stopped struggling and stood rigid, his eyes blank.

"He will stand thus until we are ready to question him," Salanoa explained as the Elder joined her. "What about the hound?"

The Elder glanced upward to where the hound struggled in the branches. "You have power over animals. Can you erase its mind of what it has seen? It is much too big to keep prisoner."

"If we shift it to wolf shape the true wolves will demand its death.

I'll need Jeanne's help with its memories. Will your wood magic hold it?"

"For now."

Salanoa went to the two humans. "We heard the explosion. Are you both all right? Jeanne looks dazed."

"Just...dizzy," Jeanne said slowly. "What was that globe?"

"Globe?" Salanoa caught sight of the empty circle where once a tree and bushes had been. Her eyes narrowed. "A transfer globe," she explained grimly. "The witches must be certain you are here to entrust one to a goblin. When broken, it transports whatever stands within its range immediately to the castle." She directed her pendant at Jeanne. "You probably inhaled some of the smoke—it makes one dizzy and disoriented."

"It was my fault it spotted Jeanne," Peter confessed. "I was looking for her and disturbed her illusion."

"You didn't mean to, Peter," Jeanne said. "It's all right."

Salanoa sighed. "You two are still not ready to work as a team. And now we have no time to teach you."

Hooves pounded along the trail and Elin burst into the clearing, followed closely by Hahle and Renw. "Peter! Jeanne!" Elin pulled up sharply. "We heard the noise. Are you all right?"

The hound shrieked from above. Elin and Hahle started at the sudden noise, but Renw whirled and bolted into the underbrush.

Hahle reared. "Come down here and say that!" he taunted the hound.

Elin peered into the shadows after Renw. "Peter, Jeanne, could you teach Renw to disbelieve his fear? I hadn't realized how foolish we looked."

"It had best be done tonight," the Elder said, helping a still coughing Leereho over to Salanoa, "for at daybreak you will leave here."

"So soon?" Elin asked, dismayed. "Neither of them is ready."

The Elder glanced at Salanoa. "I have heard disturbing reports. And you can see for yourself that this is no longer a place of safety for them."

"The witches sent only a transfer globe," Salanoa agreed, "but they could have sent an army. So far we have them worried enough to raid villages and attempt to capture or kill the remaining wizards. Every unexpected action we take confuses them that much more, leaves them much more open to attack. They would expect us to gather and keep our power tightly together to attack them."

"So we'll do the opposite," Peter finished. "I hope you're right, Salanoa." He eyed the goblin. "Let me know if his witch is…" he glanced at Jeanne, hesitated and ended lamely, "…the dryad's witch." He ran into the trees. "C'mon, Elin, let's find Renw."

Jeanne looked after him suspiciously. *What's he hiding*? she wondered.

* * *

In the darkness before daybreak, two humans, an elf, and three Windkin entered the softly glowing Glen. Renw pranced with delight. "No reins! No more reins!" Hahle and Elin exchanged amused glances behind him.

Jeanne studied the elf beside her. "Leereho, where's your bow? You didn't leave it behind because of me, did you?"

"I acted without thought. Now I will think," Leereho replied cryptically.

Peter spared a moment to wonder what they were arguing about, then gazed in wonder at the young trees already towering high above their heads. The Glen had recovered rapidly, and its strangely beautiful trees reflected the magical glow. In the center of the Glen was a tall tree with wide, silvery-shining leaves. The Elder, the Windrunner and Salanoa waited at its base.

"The day that the witches invaded our land," the Elder said slowly, "the Glen of Ancient Voices whispered one riddle.

> *When at the last door humans appear*
> *To one the Name-thief's Bane will awaken.*
> *Then those bound by Change will lose the fear*
> *And the power of the Three be shaken.*
>
> *For the Heart-sharer before the crystal throne*
> *Must the lost name with fire be spoken.*
> *The doom of the false for the dead shall atone*
> *And two curses of hate be broken."*

"Graylod's legend!" Leereho whispered. "I did not dream it came from here!"

"*Two* curses?" Peter asked.

The Windrunner snorted. "We now understand the first part of the Voices' prediction, but we can only guess at the rest. You humans have two choices. Either attempt to solve the riddle, by going to their castle, or give up the quest, now, and we will try to hide you."

Peter shook his head. "We can't hide from one witch, it seems. I'm going on. Stop scowling at me, Jeanne. I was only wishing that you would stay behind, I didn't say it."

"Well, then, don't, because I'm coming along. We'll solve the riddle."

The Elder bowed to them. "The quest is yours. Leereho," he continued, drawing five white sticks from beneath his cloak, "I have obtained these from the Tree of Life. Their magic should help against the white hounds."

Leereho looked awed as he accepted the gift. "Roots from the Tree of Life," he said in a hushed voice. He placed the dried roots in his belt pouch with as much care as if they had been precious jewels.

"We have done what we can to protect and prepare you," Salanoa said. "The gathering will be dismissed tomorrow, and mayhap in the dispersal of wizards the witches will overlook two humans."

"We hope," the Windrunner muttered. "Run with the Wind."

Salanoa drew a symbol in the air before them that glowed green before fading. "May the Green go with you, for all of our hopes do."

* * *

The company moved quietly and quickly through the forest, since Peter and Jeanne could now keep to the swift pace the elf set. The sun was directly overhead when they reached the edge of the woods. Hahle glanced through the thinning stands of trees out to the plains. "We'll stop here and rest a while," he said as the others joined him.

"Good," Leereho agreed. "We'll need to gather firewood and water before we reach the desert."

"You mean we have to carry wood, too?" Renw grumbled. "Scouts usually travel light."

Leereho started gathering the dry wood on the ground. "We are not on a scouting expedition, partner. Nor are we in any hurry. The desert is a good place to hide, for those who know it well."

"As we do," Elin agreed. The stallion moved to the side of Jeanne, who stood silently watching a grove of trees off on their left. "Something troubling you, Jeanne?"

"A little." She indicated the grove. "What's over there, Elin? I feel...drawn to that place."

Elin glanced uneasily toward the grove. "The Mirror of Truth. I'll take you there, Jeanne, but you must promise not to drink of its waters."

"I promise, Elin, but I'd rather go alone." She glanced over at Leereho and Peter, who were gathering wood. "Is there some place where I can fill the canteens?"

"From the stream that feeds the Mirror." Elin waited as she collected the water skins from the other Windkin's packs and rejoined him. "You will be careful, Jeanne?"

She nodded. "I promise, Elin." She stepped carefully through the brush, making her way to the silent stand of trees.

Peter and Leereho busily gathered dead wood. "The desert is not far," the elf said as he worked. "Just beyond the plains. The nights will be cold, and the wood we gather now must serve until we cross the desert."

"How long should that take?" Peter tossed a fallen branch on the growing pile of wood.

Leereho looked up at the sun. "Normally about two days, riding a Fleet One. The last time Renw and I went through, the witches were not bothering to patrol there. If that is still the case, we can take the long way through and stop at a few of the oases."

Peter glanced over to where the Fleet Ones were grazing. "Why do the Fleet Ones live on the desert?"

Leereho followed his gaze. "They are guarding that which was theirs. The desert was not always the way it is now. Once Windgard was the most beautiful place ever seen. Plains stretched in every direction, ribboned with streams and dotted sparsely with trees. The witches changed all that and left only a few strips of fertile soil to mock the owners. The Fleet Ones were forced to come to us for help, volunteering their services in exchange for the few water spells we could remember, for they did not want to leave their land, only exist off it until the witches could be destroyed. Their life is harder than the rest of the Folk, for until now the witches left us our land."

Leereho started tying up bundles of wood, dividing the pile into three portions and making compact bundles to lash behind the saddles. Peter looked out at the plains. "Is that all we need now, Le?"

"Just water." Leereho looked through the trees. "And it appears that Jeanne has gone for that. Alone, again."

"Will you stop harping on that? Between her powers and the ring of Calada she's safer than she was back on Earth." He let his mind reach out to sense Jeanne's. "She does seem upset about something, though. Maybe I'd better find her."

"Where is she?"

Peter concentrated. "Beyond that grove of trees," he said, pointing.

"That grove," Leereho said thoughtfully. "There was a legend." He thought a moment. "It has been so long since I have been home, I have forgotten what lies in these woods."

"You have forgotten the Mirror of Truth?" Elin asked as he joined them.

"That accursed place? Call it instead the Mirror of Possibilities! I thought the Council had sealed it years ago."

Elin studied the angry elf. "What queer ideas you elves have of Truth. Must a deed have only two results? Could it not instead lead to a wide range of possible futures, each dependent on other factors?"

Peter glanced from one to the other. "What are you two talking about?"

"And you let Jeanne go to that place?" Leereho said angrily.

"She had a right to consult the Mirror. She promised not to drink of it, so you need not fear the Visions of Tela. Peter, the Mirror of Truth is a pool that sometimes shows visions of the future. The visions do not always come to pass, because the future is dependent upon the present, and what is done or left undone affects what will be."

"And Tela?"

"An elf long ago who found a pool when he was thirsty and drank of it, not knowing that it was the Mirror. For the rest of his life he saw visions of the possible future, each one dependent on the results of his actions."

"So he went insane," Leereho said bitterly.

"And Jeanne's over there!" Peter ran towards the grove.

He found her just leaving the grove. "Peter!" she said, putting down the filled water skins. "Come here." She led him through the line of trees. "Look at that," she ordered.

Peter obediently looked. At the bottom of a gentle slope was a still pool. Mist drifted across its surface, even though the sun was directly overhead. "It's quiet now," Jeanne said uneasily, "but not two minutes ago, in the water, I saw you and...and a castle, and you were in the dungeon."

"Aw, Jeanne, did you have to tell me? That's not a great future for me." Swiftly he told her what Elin and Le had said about the Mirror.

Jeanne glanced at the water thoughtfully. "It's a possible future, then. That's a relief. We can do something to prevent it. I wonder if we can both see the same future. C'mon, Peter." She slid down the slope, while Peter watched her from the top. She looked up at him. "Come on, Peter. I have to know if you can see anything."

Peter frowned, but he followed her down the slope. "Okay," he said, "but I'm beginning to agree with Le about this. What did you do?"

Jeanne picked up a pebble. "Watch the ripples," she ordered. Peter sighed and watched the water. She tossed in the pebble.

Peter stared at the ripples and saw only the water spreading out. And then... Peter shook his head. It seemed but a second's brush of strange whirling emotions and half-seen images, but when he glanced at Jeanne, he could tell that she had seen something. Her face was white, and she tried twice before she could speak.

"You...you didn't see anything?"

Peter shook his head. "Not a thing."

Jeanne bit her lip and picked up a pebble. "Here, you try it."

Peter took the pebble and tossed it in the water. The ripples slowly spread out, moving farther and farther away... Suddenly he saw a figure lying still on the sand almost at his feet. He looked closer and, seeing that it was Jeanne, apparently asleep, reached out his hand to touch hers. He recoiled in shock. Her skin was icy cold! The image suddenly dissolved, but his hand still felt the coldness of the touch.

"Well, did you see anything?" Jeanne demanded.

Peter stared at her. "Didn't you see anything?"

Jeanne shook her head. "No. Did you?"

"I'm not sure," he lied. He picked up another pebble. "I'll try again."

This time the vision was only a glimpse, a slight impression, and then it was gone. Peter had to swallow twice to dissolve the lump in his throat.

"Peter?" Jeanne was too angry to feel her fear growing. She knew he had lied to her before, knew it as clearly as if he had told her. And yet why hadn't he told her the truth? Could he have seen something that might happen to her, just as she had seen three horrible things that might happen to him? She didn't want to think about that.

Peter shook his head. "No, nothing." Not for anything in the world would Peter tell her that he had seen her sitting dejectedly before a dull red fire, her hands bound behind her back. He shook his head again, but the memory lingered. "No, nothing at all," he repeated with a weak smile. He knew she didn't believe him, but he could tell that she was frightened by her visions as well.

Jeanne turned and started back up the slope. "We better get the water back before Hahle decides to leave without us." Peter could sense the effort it took for her to keep her voice light.

He followed.

CHAPTER 11

SAND, SHADOWS, AND SPECTERS

"Hahle, pride in your home is one thing," Peter declared. The stallion stopped in the deep shadow of a dune and his rider dismounted, still arguing. "But for you Fleet Ones to stay here, with the flame witch and her spells burning your land, blowing sand so deep that you can't even walk, hunting down your oases, and sending her hounds to chase you whenever they're bored is nothing but sheer stubbornness!"

The sands, turned blood red by the dying sun, stretched endlessly, interrupted only by a few large dunes. Peter glanced back along the hoofprints to see Elin and Renw plodding through the deep sand, then pulled his cloak out of the pack and shivered into it.

Hahle stomped a hoof. "No witch will chase us from Windgard. We manage to survive, with the Folk's help."

"There's something hiding not too far from us," Jeanne reported as she and Elin joined them. She dismounted and scanned the desert before them, giving an uneasy glance at the distant dunes. "A hound, I think, but it seems to be waiting. There might be more coming."

"We had better keep moving, then," Leereho agreed, eyeing the fading red of the sky.

Jeanne hesitated, remembering the Mirror. One future had shown sand and hills against a starry night sky, and now above them the last traces of red were swallowed by star-speckled black. "Night," she whispered to herself in growing horror, "and dunes. Oh no, it's happening!"

A shriek rose out of the night and passed over their heads. Leereho and Peter exchanged glances and scrambled into the saddles. Hahle studied a dark shadow that blotted out the stars as it circled above them. "Shall we act frightened to fool that braggart?"

Renw shivered violently. "It won't take much acting on my part."

Elin chuckled and ground one hoof suggestively into the sand. "Just keep in mind what you would do if you caught it on the ground." He tossed his mane. "Get on my back, Jeanne. We can outrun it."

"Not in this sand," Jeanne said quietly, the ring glowing as she fastened her cloak about her neck. "Besides, there's ten...no, thirteen goblins heading towards us from the south."

Hahle groaned. "We can't go back. We'll have to head eastward and swing around them. Hurry, Jeanne."

Jeanne stepped away from Elin, her eyes seemingly observing the distant approach of the goblins. "No, wait, I can handle them. They're not moving too fast."

"The Hound Riders have poor night vision," Leereho said. "They will depend on the hound to lead them to us."

"Their main problem at the moment is the giant land crab they think is blocking their path," Jeanne said mischievously.

"Land crab?" Leereho puzzled.

Elin chuckled. "What are you doing with your illusions, filly?"

Peter stirred uneasily in the saddle and squinted eastward. "Why do I sense trouble coming from the east," he muttered to himself, "if the goblins are in the south?"

Hahle ignored the mutterings of his rider. "Mount up, Jeanne. Here comes the hound again."

Suddenly a violet glow shot down at them from above, flooding their hiding place with the strange light and revealing the hound poised above them, a deep violet globe clutched in one taloned paw.

"C'mon, Jeanne!" Peter yelled.

Jeanne stood her ground, staring fixedly at the hound. "Oh no, you don't," she muttered fiercely. "You won't catch me with that old trick!"

The sharp beak opened and a grating shriek washed over them. The hound hovered above them, visibly puzzled at Fleet Ones that did not run from it. It shrieked louder, not seeming to notice its claws closing tighter and tighter about the globe. The sphere cracked under the pressure of the hound's grip and exploded. The hound vanished, magically flung through space to the castle.

"Good idea, Jeanne!" Peter cheered. "I didn't think you could control it that quickly. How are the goblins doing?"

"Still trying to fight the crab, so we should be able to slip past them while they're preoccupied. Uh-oh, I spoke too soon. Now there are about five trolls coming from the east."

"Get on my back, Jeanne," Elin ordered. "We can't stand here."

"And you can't run in this sand," Jeanne retorted. Her eyes looked across the distance. "Darn! The goblins must have discovered the illusion. Now they're coming, too."

"We can't go back, and we can't go forward," Hahle grumbled. "Jeanne, will you come or must we drag you?"

"Those trolls have sharp eyes," the girl replied absently. "They just walked through the first illusion I threw at them. The goblins are suspicious, too. But let's see if they walk past this!"

Leereho drew his sword. "I can hear them."

"Hear them! I can see them!" Peter hissed. "Here come the trolls!" A slight movement by one of the near dunes caught his eye. Two white Fleet Ones trotted out from behind the ridge of sand. The elfin riders looked uneasily at the approaching trolls, who stopped to stare at the elves.

"*White* Windkin?" Elin muttered.

"Those near-sighted goblins have to see them, too," Jeanne whispered. The ring sparkled faintly as she swung up into the saddle. "I need help, Peter. Believe in that illusion, please! I can't hold both an illusion over us and that one, too."

Peter added the strength of his belief to her illusion. The elves' mounts whirled southward to retreat, then turned and galloped to the west as the goblin patrol surged out of the darkness. The two patrols merged in yelling pursuit of the escaping images, passing the six hidden under shadows and illusion.

"Let's move out as fast as you can!" Jeanne urged. "I can't hold it too much longer!"

The Fleet Ones plunged southeast, picking up speed when the drifting sands cleared and their hooves found solid ground. Soon the patrols had been left far in the distance and the Fleet Ones slowed to a walk. Jeanne sighed and leaned over Elin's neck.

"Tired, filly?" The stallion slowed his pace to a gentler stride, keeping Hahle and Renw in sight. "What were you doing back there?"

"Preventing a possible future," Jeanne said wearily. She straightened and rubbed her eyes, feeling sore muscles complain with the motion. "In the Mirror we ran from goblins straight into trolls. Hahle and Peter were badly hurt before we could fight our way free."

"But that didn't happen," Elin said slowly. He made an exasperated sound. "Why didn't you tell us?"

"Because I didn't know if what I was doing would prevent that future or cause it. All I could do was delay until the trolls appeared and hope that by then the battle had been prevented." She started as a figure loomed out of the night. "Oh, Peter, you move so quietly! Are we stopping yet?"

"No, Hahle wants to see if we can reach an oasis. Le and I decided to walk for awhile, so Renw went out to scout ahead." He peered up into her face. "You look tired," he said, concern and a hint of anger in his voice. "I sensed you were overdoing it back there. What were you trying to prove?" He caught her hand. "Where's the ring?"

She pulled out of his grasp. "In my pouch. I felt it draining me so I put it away."

Elin shook his mane. "The ring shouldn't drain you. Do you sense anything around us?"

"I can't even sense Peter at the moment. I did pick up a sort of *hunger* when I had the ring on, but that could have been anyone."

"Do you still feel drained?" Elin prodded. "We could have a white hound following us."

"A what?"

Peter felt a chill creep up his spine and glanced past Elin. "Elin, Jeanne, look out!" he yelled, pulling Jeanne out of the saddle.

The ghost drifted lazily over Elin's back and swooped down at the humans. Peter grabbed Jeanne's hand and pulled her after him. The spirit floated in pursuit, ignoring Elin's attempts to hinder it.

"Hahle!" Elin called. "Le, I need a fire! It's drained enough energy from Jeanne to be attuned to her but not enough to become solid!"

Leereho waited until Peter and Jeanne had passed him, then stepped before the pursuing shade and pulled a small stick out of its airtight container. The stick blazed and Leereho thrust its tiny flame towards the ghost. The spirit shuddered and backed away. "Peter," Leereho said, his attention on the ghost he was keeping at bay, "you better get the firewood and start a few fires. The Fleet Ones are too tired to run any farther tonight."

"We could outdistance that white hound easily," Hahle argued, "but where one appears others are not far behind." He looked into the distance as Peter pulled the saddle and bundle of wood off the stallion's back. "I hope Renw hasn't been trapped by those life drinkers."

"Renw is a swift runner," Leereho said calmly, shifting to keep the burning stick before the frantically dodging spirit.

"Jeanne, look out!" Peter warned, scattering the wood as he rushed towards her. "Here comes another one!"

Jeanne, her hands filled with Elin's saddle and pack, stumbled backwards and fell, the heavy load landing in her lap. Elin reared, interposing his body between the filmy shape and the struggling girl. The specter floated under him, groping for Jeanne, and blundered into the intervening Hahle.

Jeanne stifled a cry as the phantom touched Hahle. For the briefest of moments, she was part of Hahle, feeling an icy burning sensation sweep through his body. Hahle uttered an inarticulate sound and crumbled to the ground before her.

"Hahle!" Peter yelled.

"Get some fires going before more come," Elin ordered. "I can keep it away from Hahle now that it's solid." He grabbed the shapeless spirit with his teeth and flung it away, out over the sands.

"Elin, he's ice cold! What did that ghost do to him?"

"Later, Jeanne." Elin caught the returning spirit and flung it to the ground. His hooves battered it into the sand while it tried to flow away from the pounding.

Jeanne stared at him. "I don't sense...it doesn't feel any pain, Elin!"

"Help Peter with the fires!"

Peter was slowly completing a large ring of fires with themselves in the center. With Jeanne's help he closed the ring, forcing the two ghosts out into the fringe of firelight. He looked from the flames to the ghosts. "Why are they afraid of fire?"

The rumble of pounding hooves sounded out of the night and Renw's voice called, "Look out! Here I come!" The stallion leaped the fires and landed safely within the circle. The three spirits that had followed him stopped when they reached the light and began prowling along the barrier, seeking a weak spot.

"The hungry ones are out in full force tonight," Renw breathed heavily. "I almost didn't make it back."

Jeanne caught her breath, and Peter turned at the faint sound and froze. Resembling pulsing ameba, specters floated out of the night sky, heading unerringly towards the fires. Peter counted twenty-five phantoms prowling about the ring of flames, jostling each other in hurried retreat and advance as the light touched them. Peter retrieved the wood from Renw's pack and checked the fires.

Jeanne knelt beside Hahle and draped her blanket over the cold body. She put on her ring and rested her hand on the still neck. "Elin," she said worriedly, "he's barely alive. What did it *do* to him?"

Elin sighed. "Drained him of some of his life force. The first touch stuns and the victim will usually recover." The stallion eyed Jeanne. "Unless the spirit managed to drain its victims from afar, as one did to you." Peter suddenly remembered the Mirror of Truth. At least his first vision didn't seem to be coming true.

"There is no recovering from a second touch. Luckily, with the first touch the spirit absorbs enough life to become solid, and since it can then harm no one but the original victim it can be kept away."

"And it doesn't feel pain," Jeanne whispered.

"Nothing but hunger," Elin agreed, "hunger for life. If it wasn't for them fearing fire, or light, there would be no refuge from them."

"So Renw once told me," Leereho agreed. "But these hungry ones never existed before the witches' arrival. Is this also the result of their spells?"

"The witches did not willingly create these beings," Elin explained. "The spirits are those of this land's people who died serving Evil, either willingly or Changed. Their curse is to still follow the Evil they served in life and they appear whenever Evil appears in our land."

Leereho stared at the prowling ghosts and shivered. "Once I might have become one of them."

Renw stamped his hoof angrily. "Stop that, partner. Jeanne, don't look so frightened. Hahle will recover with the rising of the sun."

"If we survive that long," Peter muttered. He felt a frigid blast of air and found that several of the wraiths were clustering at the edge of one fire's light. The flames wavered as if by a gust of wind. Peter went to rescue the fire and stepped into a wave of coldness that cut to his bones. "Now they're trying to put the fires out!"

Ice slicked parts of the burnt wood, and Peter added dry twigs, coaxing the fire back to life. The flames struggled up from the embers and the spirits retreated to another fire. "I'll get the one over here," Jeanne called. "Le, they're working on one by you."

Peter moved to another flickering fire. He glanced up at the wraiths swarming scant inches from him, kept distant only by a small dying fire. "Vultures," he said. "Leave us alone!" He focused his power and launched it into the cluster of ghosts. One spirit trembled, its filmy shape dissipating like fog before sunlight. He felt a wailing cry in his mind as it dissolved.

"Nooo," a human voice echoed.

Peter whirled as Jeanne staggered back from the fire she was tending and collapsed. Elin hurried to her and dragged her limp body away from the flames.

"Stay with your fire, Peter," the stallion ordered as Peter started towards them.

"Elin, what happened?" Peter demanded.

The stallion's eyes were full of anger. "Thank the West Wind, she's only fainted. Don't you know better than to kill in the presence of a Sensitive?"

"But I didn't mean... How did I..." Peter stammered. He caught his breath. "Is she all right?"

"Just stunned for the moment."

Peter turned back to the fire and shook a stick at the phantoms hurriedly flowing away from him. "How could I kill something that's already dead?"

"By depriving it of belief in its own existence." Elin's voice calmed. "I apologize for my anger, Peter. That blow would have only stunned a normal being. The spirits' link to existence is a fragile one, dependent on others' lives."

"Nice to know that I've got the perfect defense, even though I can't use it."

"No, Peter," Jeanne said in a trembling voice. She slowly sat up and raised a shaking hand to her head. "Use it if you need to. Just warn me first, huh?" She feebly pushed Elin's nose away. "Don't fuss over me, I'll live. Wow, Peter, your bolts are as powerful as Salanoa's." She nursed her head in her hands. "Have I got a headache!"

"Sorry, Jeanne." Peter looked past Leereho to regrouping spirits and a wavering fire. The wraiths fled at his approach and gathered at the opposite side of the circle. "Anybody have any ideas about how to keep these fires going? We're going to run out of wood at this rate."

Leereho stared at Peter, and the boy could sense a memory struggling behind the elf's eyes. "Fool that I am!" the elf suddenly exclaimed. He rummaged in his belt pouch and tossed Peter a short root that tingled with a faint electrical shock when the boy touched it. "Magic from the Tree of Life. Put them in the fires."

As soon as the root touched the flames, the fire flared up brightly and the ghosts scattered in confusion. The five roots were placed evenly about the circle and the separate fires suddenly merged to create a solid ring of flames.

Peter watched the fleeing spirits with satisfaction. "I don't think they'll be back tonight."

"Good," Renw yawned. "I need some rest after all this excitement."

* * *

The night passed slowly. Leereho stared out over the silent sands, his hand on his sword. In the fiery circle, only he stood awake and on watch, since he needed no sleep. He scanned the night sky, waiting for the first dark shape to blot out the stars. The flames were a protection against the ghosts, but their brightness could be a beacon to any other enemies that roamed the desert.

He whirled, his sword whispering out of its sheath, as a low moan came to his ears. As the slight sound was repeated, he moved back from the fires and went among his sleeping companions, bending over one blanket-wrapped figure. "Jeanne," he called softly. He hesitated, unsure as to whether she was dreaming or sensing an approaching danger.

* * *

Jeanne stirred in the depths of her dream. The scene had changed so that she was no longer alone in the desert, surrounded by hovering white shapes projecting their torment at her. Now she stood in a large empty space of violet. Beside her was a shadowy, indistinct figure that could be either dwarf or elf. The emotional pattern, she suddenly realized, was that of the ghost that Peter had killed, but the incessant hunger was gone and instead the emotions had the altered quality of the Change.

She willed to see and slowly the violet space about her solidified into an enormous room of light. Sparkles of violet danced in the crystal floor and mirror-bright walls. Before her, three high-backed thrones on a dais materialized out of the shimmering wall. One was draped in shadows, the next was red stone sculpted into the likeness of leaping flames, and the third was cut from a massive yellow crystal.

She turned her attention from the empty thrones back to the silent being beside her. Her probe had revealed none of the inner struggle and torment that she remembered from Leereho's Change, nor the undercurrent of fear and pain that had been the dryad's. This being's emotions had a curious overlay of acceptance, as if he considered the Change normal.

Jeanne sensed emotions before her and turned to see violet shadows occupying the thrones. She cautiously probed and found that two of the shadows had primitive, superficial emotional patterns, quite unlike the complex and confusing tangle of the third's. Uneasy at that discovery, she withdrew her probe as the blurred shadow on the crystal throne rose and descended the dais. The being beside her knelt, broadcasting such waves of intense adoration and devotion that Jeanne wanted to shake him.

The shadow drifted to stand before the fawning figure. Jeanne caught an instant of smug satisfaction and superiority that set her teeth on edge. Determined to see just what the shifting shadow concealed, she gathered her strength and willed to see behind it. She saw for only a second—and screamed in horror.

CHAPTER 12

MISTS AND VISIONS

She awoke still screaming and found Peter shaking her. He released her when he saw that her eyes were open and sank back on his heels to watch her. She looked about a little wildly and saw neither a witch nor ghosts, only her friends about her.

"You all right now?" Peter asked.

Jeanne caught her breath in a sob and nodded. She shivered violently and Peter threw his blanket about her shoulders.

"Feel up to telling us about it?" he asked as he settled himself again. When she remained silent, he continued, "You really had this place in an uproar. I thought goblins or something was attacking."

"I'm sorry," she said softly. "I had a nightmare."

"Some nightmare. You know, I never heard you scream before, not even back in the caverns. Should have screamed back then," he mused. "Probably would have frightened the witch away."

"Not *her*!" Jeanne shuddered.

"Was that what it was about? Le said you were talking about ghosts for awhile."

Jeanne nodded. "That, too. Oh, Peter, they're in such pain! They need living things, but just being near life tortures them so!"

"You listened in earlier, didn't you?" Peter scolded.

She hesitated. "Just a little. But in the dream—it was horrible! I couldn't shut them out and they kept broadcasting it over and over!"

She glanced up at Elin. "You're wrong about the Changed Ones, Elin. I don't think all of them become ghosts. Those who try to fight it, like Le, probably don't. But the one I was with deserved it!"

Leereho looked bewildered. "The one you were with? What do you mean?"

"In my dream," Jeanne explained hurriedly. "It was the ghost that...died, only it was before he became a ghost, while he was still a Changed One." She shook her head at the memory. "He adored her, even without the Change's influence. He practically groveled at her feet and after what she had done to him, too! He didn't fight!"

"So that's where the witch came in," Peter observed, translating her explanation. "What was so frightening about that, Jeanne? We ran into one before."

"This time I saw beneath the shadow." She took a deep breath. "And she saw me!"

"Which one?" Peter prodded. "What did you see?" He stopped and held his head. "What am I saying? Nightmares are never real."

Leereho shook his head in bewilderment. "Are all humans as contrary to magical laws as you two? Jeanne, only a few of our seers can see another's past, but never in dreams. First they have to be touching either the person or a belonging, and then–"

"Fine, then you tell me what I did see." Jeanne rattled off a description of the room in her dream. "Is that place real?"

Leereho staggered back against Renw as if she had struck him. She could feel his mind whirling with remembered pain and regretted her anger. "That is the witches' throne room! But how did you see it?"

Jeanne huddled inside the blanket. "I don't know! If it was a vision of that ghost's past, then why could I use my powers as if I was actually there?" She paused, remembering. "The witch acted as if I was."

"No, Jeanne, you were here, not at the castle," Peter disagreed.

"But then how did I see all that? My powers don't include visions."

"Oh, my lamentable memory!" Elin snorted. "You may not have that power, Jeanne, but sight of the future and of the past is one of the attributes of the ring of Calada. First it showed you that ghost's past, then switched to the future, to when you finally meet the witch."

Jeanne looked reproachfully at the ring on her finger. "Sneaky thing. Now I'll be getting nightmares every night?" She shivered and, pulling the ring off, stuffed it into her belt pouch.

"What did you see, filly, that frightened you so?"

She stared at their protecting circle of flames and listened to the crackle of the fires. "I didn't expect her to react so quickly."

"Who?" Peter asked.

Jeanne looked at him. "I think you know who. What witch did the dryad and the goblin serve, Peter? You never said if Salanoa told you, and I think she did. Do you know who sits on the crystal throne?"

Peter hesitated. "A human," he finally said.

"A human witch!" Leereho exclaimed. "But the Watcher is the only doorway to the human lands and, aside from those of the Wise, Jeanne is the first human female to enter since the last war with the Shadow Land, ages ago!"

"So who says that she wasn't here all along?" Jeanne argued. "She certainly looked ancient!"

"Ancient, Jeanne?" Peter asked. "The witch that the dryad and the goblin remembered was old, but not ancient."

"They saw the illusion she hid behind," Jeanne said firmly. "I got the impression that she was older than she looked, and she looked to be over a hundred at the very least." She frowned thoughtfully. "She wasn't surprised or frightened to see me. Just expectant, as though she had been waiting eagerly to see me, and her eyes had a strange kind of...of hunger. I know it seems silly, but I felt caught in those eyes, like I was being pulled out of myself. I guess that's when I screamed."

"Blessed Wind," Elin breathed. Jeanne could feel the horror grow in the stallion.

"What is it, Elin?" she asked, climbing to her feet and going to his side. "Elin?"

The stallion stared into space. "I am a student of the magical arts," he said in a dead voice. "I studied under Kelan, Lore-Master of the Folk, he who was killed in the Battle of the Seven and the Nine, and from him learned the tally of those banished to the Shadow Land. But never, of all of them, did I think that the bane of humankind would return to plague us!"

"Elin!" Jeanne tried to break through the wall his mind had retreated behind.

The Windkin shook himself, and the sudden concern in his eyes frightened Jeanne more than his withdrawal. "Jeanne, the only human witch I know of that could have lived this long is Vana the Immortal."

"Elin, don't tell her any more," Peter ordered, moving to her side.

"Why not?" Jeanne demanded. "Peter, you've been hiding something from me ever since we left the Glen. Who is Vana? What did Salanoa tell you about her?"

Peter looked uncomfortable. "Jeanne, you don't want to know. Trust me, huh?"

Jeanne's eyes flashed. "You're trying to protect me again, and I don't like it! Let me remind you, we both have equal powers and we both pull our own weight on this team! Elin, who is Vana the Immortal?"

Elin looked uneasily at Peter. "She must know what she faces, Peter," he apologized. "Ignorance would be a greater harm than protection." He turned to the waiting Jeanne. "Vana is not her true name, of course. Perhaps a few wizards might remember it. She is not actually immortal."

"Let me continue, Elin," Peter said suddenly. "Jeanne, I..."

"Vana the Immortal is not actually immortal," she prodded.

Peter nodded. "I had to use my disbelief on Salanoa to get her old memories of Vana. Of course, we didn't know at that time who was the witch, but after Salanoa remembered Vana, it explained a lot of questions that were bothering me."

"Stop trying to change the subject!"

Peter took a deep breath. He reached out and took her hand. "Now you can be sure I'm not lying," he explained. He glanced uneasily at Elin and sighed at the stallion's nod. "Brace yourself, Jeanne. Vana the Immortal is called the Immortal not because her body lives forever but because, back in the days when humans lived in this land, when her original body grew old, she...took another one."

Jeanne's hand jerked in his grasp. "Someone else's? How could she?"

Peter shrugged. "Does it matter? The fact is, she did, and she continued to capture a new body every time the one she inhabited grew old. What scared me is if you... I mean, she..." He caught his breath. "Vana is probably looking for a new body, and it has to be human."

"No." It was a tiny protest, then the total realization hit her. "NO!" Jeanne struggled to free her hand. "Peter, she saw me!"

"It was only a vision!" Peter caught her shoulders and forced her to look at him. "She won't get you with me around."

"Or me," Elin added.

"Or any of us," Renw inserted.

"I..." Jeanne took a deep breath. Peter could sense the wild terror in her diminish as she took control of her own emotions. Somehow she seemed to retreat from him even as he held her. "I'm sorry," she said softly. "I'll be all right now."

"You sure?" he asked, surprised. He hadn't expected her to be so calm and wondered how long she could hold that stillness. Peter remembered the difficult time he had had hiding his fears from Jeanne when he first learned about Vana.

Jeanne nodded with a faint smile. "I've read enough stories. I guess I should have foreseen it."

"You just did." *Ooops*, he thought, sensing a faint crack in the stillness.

Jeanne looked at him, at all of them, and Peter could sense the boiling tumult behind her gaze. She tried to pull away from him and her mental block snapped into place. "Please, everyone, I...need some time to think."

Peter tried to probe past her block, then nodded and released her. Renw and Leereho moved away, and Elin nudged her gently before trotting away without a word. Peter retrieved his blanket and settled himself on the ground, his back to her.

"Peter, I'm sorry. I just have to face it in my own way." She caught the touch of reassurance he sent her and smiled as he wrapped himself in his blanket and tried to go back to sleep.

The smile left her face as she looked out across the desert and felt fear seeping out from under her mental control. Salanoa spoke in her memory. "*Control fear. Never let terror rule you, for it is the favorite weapon of the Shadows.*"

Jeanne settled herself cross-legged on the sand and, closing her eyes, felt once again the incessant tug of a horribly ancient mind. She let go of her thoughts as Salanoa had taught her, draining her mind of all but the touch of sand against her palms and the faint scent of wood smoke.

*   *   *

"Jeanne, come back."

Peter's voice broke the spell of quiet. She opened her eyes and saw that the fires were subdued and dying and the eastern horizon was streaked with red. She turned her head, feeling the complaint of stiff muscles, and met Peter's concerned gaze. "You were so far away," he said, handing her a steaming cup of *serwasn*.

"Not very far." She breathed in the minty scent of the herbal tea and studied the Windkin breakfasting on grain from the packs. "Hahle hasn't recovered yet?"

"The sun will be up soon. Jeanne, are you angry with me for not telling you sooner about Vana?"

"Can't you tell I'm not?"

"Your block is still up," he said mildly.

"Oh." She laughed nervously. "Old habits, I guess. I used to feel so protected back on Earth, hiding behind my block. Hiding from myself," she added bitterly. She stared into the depths of the beverage. "Peter, I'm scared, but I'm not angry at you. You meant well. But even if it frightens me, I'd rather be warned."

"I'll keep that in mind. You're a brave girl, Jeanne."

"Brave! Trembling in my boots is a better description." She blew the steam off the cup and sipped the *serwasn* slowly. "What else do you know about Vana? How was she ever stopped? If this land follows the stories I've read, she should have obtained the memories of every life she took. That would have made her difficult to find."

"Vana has a long twisted tale that winds through several kingdoms' histories. Elin could probably tell it better."

"No, Peter, you tell it. Elin would pull in half a dozen other tales and I'd never figure out half of them. Besides, we haven't talked together like this for ages." She glanced at him over her cup. "What ever gave you the idea of going through Salanoa's memories for Vana's identity?"

"Let me tell you the story of Vana's unmasking and I know you'll guess some of the questions I needed answered. All right? Once upon a time—"

"Peter!"

"Once upon a time there was a human kingdom where the Mist Lands now stand. The king and his young queen had always had a fair trade policy with the Fleet Ones of Windgard. The Fleet Ones would send volunteers to help with transportation—provided the volunteers were treated well—in exchange for grain that the humans grew.

"Suddenly that policy changed. Fleet Ones were hunted and enslaved by the humans. The Windrunner of that time was a good friend of the queen and went to see her to ask for an explanation of her husband's strange behavior. The Windrunner found her friend, but somehow she sensed that this was not the queen she knew. A stranger was inhabiting her friend's body. The Windrunner barely escaped from the queen with her life. She went to ask the Fleet Ones' friend, the wizard Graylod—"

Jeanne choked on her tea. "Graylod!"

"Wizards are very long-lived, it seems," Peter explained. "No one knows for sure how old Graylod, or even Salanoa, is. Anyhow, the Wise had been searching for Vana years before the Windrunner discovered her. It seems that too many queens and influential women had changed suddenly over the centuries. Her trail was easy to backtrack, since she stayed in some kingdoms over several generations, and, once the wizards discovered her true name, they devised a name spell to take away her powers and trap her forever in one body.

"When the Windrunner found Graylod, the wizard rushed back with her and cast the spell. They couldn't kill Vana, of course, because the king had absorbed enough lies about Fleet Ones to doubt the Windrunner. The queen's death would have only started a war. She was trapped, though, and she knew it. Soon afterward Vana vanished, and the Wise believed she had gone to the Shadow Land to find a way of breaking the name spell."

"And now that she's broken it, she's out to punish those who put the spell on her," Jeanne said slowly. "That explains why Windgard was turned into a desert and the witch hounds chase the Windkin for sport. And that fear curse put on the Windkin. Vana's idea of revenge."

"It took me a while to think of the revenge motive since the curse seemed to have erased curiosity along with memories," Peter said. "I asked the Windrunner, the Elder, Salanoa, Le, Hahle—everyone I could about the desert and not one person thought it odd that only the Fleet Ones had their land destroyed or that, with a whole land to range through, the ghosts stayed on the desert."

"No, that's the best part of revenge—when the victim doesn't know why he's being punished," Jeanne mused. "The Windkin were punished, and Graylod was captured."

"Right, Graylod was captured—the *only* wizard captured. Vana's been systematically killing all the other wizards she can find."

"Why? Why is she killing them? She's already taken most of their powers away with the curse."

Peter shrugged his shoulders. "No one seems to know."

Jeanne eyed him suspiciously. If no one seemed to know, what was he so smug about? Aloud she commented, "Peter, sometimes you can be more mysterious than a certain elf engaged to a particular wizard."

He looked at her in surprise. "I don't see how you can call the Elder mysterious when practically everyone at the gathering knew about him and Salanoa."

"Uh huh, and everyone was so busy gossiping about them that no one realized that their real reason for being absent from the gathering so often was to train us." She suddenly paused and looked absently into space. Putting her cup down, she rose and started folding the blanket she had borrowed from Leereho. "Le's back. Was he scouting? And

Hahle's coming around."

The stallion stirred as the sun peeked over the horizon. He lifted his head and looked about blearily. "Didn't we make it to the oasis?" he asked in a groggy voice.

"Of course not," Renw snorted. "What were we supposed to do, drag your oversized carcass there with half the white hounds in existence hanging around? If you have to play the hero, Hahle, next time do it near a supply of wood and water."

"Don't pay any attention to him," Jeanne ordered as she pulled her blanket off the black stallion. "I appreciate the rescue. Thanks, Hahle."

The stallion struggled to his feet and nuzzled her unsteadily. "So long as everyone is all right," he murmured thickly. "Isn't anyone going to offer the hero some water?"

"You can have my water skin," Leereho offered as he stepped between the dying fires. "Or, if you can walk, the oasis is only a short distance away."

"One skin of water won't quench his thirst," Renw commented. "He'll walk. Won't you, Hahle?" he added, coming alongside the other stallion. "Just lean on me if you feel woozy. Don't worry, Jeanne, it's nothing for you to heal. He'll be fine once he starts moving. Move, Hahle."

"Is this any way to treat a hero?" Hahle muttered.

"But..." Jeanne tried.

Renw steered the black stallion between the fires. "I'll be back for a share of the gear once I get this old plodder to the oasis," he called.

"Old plodder!" Hahle snorted.

"Whoa! Don't knock me over, Hahle!"

*   *   *

Twilight found them deep in the heart of a barren forest not far from the fringes of the desert. No life sheltered under the desiccated trees; the slightest breeze set branches rubbing together with an eerie creaking sound. Jeanne tried not to look at the brown wasteland.

"By tomorrow evening we should be in the Mist Lands," Renw mused, glancing over at Leereho, who was heating *serwasn* over their tiny campfire.

Leereho nodded. "Since Hahle took us through Dune's March, the most direct path through the desert, we should be able to use our old base in the foothills if we need shelter tomorrow night. We probably will, unless any of you like sleeping out in the snow."

"Snow?" Peter asked. "We just came through a desert! What kind of mixed-up climate has snow next door to a desert?"

"Witches," Renw snorted. "The flame witch prefers heat, and the Dark One prefers shadow and cold. The Mist Lands, just to suit her, are shrouded in a gray mist through which the sun never shines. Which is a help to us, since the hounds will never see us through the mists."

"The witches could always lift the mists," Peter argued.

Renw snorted again. "Why should they? The mists are the only defense for their castle. They're so sure of themselves that they don't even bother to patrol the Mist Lands or place guards on the castle walls."

"The castle is defended by the curse," Leereho disagreed. "Of all the Folk, only you Fleet Ones can go near it without being weakened."

Peter poured himself a mug of *serwasn* and let Renw and Leereho continue their argument without him. Jeanne had found a semi-comfortable tree to lean against, and he settled himself on the ground near her. The girl nodded to him and silently sipped her *serwasn*, but Peter could sense that her mind was far away. "Anyone following us?" he asked softly.

Her dark hair rippled as she shook her head. "Not for miles. At my farthest range I can sense goblins or trolls back on the desert, but they're too far away to cause any trouble right now."

Peter glanced at the fingers curled about her mug. "No ring? Have you been getting any more visions?"

Jeanne shivered. "No, thank goodness. But the way those two patrols headed straight for us, I wondered if maybe they were tracking the ring. I could always sense Salanoa's pendant."

"I never thought of that," Peter said, dismayed. "No, that can't be it," he corrected himself. "The Dark One found us before you had the ring."

"Then how are they finding us?" Jeanne mused. She drained her mug and leaned back against the tree, staring up into the starry night sky. "Do you realize how long we've been here? Our parents have probably given up hope."

Peter shook off his homesickness with an effort. "Just don't you give up hope. 'Belief is a good part of magic,' remember?"

* * *

The next day the six came to a strange division line running from horizon to horizon. On one side of the invisible line stretched the brown and gray wasteland while on the other a solid wall of gray mists hovered over the snow-covered ground. Jeanne bent and gathered a handful of snow. "Brr," she shivered, packing the snow. "I can't see anything through that mist. Wish we didn't have to go in there." She hefted the snowball.

"No, Jeanne!" Peter dodged the snowball, then bent to make his own.

"You humans can't see?" Renw said worriedly. "Elin and Hahle will take you, then. Our eyesight isn't as good in this murk as Leereho's—and don't start bragging about elfin sight, partner—but at least we can see enough to walk." He snorted in surprise as the snowball intended for Jeanne hit him in the ribs.

Jeanne laughed and darted around the stallion. "What happened to your reflexes, Peter?" She scooped up more snow and dashed away.

"They're just fine," Peter retorted as his next snowball hit her back. He laughed, forgetting to duck, and a wad of snow splattered over his shoulder.

Hahle and Elin watched the snowball fight with interest. "Is this a human ritual?" Elin inquired politely as the battle raged around him.

"The Folk's children don't have snowball fights?" Peter stopped to ask. He felt snow accumulating on his back from two more direct hits, but ignored that, waiting and watching out of the corner of his eyes for Jeanne to emerge from hiding behind Hahle. When she finally did, he whirled and pelted her with his supply of snow. Jeanne laughed as she withdrew behind the black stallion again.

"Possibly in the colder regions," Renw said absently. He stepped up to the now-muddied borderline of grass and snow. "We'll scout ahead and leave a trail for you to follow." The roan vanished into the swirling mists.

Leereho hesitated, half in and half out of the gray wall. "Do not get too far behind us. Snow falls at a witch's whim and it is much too easy to lose trails in a storm."

Peter eyed Jeanne. "Enough?"

"Enough," Jeanne smiled, dropping her last snowball.

"We'll be along as soon as we brush off some of this snow," Peter said to Leereho. The elf nodded, and the gray wall closed behind him.

"You missed some on your shoulder," Jeanne said, coming up behind him and scraping snow off his cloak. "I don't think Hahle will appreciate you dripping ice water all over him." She shook her own cloak once more for good measure, then swung up onto Elin. Hahle and Peter followed them into the gray wall.

Once inside the mist, Peter lost all sense of direction. He was in a thick, clinging sea of gray, so dense that he couldn't even see the Fleet One he rode. Instinctively he tightened his grip on Hahle's mane and only relaxed it at the Windkin's indignant complaint. "Sorry, Hahle," he apologized. "You can actually *see* in this?"

"Not too far," Hahle's voice came from out of the grayness. "But enough to follow the trail. Elin, either slow down so I can see you or stop muddling the trail!"

"I have a feeling that this mist was intended to be more of a defense against humans than the Folk," Jeanne commented. Although she couldn't see him, she sensed Elin's surprise.

"Possibly," the gray and white stallion agreed thoughtfully, "although you are the first humans to come this far on your own."

"Was that supposed to be a compliment, or are you trying to scare us?" Jeanne peered through the mist uneasily. The clinging fog coiled about her like a live thing, and she recognized the magic that had created it as being akin to her own illusions. Although her senses assured her that there were no enemies lurking in its depths, she didn't like riding so blindly into the witches' own land. By touch she found her belt pouch and donned the ring. After scanning the fog with her heightened powers and sensing only Leereho and Renw in the distance, she concentrated for a moment on the gold band. The rainbow brightness expanded and the mist retreated before it, rolling back from the glow until Elin stood within a fog-free circle.

Elin stopped in bewilderment and watched the gloom warily. Jeanne patted his neck and slid out of the saddle. Her boots crunched faintly through the packed snow as she explored the limits of the ring's light. Elin watched her and nodded in comprehension as the clear area stayed centered about the girl. "I had forgotten the ring again. You don't sense any trolls about?"

"No other life out there except Renw and Le," Jeanne said. She stopped at a sudden thought. "You know, I haven't sensed any small animal life since we left the Glen."

"None are about," Hahle explained as he entered the lighted clearing. "When the witches came, the small life either fled elsewhere, away from Windgard and the Mist Lands, or died when the enchantment was cast."

Peter blinked as Hahle stepped farther into the clearing. "Hey, I can see! Your powers certainly come in handy, Jeanne."

Jeanne gave him an odd look and Peter caught her flash of irritation. Before he could ask, she whirled as if to a sudden sound and scrambled back into the saddle. "Leereho's very worried about something."

Elin's nostrils expanded to catch the icy breeze. "I smell a storm coming. Leave the ring glowing, Jeanne, we can move faster through this murk with it."

The two Fleet Ones followed the marked trail quickly. Soon Jeanne could see the dark shapes of the foothills closing about them. Hahle fell back so that the Windkin moved single file along the narrowing path. Jeanne stifled a gasp when she noticed that the trail ran along the bottom of a deep gorge. Massive boulders were tumbled over the ground like spilled marbles and, looking up, Jeanne could see the outcroppings the rocks had fallen from looming over them on both sides.

Tiny bits of stone clinked down from the giant slabs of rock overhead, the sound echoing sharply in the sudden stillness. The Fleet Ones' unshod hooves stepped quietly, almost daintily, through the rocky clutter littering the trail. The rock walls creaked as a chill wind whistled down the narrow gap. The ground sloped upwards.

Finally the long stretch of rock ended. The path widened as it left the gorge and Hahle moved up to Elin's side. Jeanne released her tightly held breath in a sigh of relief. "Rocktooth Pass is dangerous," Elin agreed, "the most dangerous of the passes leading into the Mist Lands. But now we have entered the Darkling Valley. On the other side of the valley are the Mountains of Illusion, and among those peaks stands the castle."

A tiny snowflake drifted down. "Leereho and Renw are still far ahead," Jeanne said worriedly. "Do you think we'll make it to their cave before this storm hits?"

"The winds smell of magic," Elin said thoughtfully. "There's no predicting when a spell storm will come. Hahle, we'd better take the risk of a gallop." He lengthened his stride.

"Don't blame me when you break a leg on a patch of ice," Hahle muttered gloomily as he followed.

More snowflakes drifted lazily on the chill winds. Still the trail ran on into the mist.

"The snow will cover our safe trail," Elin panted.

"I can guide us to Leereho and Renw, but only the most direct way," Jeanne answered. "They're off to the left, and upwards."

"And the trail leads to the right," Elin observed. "Renw must have had a reason for going such a roundabout way."

The biting wind swirled about them, and the storm hit with its full force. The Fleet Ones stopped as snow and sleet lashed into their faces. "We can't go that way," Hahle shouted over the howling wind.

"We have to," Peter yelled back. "Jeanne, can't you do anything?"

The flash of anger he had noticed before suddenly flared up in the girl. "Stop believing everything you see, Peter!" she exploded. "This is a magical storm! *You* do something!"

"I can't disbelieve an entire storm!"

"So who asked you to? A small area of disbelief is all we need."

Peter closed his eyes and his mind against the storm. There was no storm, no wind, no snow. He felt the force of his disbelief build up inside him, then cast it outwards.

"Nice going, partner!"

Peter opened his eyes and found that they were once again standing in a cleared area lit by the glowing ring. At the outer limits of the ring's glow, the storm buffeted against the invisible wall of his disbelief.

"How long can you hold the storm back?" Hahle asked worriedly.

"Long enough to get where we're going, I hope," Peter glanced over at Jeanne. "Lead on, partner."

"Off a bit to your right, Elin. I'll let you know when we're even with Leereho and Renw."

The storm's fury lashed uselessly against Peter's force field as they moved on. The four travelers skirted the edge of a small frozen lake, then headed left along its shore and up into the hills.

"Leereho and Renw are inside this hill," Jeanne said finally as they stood on a gentle slope, "but I can't be sure where the opening would be."

Elin sniffed at the snow, then raised his head. "Lower your barrier, Peter. I need the wind."

The storm engulfed them and Elin snorted in satisfaction. "Ah, this way."

They followed him and were soon inside the small limestone cave. A fire crackled cheerily in one corner, its smoke drifting lazily out a small hole in the ceiling, and from the back came the murmur of an underground river. "A little damp, as caves go, but it's our best-equipped base," Renw said as he showed them about.

"We thought you were lost when the storm hit," Leereho said, starting to unsaddle Hahle. "We were about to go out after you when we felt Jeanne's touch and knew you were all right."

"How long do you think this storm will last?" Hahle asked, looking out at the gray-and-white-whipped mists.

THE CRYSTAL THRONE

"No telling," Renw snorted. "Sometimes a storm will last for weeks and other times maybe only a few hours. But we'll be safe enough here."

* * *

The storm howled outside the cave for two days more, covering the valley with a fresh blanket of white. The six passed the time in their own ways. Leereho and Elin exchanged stories and argued the truth of legends while Hahle and Renw tried to find the source of the underground river. Peter gave up on that search after an unsuccessful day and went back to experimenting with his powers. Catching Jeanne's amused gaze on him after he had mindlessly entangled himself in the blankets, he knew that he wasn't the only experimenter. He scowled at her as he untangled himself and snapped a small barrier of disbelief around his mind so that she wouldn't control him again.

He wandered over to the cave's entrance for the tenth time that day and stared out into the mists. The raging storm still looked as if it would never let up. He gathered his disbelief and flung it outside of the opening, watching in satisfaction as the storm drew away from the hillside.

"Playing again?" Hahle snorted behind him.

"Just testing. Now we don't have to follow Elin and Jeanne just to see where we're going. I can push the mists back farther than the ring."

"That won't do much against the witches."

Peter smiled. "You'd be surprised what it can do, if I can get it to work right. Jeanne, could you help a moment? I need a spell to... What's wrong?"

Jeanne stood beside them, but he sensed that her mind was out searching the mists. She shook her head. "I can't tell for sure. I get an impression of life out there, but I can't tell how many or how close. The impression is clearer without the ring, too, and that isn't normal."

"Could the magic in the storm be affecting the ring?" Peter asked.

"We've been here three days and I didn't get this distortion before. There's magic out there, all right, but not from the storm. And I don't like it one bit."

* * *

Late that night, when the storm was finally beginning to die down, Jeanne was still watching from her post by the cave's entrance. "Have they come any closer?" Peter asked as he moved to her side.

Dark hair rippled as she shook her head. "Still in the same spot, wherever that is."

"Go get some sleep, I'll watch for awhile." She gasped suddenly and caught his arm for support. "Jeanne, what happened? Are you all right?"

She pushed the hair out of her face with a trembling hand. "Someone just died out there, Peter."

He felt the pain in her mind and tried to calm her. "So there's one less troll, Jeanne. Don't let it hurt you so."

"You don't understand, Peter. He was of the Folk!"

He stared out into the mists. "The Folk? Did the Elder send someone after us? Is that the magic you sensed?"

Jeanne followed his gaze. "No, that magic is all wrong, all warped and distorted. I don't like it. It feels like a jumbled version of the spell creating the mists. I wish I knew why he was out in the center of it."

CHAPTER 13

THE VIOLET FIRE

Early that morning, Jeanne awoke suddenly, her senses jangling a warning. Still half asleep, she scanned for the source of danger. With a sense of relief she found nothing and tried to fall asleep again. The next second she sat up, her mind reeling with surprise.

She had felt nothing! No patient alertness from Leereho, not even the blurred muddle of dreams—and as she glanced about the cave she saw that all were asleep. For a moment she feared that her emotional block had sealed her off from her companions, but when she tried to touch them with her mind, she sensed the magic holding them captive in sleep. She spotted Leereho at his post by the entrance and hurried to the side of the silent elf. "Sleeping, like everyone else," she whispered. "Oh, Leereho, the spell has to be strong to affect you, too!"

Silently the girl edged toward the entrance of the cave, all her senses tensed. She shivered as the magic beat against her shield, striving to dominate her as it had her friends. She activated the ring's glow and the rainbow light pushed the clammy touch of the distorted spell away from her.

She tried to probe the mists outside the entrance, but, like last night, the impressions she received were not clear. She sensed intruders but had no idea whether they were waiting for her outside the entrance—or were even aware that the cave existed. Her probe answered one question. *Drat, the illusion I put up to hide the cave's entrance is gone. No hiding from them then. And I can't let whomever it is inside, not with everyone so defenseless. It's up to me. I either have to stop them or draw their attention away from the cave.* She hesitated as her eyes fell on one blanket-wrapped figure. *Peter's not going to like this.*

She stepped cautiously out of the cave, her powers gathered and ready. The wind whipped her cloak about her, and her hand moved automatically to hold back her loose hair. Her wariness grew as she noticed that the spell was beginning to affect even the ring of Calada. The protective glow holding back the mist was starting to shrink back towards her. She clamped down on her fear and forced herself to stride boldly down the hillside, away from the cave and deeper into the heart of the magic. As she walked, she noticed a light out of the corner of her eye, but she could not look at it directly and see it.

She turned her head to catch sight of it again. Yes, it was a light, flickering like a torch, but what torch could stay alight in a wind like this? Suddenly the light was blotted out, and the sudden return of emotions inside the cave overwhelmed her before she could block them. Jeanne gasped as she noticed that the light was fading from her ring, flickering almost as if the magic was being drained. The mist closed about her, and she sensed the source of the warped spell drawing nearer.

She heard a sound behind her and whirled, her mind seeking its cause. She sensed Leereho emerging from the cave, but then the twisted magic sprang up and snapped into place like the bars of a cage about her. She opened her mouth to shout a warning when a heavy hand clamped over her mouth.

* * *

Peter slowly climbed out of the sleepy daze enveloping him. For some reason, the thick fog of sleep seemed unusually unwilling to release him today. He had been dozing on and off all morning, and each time he decided that it was time to get up, another side of him wanted to sleep for five minutes more. He was about to agree with the sleepy side again when suddenly he was rudely awakened.

Peter sat up and shook his head. The feeling had lasted only a few heartbeats, but somehow he could not dispel it. That strange upsurge of emotions had certainly not been his, more like a cry directed at him. A cry filled with hopelessness, despair, and a fear so sharp and intense that it had felt like a shout. Peter caught sight of a discarded blanket and shot out of the cave.

He tripped over Leereho outside the entrance. The elf was dazed, and a swelling lump on the back of his head explained why. "Where's Jeanne?" Peter demanded, looking about worriedly. The Fleet Ones pushed past him and spread out over the hillside, studying the snow for tracks.

Leereho shook his head painfully. "Goblins. Two of them had Jeanne, and I did not see the third."

Peter concentrated, reaching for Jeanne's mind, but the normally clear linkage was confused and indefinite. He was aware that she was alive, but not where she was or whether she was hurt. His fears threw the memory of his last vision at the Mirror of Truth at him, and he knew that its foretelling of Jeanne as a bound captive had come true. "We can't let Vana get her hands on Jeanne! Which way did they go?"

Suddenly an explosion of light ripped through the gray mists. A rising spout of rainbows, as blindingly brilliant as a Roman candle, lingered for a moment on the horizon, and then faded from view. "I'll start there!" Elin yelled and dashed into the mists.

"That fool will break his neck one of these days," Hahle muttered, "and I'll have to drag him home. Hurry up, Peter. Renw will care for Leereho."

Peter helped the elf to his feet. "No patrols, huh?" he growled as Renw moved alongside to help Leereho into the cave.

Leereho held his aching head. "Goblins should not be on patrol in the Mist Lands. Trolls would. I do not understand what goblins would be doing here."

"They captured Jeanne and slugged you. What more could they do?"

Peter scrambled onto Hahle's broad back, then saw Leereho pulling himself onto Renw. "Le, what are you doing? You can't ride with a lump like that on your head."

"I only saw three goblins, but there might be more. I am coming along."

"All right, partner," Renw reluctantly agreed. "But if you fall off, we're stopping right there."

They followed Elin's and the goblins' tracks through the snow and soon caught up with the stallion. "What's a statue of a goblin doing in the middle of the Mist Lands?" Peter asked as he slid off Hahle.

"I wonder if we will ever discover all the powers of Calada's ring," Elin mused as he studied the still figure. "This is no statue, Peter. The goblin is time-trapped."

"Why didn't she just freeze the others in time as well?" Hahle snorted. He studied the snow. "The tracks aren't heading for the castle, but those goblins are in a big hurry. We should be, too, if we want to get Jeanne back safely."

"The ring only acts when Jeanne is threatened with physical danger," Elin said thoughtfully. "Peter, look at his extended hand. He seems to have something in it."

His skin crawling at the touch of the cold flesh, Peter pried the bony fingers open. "It's the ring!" He started as the dulled ring moved toward his reaching fingers. "Hey, it's trying to get to Jeanne! We can use it to find her."

"We've got other problems right now," Elin said. "The goblin is recovering. Peter, get back behind Hahle and close your field about us. I don't want him to see you. Leereho, you'll have to ask the questions. I doubt if he could understand us."

The goblin shivered and blinked. Catching sight of the three grim-looking stallions hemming him in, he tried to shrink away. "Garv, help!" he squeaked. Leereho calmly removed the goblin's sword and dagger as the bony creature attempted to reach for them. "Don't hurt me! I'll tell you anything you want!"

"What are we supposed to do with *him*?" Peter whispered to Hahle.

The stallion stamped one hoof suggestively. "We'll think of something."

"We don't mean to hurt no one," the goblin said hastily, eyeing Hahle. "The Flame Witch, she just told us to catch people and bring them to her. And if we found any wizards, we was to bring them especially to her and not let the Other know."

"How did you find us?" Leereho queried, tapping his fingers on the hilt of his sword.

"The fire points toward magic stuff like that ring, it does. So we left Nif with our other prisoner and me and Garv and Bur, we come over to see who's there. The fire makes you Folk nice and weak, so's you're easy to catch. Bur, he hit you. I'd be glad to lead you to him."

"What a little snitch!" Peter said disgustedly. Hahle whacked him with his tail and the boy bit back his additional comments.

"Bur didn't have to hit you," the goblin continued, "but we had our hands full with the wizard." He rubbed the side of his jaw at the memory. "She hit me a good one, she did."

"Good!" Peter muttered. Hahle choked.

"The fire?" Leereho asked, trying to get more details.

"The Flame Witch gave us a spell so's we could see through the mists. Comes in real handy, it does." He looked slyly at the Fleet Ones. "You got a spell, too. Don't look like the one the sparkly ring had, no, it don't."

Leereho deftly sidestepped the question. "There are four of you, then? If you are lying, the Fleet Ones are swift with vengeance."

The goblin shrank back inside of himself. "Only four of us, yes, noble one. Don't let the Four-Footed Ones hurt me!"

"What other powers does your fire possess?"

There was a gleam in the goblin's beady eyes that Peter didn't like. "Powers, noble one? Just the ones I told you. I'd be right glad to take you there so's you could rescue the wizard."

"I'll just bet you would," Elin said. "Leereho, you and Renw better stay here with our friend. I don't trust him, and you won't be any help with your head and the fire's drain. Peter, damp your field until we're away from here."

"Here, now," the goblin said uneasily. "What's he saying?" He squeaked as the mist shut about him. "I can't see! Don't hurt me, noble one! I done told you everything you wanted!"

The protests died in the distance. Peter leaned over Hahle's neck. "I felt like hitting him myself. What a slimy character! You realize that he was hiding something about the fire."

Hahle nodded. "We didn't have the time to frighten him into confessing it. We're counting on you to protect us, Peter. The fire only controlled you before because you weren't on guard against it."

"I know. And Jeanne was." He felt the ring tugging inside his belt pouch. "We're getting closer."

The stallions clambered up a frozen rise. "Hahle, look, there's the fire!" Elin exclaimed.

Peter peered through the mists. "What fire? I don't see anything."

"It's golden," Hahle said in a dreaming voice.

Peter looked at the stallion uneasily. There was an odd tone in Hahle's voice, yet somehow it held an elusive familiarity. He caught sight of a light out of the corner of his eye. The light winked out when he faced it, and reappeared when he turned his head. "There it is," he agreed. "But it's not golden, more like a dull red. Hey, will you two slow down? We want to sneak in, not barge in on them."

The Windkin trotted forward silently. Peter's uneasiness rose. "C'mon, enough joking. Stop! Whoa!"

He stopped pulling at Hahle's mane. "Why, that lying goblin! This is what he was hiding!"

Concentrating carefully, he mentally placed a barrier around each of their minds and then clutched wildly at Hahle's mane when the stallion came to an abrupt halt. "What happened? My mind feels like it's been turned inside out."

"The fire has vanished," was Elin's groggy comment.

"It's still there," Peter said grimly. "Our goblin friend neglected to warn us that it hypnotizes you if you see it straight on. Only I had my shield up so tightly that I could only see it by looking sideways at it."

"So you weren't affected, thank the Wind, or we would have walked straight into their welcoming arms." Elin stamped a hoof angrily. "No wonder he was so willing to lead us to his friends!"

"It does give us a good way to sneak in, though," Peter mused thoughtfully. "You two feel like doing a bit of acting?"

Elin saw his line of reasoning. "It might work at that, but all three of us aren't going to walk boldly into that trap."

"Of course not!" Peter agreed. "You two walk in as if you're still caught in its spell, and I'll sneak in behind while they're watching you."

"I don't like that," Hahle disagreed. "How about Elin going in the front and Peter and I sneak in the back?"

Peter suddenly realized why Jeanne so disliked being protected. "Don't you think I can protect myself, Hahle?" He slid off the stallion's back without giving him a chance to reply. "Wait five minutes and then start moving. And whatever you do, don't look at that fire straight on! I don't want to have to rescue you as well as Jeanne."

Hahle and Elin exchanged glances. Elin's ears twitched, and he gave a snort of laughter. "And you wonder why I can't control *my* human!"

Peter plunged on into the mists, keeping his bearings by observing the fire out of the corner of his eye. The field of disbelief extended far enough ahead of him so that he could avoid tripping over any stones or falling into the hidden gullies. The ring tried to pull him sideways as he gave a wide berth to the camp. He didn't dare risk going close enough to see if he could spot Jeanne for fear that he would be observed, but from what he could see through the obstructing mists, the camp was quiet.

He settled himself into position on the frozen ground and waited for the Fleet Ones to arrive. The camp was almost too quiet. A feeling that he had overlooked something nagged at him like an incessant mosquito, but he dismissed that worry as the sound of the Fleet Ones' hooves came to his ears.

He crawled closer to the camp, feeling the ring trying to roll out of his belt pouch, and controlled his instinctive aversion when the red fire suddenly appeared in the mists ahead. *I must be inside its range of influence*, he decided when the fire did not affect him as it had the Fleet Ones. With the aid of the firelight, he located the three shadowy figures that were the goblins off to his left. The ring tugged him to the right of the fire and he could dimly make out the outlines of Jeanne seated there.

Confident in his bearings, he snapped off his field of disbelief. Instantly he realized his mistake. The magical fire whipped unerringly in his direction like a striking snake.

"Peter, look out!"

Peter scrambled to his feet and drew his sword at Jeanne's cry. He turned as the largest goblin he had ever seen lunged out of the mists at him. The bony creature stood over six feet tall and lifted a huge spiked mace with ease.

Peter dimly heard the thunder of hooves and Elin's scream of challenge back by the fire as the goblin swung the deadly weapon at him. Peter dodged out of the path of the blow and swung his sword. The goblin casually blocked the swing with his mace, and the blade caught between its spikes. With a sudden yank, the goblin jerked the sword out of Peter's grasp and sent it sliding across the frozen ground. The goblin gave a barking laugh as Peter drew his dagger.

"You're caught, elf. And those honor-bound Fleet Ones can't help you while Nif holds a sword to the little wizard's throat." He hefted the mace and stepped ponderously toward the boy.

Peter readied himself for the attack. His knife looked ridiculously small against the mace, but his sword was out of his reach. Snow creaked behind him.

Alarmed, Peter started to turn when something smashed against the back of his head. He fell into a pain-filled blackness.

* * *

The first thing Peter noticed when he regained his senses was that his arms were cramped. The next items of interest were that his arms were securely tied behind his back and that his head was throbbing. For a few moments his mind held the blurred muddle of a flaring fire, a barking laugh, and a huge mace, and then his memory returned in full. He groaned aloud as he realized how easily he had been captured.

A sympathetic touch crept into his mind and the throbbing pain subsided to a dull ache he could ignore. His eyes flew open, and he saw Jeanne seated a short distance away, her concerned eyes watching him.

"That's all I can do for you now, Peter," she whispered swiftly. "I can't heal it completely until I can reach you, my power is too low."

"All!" Peter peered through the shadows at her. Jeanne was pale and her exhaustion was evident even without the sensory linkage. "You did too much. Save your strength."

Jeanne glanced nervously over to where the goblins huddled around a normal fire. "Speak English—they understand the Common Tongue, too."

Peter lowered his voice. "Are you all right?"

"I'd be great if that fire would suddenly go out. It's draining me, but not as badly as when I had the ring. The stupid spell drains anyone with magic so they keep prisoners here and try to keep their distance. It drains them, too."

Peter looked at the fire before him and noticed that at this close range the flames were violet instead of red. Although the flames burned brightly, he didn't feel any warmth on his legs. He stared into its depths. "I don't feel any drain."

"You wouldn't. This is a time when magic can be a curse instead of a blessing. What are you smiling about?"

Peter glanced over at the goblins. "I was just thinking what a dummy I am. I'm believing everything I see again." He stared into the fire. "Why didn't you wake me up instead of going outside on your own?" he asked, keeping his eyes on the fire.

"I knew you'd be mad about that. I couldn't reach anyone. It felt like I was sealed off behind an invisible wall. I'm still trying to figure out why a torch has that effect and a fire a hypnotic one. Must have something to do with the size of the fire."

"Jeanne, don't start discussing magic or we'll be here all day." The flames began to flicker.

"Sorry." Jeanne glanced worriedly into the shadows. "I wish there was some wildlife I could summon to help us. I don't like working with goblin minds. If you knew how hard it is to influence an intelligent mind in a contrary direction without it realizing the interference—and this fire isn't helping."

"It didn't take you all that long to control me that one time," Peter said, keeping his eyes on the fire.

"You shouldn't pace so much. All I had to do was direct your pacing so that you'd trip over the packs. I've got more complicated directions to give this time and so far I can only influence Bur, and Nif a little. That Garv is different."

"Maybe you can't control three minds at once."

"Maybe. Careful, Garv is looking this way."

Peter let the flames spring up again.

"Do you think you can put it out?" Jeanne asked eagerly.

"Not completely, I'm afraid. It's linked to someone's mind and I'll have to break the linkage first."

"Whose mind? Not the Flame Witch's?"

"No, someone close by." Peter's gaze swung to the other fire.

"Garv, I'll bet. That's why I can't control him! Where is he? Oh!"

An enormous shadow fell over them. "Bur, I told you to keep the prisoners apart, not side by side!" Garv bellowed. He picked Peter up as if the boy was a sack of grain and dumped him across the fire from Jeanne. The goblin leaned over and gripped Peter's chin, staring intently into the boy's face. "You're not the elf from the cave." He released his grasp and stepped back to study his captive. "Too young to be an elfin warrior, and the spell didn't bother you so you're no age-changed wizard. A troll once told me that the Dark One is looking for a human and now I have you." He glanced thoughtfully at Jeanne. "A human and a wizard. The Fiery One will be quite pleased with me. Bur, get over here!"

A goblin in a tattered violet uniform shambled over to them. A long scar ran down the side of his bald head and his eyes held only blankness in their depths. "Hurt, smash?" the pathetic figure asked eagerly, waving his short club.

"Sit, Bur," Garv commanded. The bony creature flopped onto the ground behind Jeanne. "Watch them, Bur. If they try to get away or talk to each other then you can hit them."

"Hurt, smash," the goblin agreed happily. He braced his club on end in the snow and leaned on it. Garv eyed his silent captives thoughtfully, then turned on his heel and strode back to the other fire.

"An odd thing about Bur," Jeanne started when Garv was out of earshot.

"Shh!" Peter hissed, glancing at their watching guard.

"Is that he can sleep with his eyes open. He's not usually prone to sleepwalking and he's very bad at knots, so it's taking me longer than I expected to get free." The goblin slowly bent forward and fumbled at the ropes around her wrists. "Don't look so shocked, Peter. I didn't know how long you'd take to find me, so I thought I'd start working on my own. If you had given me some warning before your raid, I might have been able to do something to help instead of being the helpless captive."

THE CRYSTAL THRONE

Peter looked at her in admiration. "Can you put Nif to sleep, too?"

"Bur is a better subject for sleepwalking. Nif likes to argue. I don't think Garv has had a quiet moment since I got here."

As if to agree with her, Peter could hear the goblins shouting at each other. "I don't care if the Flame Witch is going to be pleased with us! That doesn't help us find our way back to the castle! We're lost, you big lumbering oaf!"

"Will you stop going over and over that!" Garv roared back. "The hounds were supposed to guide us!"

"So who's the oink-headed idiot that had to land in the desert? We're lucky the cursed life drinkers were satisfied with the hounds!"

Bur started awake. "Hurt, smash?" he asked dazedly.

"You're sound asleep," Jeanne said firmly. The goblin bent again to the knots.

Peter sensed the weariness weighing on her. "I've got the ring in my belt pouch. Would that help?"

Jeanne had twisted around, trying to see how well Bur was progressing with the knots. "Hmm? Oh, so that's why the fire pointed at you. Didn't you know that they found us by tracking the ring? You must have, if you have it now. Rev is a talkative fellow."

Peter peered across the flames at her. "You're getting awfully talkative, too. What's the matter?"

She bit her lip. "Sorry, Peter. I've got to stay awake somehow. The ring wouldn't help me, not until we get out of the fire's range. I was so glad when Rev went against Garv's orders and stole the ring. I couldn't do anything with it on."

"Sounds like a powerful spell to give a mere goblin," Peter observed, staring once again at the violet flames.

"I don't think this is the spell she gave him. The way the spell is structured now, it would affect a witch worse than it has any of the Folk. The spell she gave him must have just been a simple one to see through the mists, and Garv somehow garbled it. It's the most distorted spell I've ever sensed. No one with any magic could use it."

Peter was thoughtful. "It would affect a witch worse, hmm?" He went over the spell linkage in his mind. "All I need are the words," he muttered softly, glancing at the big goblin.

"Just a little more, Bur. That's a good goblin." She shook the rope off her wrists and started working on the rope binding her ankles. "Sleep deeply, Bur." The goblin sat back and began to snore softly.

"You know," Jeanne said as her fingers worried at the knots, "I'd like to help Bur. He's really not such a bad goblin."

"Bad goblin? He hit me!"

"Well, someone hit him, too, once and look what it did to him! The injury is old, though, and it healed so long ago that I can't do anything with it now."

"Thank goodness for small favors! Are you going to heal every goblin and troll that's out to kill us from now on?"

"Don't be such a grump." Jeanne crept quietly around the fire and struggled with his bonds. "Got any plans for what we do for an encore? We can't just sneak off. They can use the fire to track us."

"I know. We've got to put out the fire." Peter looked worriedly down at his empty sheath. "Not that it would help any, but I wish I had my sword."

"Garv has it now. You can use Bur's club. He doesn't have a knife—they're afraid he might cut someone."

Peter rubbed his freed wrists and started on his ankles. "Never mind, it wouldn't do me any good. Do you think you can handle Nif?"

"Who do you think is keeping him arguing for so long? Garv is getting furious."

"Will you forget about the blasted hounds!" The large goblin was trying to overwhelm his opponent with sheer volume. "Who was the imbecile who put the dwarf too close to the fire! I *told* you the spell bothers the short ones!"

"What do you want me to do to Nif?" Jeanne whispered. "It might take me awhile to switch him off from arguing."

Peter fished in his belt pouch and handed her the ring. "Just put him to sleep. I want to talk with Garv."

"Talk? With Garv?" Jeanne put the ring in her pouch. "Better hide his mace first." She looked at him suspiciously. "On second thought, if you think I'm going to stand by and watch you commit suicide..." Peter scowled at her and she scowled back. "Do I have to knock Nif out subtly or can everyone know?"

"Whatever is easiest."

"Thanks." She gathered a handful of snow.

"Jeanne!"

"Don't worry, I know what I'm doing. Unlike a certain person." She concentrated on the snow as she packed it and a shimmering green light began to encase the snowball. "I'm getting too tired to project the command and I don't want to walk up to him to transmit it by touch." She hefted the snowball and glanced at him. "Whenever you're ready,

Peter. I'll have to sneak up a little closer to hit him with this."

"Uh, Jeanne?" He reached out to touch her, then remembered their contrary powers and decided against it. "Just be careful."

"I intend to be. If I miss, I won't have the time to make another of these." Her eyes darkened as she glared at him. "And if you manage to get yourself killed I'll... I'll never speak to you again!" She whirled and vanished into the shadows at the edge of the firelight.

Peter wanted to reassure her, but he didn't feel too confident himself. Garv hadn't given him any time to concentrate before, so why should he have a better chance now? He suddenly remembered something. "Jeanne," he hissed. "When the fire starts flickering, shield yourself!" Irritation, then surprise and dawning comprehension flowed along their sensory linkage, and he knew that she had guessed some of his plans.

Peter sat and watched by the violet fire, listening to Bur's soft snores. The goblin's argument grew more and more heated, until Garv's huge fists hung over Nif's head. The smaller goblin abruptly turned on his heel and strode away from the angry Garv. "I'm going to talk to Bur. He makes more sense than you do!"

Peter tensed as the goblin stamped toward him. The creature must see by now that there was only one prisoner now instead of two. Where was Jeanne?

"Nif!" a clear voice called. The small goblin turned toward the shadows and suddenly found himself facing the slim figure of his former captive. Jeanne lobbed the snowball at him. "Catch!"

Snow splattered against his chest, and the green light flowed over Nif, bathing him in its glow. The goblin collapsed, and Garv let out a sudden roar that startled both humans.

The big goblin ran for his mace. A normal snowball thudded to the ground before him, and Garv hurriedly backed away, fearing Nif's enchantment. He lunged toward the shadows, his weak eyes trying to find Jeanne, but only laughter greeted his attempts. His gaze suddenly fell upon Peter, who stood up beside the violet fire and waved casually to the maddened goblin.

"YOU!" Garv bellowed.

"Hi, Garv," Peter said lightly. "Looking for someone?" He readied himself for the goblin's inevitable reaction.

The tall goblin did not disappoint him. Garv charged straight for the human, the huge hands reaching out to grab and crush. Peter tensed and, as the goblin drew nearer, shot a bolt of disbelief straight into the heart of the violet fire. The flames vanished, except for a tiny ember glowing among the ashes, and the mists descended with a rush.

Peter felt himself shaking and tried to steady himself, to be ready for Garv's next move. He hadn't expected to be able to do *that* to the fire! He could hear the goblin swearing angrily as he groped in the swirling mists. "Maybe you could use a little light, Garv," he suggested. He felt the sweat bead on his forehead as the goblin rushed blindly past him. For his plan to work, he dared not use his own power to see in the mists, which made him as blind as the goblin. *C'mon, Garv*, he thought desperately. *Light the fire*!

Finally, the sound of the goblin's heavy breathing stayed in one spot. "*Deorc Fyr, rwit! E leoht uorar maglod rwit!*"

The fire surged upward, and Garv looked triumphantly at Peter, who was rapidly going over the spell in his mind. The goblin barked and reached for the boy.

Peter shook his head. "Sorry, Garv." He shot the full force of his disbelief into Garv's mind, aiming straight at the spell-link between the goblin and the fire. He felt the link vanish for good as the goblin staggered backward and collapsed, unconscious from the blow. "Sorry, Garv," he said again. "But, thanks."

CHAPTER 14

THE LIFTED CURTAIN

Peter glanced at the fallen goblin, then turned his attention to the coldly burning flames of the violet fire. He focused his disbelief and the fire flickered abruptly and died. No embers crawled among the ashes; with the spell-linkage between Garv and the fire destroyed, there was no mind to fuel the flames.

"Peter, you did it!" Rainbow light surrounded him as Jeanne stepped out of the mists, carrying a familiar blade. "Here's your sword." Thoughtfully, she looked down at the silent Garv as Peter sheathed his sword. "I still don't see why disbelieving a person should be so painful."

Peter glanced worriedly at her. "Are you all right?"

The girl had started to raise a hand to her head, but she glared at him and changed her hand's motion to brush back her hair instead. "Just tired. Elin and Hahle are coming, and it feels like there's a goblin with Leereho and Renw. Rev, right?"

Peter wasn't fooled by the change of subject. Why did their powers have to be so contrary? He hadn't wanted to hurt her. The cold ashes pulled at him and he turned to study them. His plan no longer felt as clever and correct to him now as it had when he was a bound captive by the fire, but still he wanted to try to rekindle the ashes. He struggled against the compulsion. How could he use a spell that would hurt his friends as well as the witches? The temptation to use the spell he had learned was overwhelming.

Behind him, Jeanne shivered as she sensed the spell's lure. The spell felt wrong, very wrong, and her instincts were clamoring against

Peter's use of it. But how could she stop him? And why did she feel that she must? A spell against magic would be helpful to Peter, even if it only duplicated his own powers. Was she jealous? Was her worry for herself instead of Peter? She shook her head and said softly, "If you want to see if it will work, Peter, do us both a favor and leave off the first three words. From the way the air trembled when he spoke them, I think they're an invocation to the Shadows, and you don't want one of those answering you."

Peter did not turn. "Oh. Whom do I invoke, then?"

Jeanne drew her cloak closer about herself and wished the throbbing in her head would go away. "I don't know the names of any of the Green, but I guess it wouldn't do any good to call on them even if I did." She knew she was stalling the inevitable, but somehow she had to try, until she could uncover why she didn't want Peter to use the spell.

Peter frowned and brushed snow over the ashes with his boot. "Why not?"

"Because, silly, even if the spell wasn't contrary to magic and thus to them, you wouldn't believe in them." Jeanne turned the ring thoughtfully and reluctantly added, "The spell is in the Old Tongue, it should work by itself. Probably would be more powerful without an invocation."

Peter nodded briskly, showing no sign of the battle raging within him. He didn't want to use the spell yet; Jeanne was within range and already exhausted. The ashes pulled at him, though, and the idea of flames answering his command was a powerful one.

Finally, he could resist no longer. "*E leoht uorar maglod rwit!*" He gasped in astonishment. A burning heat rose within him and he felt as if he was standing in the center of a huge fire.

"By the Green!" Jeanne breathed, feeling his pain. "Damp it, Peter! Disbelieve!"

Peter fought to control his thoughts as the flames surged within him. The heat abruptly vanished and he staggered and fell to his knees. "What...why?" he asked haltingly. Every breath was a stab of pain, as if his very lungs had been seared by the internal fire. He looked down at himself, expecting to see some evidence of the fire, but there was none.

Peter winced at the touch of Jeanne's hand on his shoulder and wondered why the pain hadn't vanished. He caught the wash of her fear and concern. "What are you feeling so guilty about, Jeanne?" he asked, and much to his surprise, she burst into tears.

"I'm sorry, I'm so sorry," she sobbed. "I knew I should stop you, but I thought I was just afraid for myself. After all, you don't have any magic—it shouldn't have harmed you."

Peter cautiously climbed to his feet. "But it did. I must have some magic about me, then." He caught his breath at a sudden thought. "Jeanne, how many spells did the Elders give me?"

Jeanne wiped away her tears, smudging one cheek. "Three, but I don't see what..." She stopped and met his eyes. "Oh, no!"

"Oh, yes! That was close, too close! Of all the stupid—ow!"

Jeanne bit her lip. "I can't help with the pain, Peter. It's too contrary to the ring and I need its powers to do something now. You'll have to disbelieve it."

"Pain? Disbelieve pain?"

"Pain caused by magic, Peter. There's a difference." She sat down on the ground and put her head in her hands. "I can't even stop two goblins without being weakened. What are we supposed to do against three witches?"

"Don't think that way, Jeanne." Peter reached out to touch her, thought better of it, and started concentrating on disbelieving his own aches.

"Peter! Jeanne!" Hahle dashed out of the mists into Peter's field of disbelief and braked to a halt before them with a rattle from the saddle and gear on his back. "What happened to the goblins? Are you two all right?"

"Peter's hurt. I'm just tired." Jeanne felt a warm breath on the back of her neck and turned to smile up at the gray spotted stallion. "I'm sorry about the last time we met, Elin; I didn't have Nif completely under my control yet."

Elin chuckled. "But enough to tell me of your plans before him and he unable to hear because of your powers."

"If Elin doesn't stop discussing magic at every opportunity, our people will avoid him more than they did when he first studied lore under Kelan," Hahle muttered. "We believe in leaving magic alone." He sighed and nudged Peter gently. "How badly are you hurt, Peter? We must run swiftly to the Silent Forest before the goblins recover and relight their fire."

"I'm all right," Peter said, feeling the fiery pain dwindle. He swung into the saddle. "I should know by now not to play with magic."

Elin and Hahle trotted briskly into the mists, and Peter hastily added, "There's no need for us to hurry. This group is lost and I've broken Garv's memory of the spell."

"That is good to hear," Leereho said as he and Renw joined them. "I feared we would have them either warning the witches or following us for revenge. We have dropped our captive safely tied by their fire and their weapons are broken and cast in the flames."

"Good," Peter said. "I saw more than I wanted to of that mace." As the Fleet Ones moved down the slopes of the hills towards the valley floor, he told them about his capture and their escape.

Elin chuckled. "They probably never realized how dangerous you two could be as a team."

"Speaking of teamwork," Peter inserted, clutching the saddle as Hahle slid down a small rise of ground, "next time don't go wandering around on your own when you spot trouble like that, Jeanne."

The girl sighed wearily. "We went over that already. You probably would have been able to break the spell and awaken everyone, but I couldn't. And I couldn't let the goblins come in after us. Do you know what they would have done if they had found three helpless Windkin?"

Renw snorted. "They would have killed us without hesitation and dragged Leereho and Peter away along with you, Jeanne. There is a long war between the Hound Riders and us. *We* are not arguing with your decision, Jeanne. You did the only thing you could. But why didn't they take Leereho as well?"

Jeanne shivered. "Rev and Garv argued about that. Garv had gone over to get him, and Rev was just holding my arm. So I hit him the way my brother had shown me and ran. They had seen my ring and I guess the Flame Witch had told them to capture wizards. Anyhow, they all ran after me. I should have taken off the ring then but I needed to see." She stared at the glowing ring. "There isn't much else to tell. They run very fast, but we were far enough from the cave by the time they caught me again that they decided not to go back."

She shivered again. "I don't see how you stood up to Garv the way you did, Peter. He terrified me, especially after Rev took the ring and was time-caught. I thought he was going to hit me, but then he pushed me on and we reached their fire just a little ahead of you."

She fell silent, but Peter sensed her unease. "Jeanne?"

"I feel so grimy!" she said angrily. "All the little individual meanness and cruelty and hate. And while I worked at controlling them, I couldn't shut all that out. It was like reaching for a shiny rock at the bottom of Stillwater Pond. The water looks clear, but as you reach in you discover it's all slime, and the gooey mud at the bottom won't let your hand go." She rubbed her ring hand on her trousers as she spoke. "I can't get rid of that feeling."

"You need rest, and food," Leereho commented. "Neither of you humans has eaten yet today." Renw stopped and Leereho sprang lightly from his back and began removing the roan's saddle. "We will rest here for now."

Peter looked about while removing Hahle's saddle and gear and discovered that the Fleet Ones had carried them almost completely out of the foothills while they had talked. The once sparse trees had multiplied into a forbidding forest where sounds dropped into the silent gloom without rippling the surface of its stillness. A short distance below the hollow they had stopped where the ground leveled out into the valley floor.

"Your power grows stronger with practice, Peter," Leereho commented as he started a small fire. "You were not able to push the mists so far before."

Peter nodded in faint surprise and tested his field, pushing the mists further along the floor of the valley. "Why are we stopping up here?" he asked. "There's a more protected spot below us."

Leereho nodded. "We needed to warn you about Darkling Valley before fully entering its confines. What do you know of it, Lore-Master?"

Elin shook his mane. "Not enough, apparently." He waited while Peter and Jeanne accepted the elfin journeybread from Leereho and settled themselves comfortably on the ground. "It has been shunned by the Folk since the last war, but at one time Darkling Valley held a prosperous human kingdom. The soil was rich, they say, and farms spread from one end of the valley to the other, except for the few small, scattered woods reserved for hunting. Humans and Folk dwelt together there in peace.

"About the time of the troubles between the humans and the People of the Wind, however, humans began to shun the Folk. First because magic was mistrusted, and later because of the disappearance of Vana, their queen, for so they still thought of her. That was the time of the exodus of the humans, the withdrawal through the Watcher back to your land. Those humans that remained shut themselves up in the Last Kingdom, now Darkling Valley, and cut the lines of contact with the Folk, especially with the wizards and the Windkin."

"We were angry," Leereho said. He folded his arms and leaned against a tree, watching the valley. "But we of the Folk respected the humans' wishes and stayed away, much to our later sorrow."

"Why?" Peter asked. "What happened to the humans?"

Leereho was silent a moment, and Jeanne felt an old sorrow grow again in the elf. "In the last war, this land was in the direct line of march of the Shadow armies."

"Oh, no." Jeanne's eyes misted. "They were all killed?"

"All," Leereho said. "The Folk saw the light of the burning towns against the sky and rallied their armies in time to stop the invasion at what is now the Wasted Land, but they were too late to save any of the humans."

"Is that why the land was shunned after the war?" Peter asked hesitantly.

Leereho did not look at them, his eyes still on the mists. "Partly in memory of our vanished friends, and partly because of fear. We learned that the humans, even when they saw that the invaders were of the Shadow, blamed the Folk for their misfortune and died cursing us. The curse settled on their land. Now none of the Folk can travel past the Gray Hills without feeling the hate of the dead."

"That's stupid." Peter frowned. "Why blame the Folk?"

"You keep saying 'we,' Leereho," Jeanne said thoughtfully, "but the grief is your own."

Leereho nodded. "I was a child during the Years of Withdrawal. I had playmates among the humans, whose parents finally brought them to the Last Kingdom."

"But when the Last Kingdom died," Peter said slowly, calculating the amount of years, "there was no forest here. And these trees are so old that you must be..." He looked into the elf's young face. "But you don't look old!"

"The passage of time has varying effects on the Folk. Some, like the Fleet Ones, age as you humans do. Dwarfs have a longer life, but others of the Folk live longer still. Of the Wise, those wizards who were once human age very slowly. We of the elves feel closest kin to them, for the elves, like the wizards, can be killed, but time is not our enemy. 'Elder,' to us, means old in wisdom, not years."

Hahle looked out across the valley and shivered. "Do these dead humans appear like the white hounds, Renw?"

The roan shook his mane. "No, you never see any spirits. You feel only a troubling about you during the daylight hours. At night, you can sometimes sense the dead about you, watching you, hating you. But they never do more than hate." He studied Peter and Jeanne. "I don't know if the dead will trouble you humans. After all, they were of your people."

"The afternoon will pass swiftly," Leereho said, gazing skyward. "We will rest here until the Moon rises. I would rather travel through Silent Forest at night than rest under its branches and let the dead gather about us. Sleep now, while you can."

"Until the moon rises?" Peter queried, peering upwards. "He can see the sky through this murk?"

Jeanne nodded sleepily as she settled herself near the warmth of the fire. Peter felt the hard knot of her watchfulness and worry blur into sleep. He draped a blanket over her, then leaned back against a tree. He pulled the dwindling spool of duct tape out of his pouch and checked on his Scout knife, then leaned back again and watched the Fleet Ones paw away the snow to the sparse grass underneath. He felt a question form in his mind as he watched, then sleep claimed him.

* * *

At moonrise, they resumed their march, entering the deep shadows of Silent Forest.

Jeanne pulled her cloak tighter about herself as she walked, following Leereho and Renw. For a few hours now, she had felt a vague unease building up about them, intensifying as if something unseen drew closer. The snow-covered trees loomed menacingly out of the mists as the gray fog retreated from the ring's glow, and she shivered, remembering the ancient trees of the Great Woods. The trees watched in the brooding silence, and Jeanne felt a nameless dread closing about her heart. She caught up to Peter. "Do you feel it?"

"Hmm?" Peter's eyes scanned the forest. "I can feel them watching us, if that's what you mean. What are you so frightened about?"

"That's not me, it's our ghostly relatives." The ring glimmered coldly as she walked beside him. "It's sad, isn't it, to realize that this is all that remains of the Last Kingdom. Nothing but a land filled with senseless hate. A curse of hate," she rephrased slowly. "Peter, do you think that this is the second curse mentioned by the Voices?"

"I was wondering about that earlier. But why would the death of the witches break this curse? Vana wasn't involved—she was trapped under a name spell. And even if she could have caused any trouble, why kill off all the humans? She can't steal the Folk's bodies."

"Ugh. Don't remind me."

Peter glanced behind at a slight sound. "I think you better go help

Hahle. My disbelief doesn't seem to be reaching him."

The blue-black stallion had stopped in his tracks. His eyes rolled as he flinched from the mists closing behind them. "Ai! Go trouble the sleep of the witches!" he cried. "They are of the Shadow that killed you, not us!" He whirled as if to flee, then froze in place, quivering, as Jeanne's mind caught his.

"Sorry, Hahle." She stepped to his side, feeling tiny beside the tall Windkin. "I shouldn't have had to be reminded."

Hahle's eyes rolled wildly. "The only escape from the white hounds is flight!" he urged.

"These aren't white hounds. Stop fighting me, Hahle." She felt another mind leap in fear and gathered it under her control. "Stay, Elin. Fight the terror they send, it's no different from that of the witch hounds."

"There are helmed Men behind us," Leereho said in a hushed voice. "Red light shines on their upraised swords and the banners of the Last Kingdom flutter above their heads."

"I don't see anything." Peter glanced from one to another. "I don't see any men."

"Neither do I," Elin suddenly said, "but the dead are coming." Jeanne gaped at the stallion, who had cowered in terror only seconds ago and who now stood boldly facing the fear-churned shadows. "And the only spell that can bind the dead is the one the Harper Dyl used against the army of dead set upon the—"

"Elin," Peter interrupted, "I'm beginning to see them."

Elin began murmuring in a low voice. His listeners could not catch any words, but the song his voice wove brought memories of spring and growing things and the fresh scent and feel of newly turned earth in the warm sun.

"Why do you stand there?" Renw pulled at Leereho's cloak. "Flee, the dead are marching!"

Leereho shrugged him aside. His sword flashed out of its sheath. "Beware, they attack!"

Abruptly the rainbow light vanished. "Jeanne?" Peter could dimly see the dark shapes of his companions facing the deeper shadows about them and heard Elin's voice still spinning its slow, deep spell. The sound soothed him, lulling his senses as it sang softly of rest, a peaceful sleep deep in the earth.

"NO!" Jeanne's despair-filled shout rang out in the sudden silence.

Hahle took a step forward, then stopped. "They're gone," he said in bewilderment. "They rushed toward us, and now they're gone."

"Not to Jeanne," Leereho said, quickly sheathing his sword. "She seems to be caught in a trance."

Jeanne struggled against the ring. The forest and mist had melted from about her and she stood in a trampled wheat field. Red light from burning fields shone against the night sky to the left as well as behind her, and before her, a small group of men fought a rearguard action against a larger number of trolls. There were no bright banners, no shining armor, no helms on the humans, who were clad only in cloth tunics and breeches. Few of them had swords, some had axes, but most—to her horror—swung only rakes and pitchforks against the better-armed trolls, buying time for their families fleeing behind them.

Another band of trolls trotted leisurely to intercept the escapees, and two young bowmen—younger even than herself, Jeanne realized—dropped back from the women and children and took aim at their grinning pursuers. The trolls stopped and their own archers stepped forth.

"NO!" Jeanne buried her face in her hands, unable to watch the hopelessly unequal battle, but she couldn't shut out the despair, helplessness, and anguish of the living and the dying. It washed over her in a gigantic wave, battering her against the hard, cold, gloating greed of the trolls. She felt herself being dragged down, caught in a whirlpool of fear and grief, and dimly sensed in its depths a power eagerly living on the fear and feeding the hate that rose all about her, seeking an outlet for revenge.

Her mind caught a quick picture of a hard-faced man with the golden circlet of a king about his forehead. The power she had sensed once before leaped gleefully about him as he spoke, his mouth twisting with hatred, but Jeanne heard no words, only felt the choking hate disperse in response to the king's command.

Abruptly the swirling emotions vanished. She heard snow creak under her feet and Leereho's voice saying, "She seems to be caught in a trance."

Jeanne lifted her head and stared sightlessly at the dark shapes surrounding her. With a sudden surge of loathing, she pulled the ring from her finger and hurled it far from her.

"You can't deny your destiny." Elin's voice intruded gently into her anger.

"Don't speak to me of destiny, Lore-Master!" she flared. "Not when you've been denying your own!"

"Jeanne," Peter chided. A fire wand blazed into life in his hand, and he glanced at the faces revealed in its glare: one flushed and angry, and three confused at the odd argument. *I wonder if they even heard Elin's spell.*

Elin hung his head. "Kelan did warn me that the study of lore involved more than simply memorizing legends and spells. But my people do not possess...we cannot do magic!"

"You just did," Peter reminded him.

"Who just did?" Hahle asked bewilderedly. "What did Elin do?"

Elin looked at the mists. "I did, didn't I?"

Jeanne laughed at the stallion's wondering expression, her anger at the ring forgotten. "Oh, Elin! Didn't Kelan ever tell you that magic comes from the will, not the body?" she asked, guessing what Elin had left unsaid. "By the way, who was the Harper Dyl?"

Elin's ears perked up at the question, but Hahle groaned. "No, Elin. No legends. I haven't even been able to follow this conversation. Let's go, before those wraiths return from wherever they disappeared to."

"Hahle's right." The gray and white stallion nuzzled the girl's face. "And you are right, filly. But I can't keep the dead away for long without Dyl's harp. Do you want us to help look for the ring?"

She sighed. "No need. As you said, I can't deny my destiny. Especially when it keeps coming back." Peter looked down and saw the gold band rolling out of the mists towards them.

Renw whirled and trotted on through the forest, Leereho and Hahle behind him, as Jeanne picked up the ring and activated its glow. Elin and Peter waited for her. As they walked, Jeanne told them everything she could remember about her vision. "This curse was Vana's doing," she finished. "I could sense her mind controlling the king's. The invasion wasn't her plan—not with the killing of the humans—but she certainly managed to turn it against the Folk."

"*'The doom of the false for the dead shall atone and two curses of hate be broken,'*" Peter quoted.

"We know who the dead are but who's the false?"

"It's a person's name," Elin said slowly. "I remember hearing of a tale once, but I can't seem to recall it."

Peter and Jeanne exchanged glances, and Peter shrugged. "Probably Vana. False queen, false immortal—it does fit."

But I don't, Jeanne thought. *I don't fit. I won't be much help with any doom, not with my powers.*

Her memories flew back to the last night they had stayed with the elves. She had found Salanoa in the center of the Glen, where the trees were the color of starlight. She had waited a moment, sensing the troubling in the normally serene mind, and wondered why the wizard seemed oblivious to the far from silent approach of her student. She sent a question spinning gently into the wizard's mind.

Salanoa turned and smiled faintly. "Jeanne. I should have recalled that my hurt would bring you. I only wish you could heal this ailment."

"What's wrong?" Jeanne asked, worried at the wizard's tone and still more by the fact that she had spoken aloud instead of mind to mind as they had begun to do within the Glen. "All day today you and Peter have both been acting as if I was made of moon crystal that would break at the slightest strain. Why?"

Salanoa looked away, glancing up at the glittering stars. "I fear for you, young one. For Peter, also, but mostly for you. This quest is alien to the nature of a Sensitive and thus holds the most danger for you."

Jeanne sensed the partial evasion. "Why, because I can't hurt anyone?" She considered the problem reluctantly. "You've taught me illusion casting, and a few mind snares, enough so that I can defend myself. But I suppose if I had no other alternative, I'd...have to use emotions to—"

"No!" The anger in Salanoa's voice surprised Jeanne. "Do not even consider that! Not even if there is no other alternative! You must not kill!"

Jeanne blinked. That wasn't what she had started to say. She suddenly realized Salanoa's anger was not directed at her, but at some memory behind the wizard's eyes. "Salanoa, what is troubling you?"

Salanoa looked at her out of haunted eyes. "Something that should have died long ago." She caught her pendant and her mind retreated behind a shield. "Your power has its virtue in life," she said slowly. "Use it for death and it will depart from you forever. And in this land, such a void would leave you open to the Shadows."

She did not explain further, and Jeanne had remained silent, conscious of the grief that clung to the wizard like a shadow, and wondering whether Salanoa had actually spoken to her or only to memories. Had the wizard once known a Sensitive who had killed?

* * *

The six moved steadily across the haunted land. The snow-covered forest seemed to stretch endlessly under the mists, its stillness disturbed only by the sound of their voices and the murmurs of a wide rushing stream, the ice-filmed banks of which they followed until they could find a ford. Always the vague troubling of the dead hovered about them, following close upon their heels as they marched at night, disturbing their sleep by day.

Finally, the ground began again to rise sharply under their feet. Peter noticed more pines and firs in the mists and realized that their journey was almost over.

"Humans named these the Mountains of Illusion," Leereho said when they next stopped to eat. He started drawing a map in the snow as Jeanne doled out dried fruit from their quickly dwindling supply. "The Folk left these peaks nameless, preferring to ignore them as well as the Shadow Land beyond. Of the Folk perhaps only Renw and I know this range well. Not even the Wise come this close to the castle."

"Why not?" Peter asked. "I mean, I can see why the Folk wouldn't want to travel through Silent Forest—the ghosts are even bothering us. But Graylod had that...teleport spell. Don't any of the other wizards?"

Le shook his head. "Once the curse struck, only Graylod could remember the spell—"

"—and even if others could remember," Elin interrupted, "the castle has its own defenses—another form of the curse. Those of the Folk who use magic grow weak as they approach—much as you were affected by that fire, Jeanne. There...was one wizard who tried a travel spell."

Renw shuddered. "That elf wizard. She was barely alive by the time I found her—did she ever regain her memory, Le?"

Leereho shook his head. Peter looked from the elf back to Renw. "Le said back in the cave that only you Fleet Ones can go near the castle without being weakened. Because your people don't use magic?"

Hahle made a disgusted sound, and Renw flattened his ears in disapproval. "Hahle..."

Jeanne closed the pack. "So we're entering the Mountains of Illusion."

Le gestured at the mists. "Somewhere off to the south is a road which leads to the lower gates of the castle, midway up Mount Ircis, a road strongly spell-guarded. However, Renw and I discovered one of the ancient Watch Ways that winds up the northern slope of the mountain. We were not able to follow it too far—Renw cannot climb like a mountain goat, and we were already close enough to the castle for its defenses to weaken me. I am certain that it is another path to the castle, one not often used from the looks of it. We will guide you to it, and there we must part company, for only you two can travel it."

Jeanne looked at the elf in dismay. She had known that the quest was basically hers and Peter's, but somehow she had assumed that the others would be along as well. *Silly*, she told herself, *as if the witches wouldn't notice the six of us sneaking up to their back door.* "Where are we now, Le?"

Leereho pointed at his crudely sketched map. "At the foot of the peak called the Dreamer, although you cannot see it for the mists. We should make our way through the forests of its neighbor, the Silver-Haired, before we stop again in daylight. Then we shall come, here, to Mount Ircis and the Watch Way."

* * *

"Peter, I've got it!"

"Huh?" Peter turned on the narrow path Renw had broken through the snow on the steep slope and waited as she climbed up to him. He glanced upwards and saw the elf's blond hair disappear among the trees. *When are we going to stop and get some sleep?* he wondered irritably. *We're already halfway across old Silver-Haired now and I'm bushed!*

"I've got it!"

Peter smiled as she reached him, her long hair tangled, her face flushed with the cold and the climb and reflecting the excitement in her voice. "Got what?"

"The answer to the riddle! The lost name, remember?"

Peter looked at her blankly. "You have the lost name?"

"No, no. Graylod does." She smiled as she caught the bafflement and irritation swirling in his thoughts. "All right, I'll calm down. Keep moving," she nudged him, "before Elin runs over us."

She fell silent as he obeyed and began climbing again. Finally, she said calmly, "Graylod was the one who put the name-spell on Vana during the trouble with the humans and the Windkin, remember? He knows her true name."

"So? He's also held captive in the castle. If he's still alive, that is."

"He has to be, otherwise the riddle doesn't make sense."

"*You* don't make sense. What does Vana's name have to do with the riddle?"

"Everything! Salanoa didn't remember Vana without your help, and Elin can't remember whose name means 'the false.' Salanoa told me that only those using magic forgot their spells—Elin remembers all those that the wizards can't. So why can't he remember one name, unless—"

"The curse made him and everyone else forget!" Peter agreed. He paused, recalling the riddle. "*'Must the lost name with fire be spoken.'*"

"Right! Don't you see? If we free Graylod, and you make him remember Vana's name, he can put her under the name-spell again. Vana's true name is the lost name!"

He stopped in shock. "No, it can't be so simple," he said dazedly.

"Simple? If you think freeing a wizard with three witches around is going to be simple, I'd hate to see what you consider difficult." She pushed at him until he started moving again.

"No, I mean the answer. It doesn't explain what we do about the other two witches."

Jeanne frowned as she climbed. Peter could hear the rattle of stones behind them as Elin and Hahle clambered up the rocky rise of ground. "I know. 'The lost name with fire' should take care of Vana and the Dark One, but not the flame witch. That's the trouble with prophecies, you never really know what will happen until it happens." She stared at the mists distastefully. "I'm beginning to forget what the sun looks like."

"It's late afternoon, according to my feet. I'm tired! How much longer are we—" He caught the fear rising in the girl. "What's wrong?"

Jeanne glanced uneasily about them. "Can't you feel it—that growing tension in the air? There's a great deal of power gathering. We've even lost our ghostly escort."

Leereho stood on the level ridge above them, gazing out across the mists as if he, too, shared Jeanne's unease. They came to stand beside him and the elf gasped and pointed down the way they had come. "Look!"

At first, they could see nothing but the gray mists below them. Then, slowly, as if stirred by a great wind, the fog began to swirl upwards, revealing the valley below them, rising until the mists hung like a gray curtain across the sky, blocking the light of the sun and casting night shadows about them.

"The castle!" Jeanne exclaimed.

Above them on the slopes of nearby Mount Ircis perched the brooding, violet-lit castle. From its turrets darted long dark forms with riders on their backs, gliding swiftly through the windless sky straight towards the six.

A blinding flash of violet light blazed on the ridge below them. When Peter could see again, fourteen figures had appeared out of nowhere to stand gazing upwards at their prey. The shriek of a witch hound trembled through the air.

Leereho stared down at the brightly garbed figures racing for the faint trail and his face hardened. His sword whispered out of its scabbard, and Renw pulled at his cloak. "Run," the stallion ordered. "I'll not have you fight your own people."

Three of the figures were elves, Peter noticed with a detached portion of his mind, four were dwarfs and the remainder trolls in the violet uniforms of the witches. He glanced through the trees behind them, wondering if they could indeed outrun them. *Not much of a race with hounds before us and those behind*, he thought in despair, drawing his own sword.

Jeanne studied the climbers, the ring on her finger glowing with a strange bright intensity. Peter caught the power building within her. "No, Jeanne, don't!"

His cry went unheeded as the girl flung green shimmering brightness down upon the Changed Ones. The three blond elves, closest of the pursuers, staggered and fell to their knees on the snowy trail. The four bearded dwarfs stopped, bathed in the green glow, then, in one synchronized movement, turned and spread out in a defensive line across the path, their axes glittering coldly in the faint light. The startled trolls, fear reflected on their features, came to an abrupt halt with a clatter of weapons and stared wide-eyed at the seven blocking their way.

"Jeanne, don't faint!" Peter caught the girl as she swayed dizzily and dragged her away from the edge of the ridge.

"I'm...all right."

"Sure you are. Seven at once, when it would have been less draining to throw a simple illusion."

"Those bound by illusion pay no heed to other illusions," Jeanne said in an unfamiliar voice. She flinched at the distant dull clang of metal on metal, of sword upon sword. "I only hope they forgive me for what I did to them," she said in a more normal voice.

"This way! Hurry!" Renw called.

Leereho took the girl's other arm, and they ran after the roan stallion, Hahle and Elin behind them. The snow dragged at their feet, and Peter felt his earlier weariness weighing his mind, slowing his body. A soft light glowed on his shoulder from where Jeanne's arm rested. "Be on guard, Peter." Jeanne's voice was tired, also. "They're sending both physical and mental forces against us."

Peter nodded, understanding now the source of his tiredness, and sent his disbelief out like a shield about the company. Their steps quickened.

A shriek sounded overhead, and a hard head rammed into Peter's back, knocking him off balance and sending the three of them stumbling to the ground. Peter looked up indignantly at the black stallion standing over him, then spotted the spear quivering in the rough bark of the tree beside him. "Thanks," he said, shaken by the narrow escape.

Hahle shook his mane, his eyes on the gray sky between the treetops. "They're circling higher. Hurry."

Peter and Leereho got Jeanne to her feet and started off again. The girl's face paled and her feet faltered. "Sorry." She gasped weakly. "Can't...block everything out. Someone just died back there."

Leereho and Peter exchanged dismayed glances above her head. "We have to climb higher," Leereho said quickly. "Otherwise Elin would carry her."

The shriek of a windborne hound was unexpectedly answered by the howl of wolves on the upper slopes of the mountain itself. "Now we're really in for it," Hahle muttered. "Where's your trail, Renw?"

"Not much farther."

Jeanne lifted her head. "Wolves...coming down the mountain, it feels like. Directly where we're heading."

Renw groaned. "So much for our easy and protected route. Move, people. Off to the left. We'll have to find another way up the slope."

"Renw." Leereho hesitated as the stallion met his eyes, and Jeanne felt hopelessness pass between them.

The roan turned. "I know. Maybe there's another way down."

Despair ran with them among the trees, howled behind them with wolves' voices. "They're following us, but not closing," Elin muttered, glancing back at the eyes glinting in the gloom. "Renw, we're being herded!"

The ring glowed brighter and Jeanne's grip tightened on Peter's shoulder. "Hounds ahead! *Below* you, Renw!"

Renw cast a wary eye at the gray sky, then looked before him and braked to a stop with a muffled oath. The rest of the company came to his side and stared, aghast. Four paces before them the ground dropped away sharply, plunging hundreds of feet to the raging river below. Hounds swooped and circled in the deep gorge, hovered before the cliff's edge. Peter wondered briefly where their goblin riders were. Renw started to turn, his eyes on the empty space before them. "Away from here, before—" He looked up, and his voice died.

"No," Jeanne said in a small voice.

Wolves' eyes glittered in the faint light, their dark fur making the creatures seem part of the shadows from which they crept. Peter instinctively backed up a step before recalling that the drop was behind him. The rainbow glow flickered as Jeanne tried frantically to build her weakened power, and Peter could feel her despair.

"Trapped," Hahle said harshly. He tossed his head and reared slightly. "Come, then, you grinning hounds of the dark. Come face the wrath of the Folk!"

The wolves, teeth bared in horrid grins, heads held low, edged closer. The waiting hounds shrieked impatiently, the windblasts from their wings shaking snow from trees along the cliff's edge and flattening the walkers' cloaks against their bodies.

Peter felt something wake within his memory, a power that he had felt stirring twice before. He cast aside his disbelief and waited, willing the spell to come. The magic stole into his mind, moving his body to its commands. He raised one hand, the five fingers spread wide, and pointed in turn at the wolves creeping towards them and at the hovering hounds. The air crackled about him as the spell blazed forth, casting the hounds and wolves into motionlessness, freezing time about them. Then it was gone from his mind, and Peter was left pointing at hounds hanging in midair, without any explanation of how they could stay so without falling.

"So that was the third spell," Jeanne said softly. "Good thing you only believe in magic as a last resort, Peter."

"Post-hypnotic suggestion," Peter said blankly, still staring at the hounds.

"Thank the Green for that," Leereho agreed. "Jeanne, Elin can carry you the short distance to our trail."

"I'm all right."

"Not with that group of Folk behind us charging from one battle into another," Elin replied, gazing at her sternly. She sighed and swung into the saddle. "I fear you will regret freeing them, Jeanne."

Jeanne frowned as the stallion began winding his way among the frozen wolves. "Windlord, are you a seer as well as a Lore-Master?"

Peter started after the three, then turned and glanced at two who stood as still as if time-caught. "C'mon, the spell won't last long."

Renw shook his head dazedly. "Of all the people to cast spells—"

"That's my human," Hahle said weakly. "Full of surprises."

"Speaking of surprises," Renw said as they left the statues of wolves behind them, "what's Elin up to?" The gray and white stallion was stamping an intricate line in the snow between the company and the time-caught wolves, stepping forward, mincing back, weaving a tortuous pattern that pulled at the eyes.

"Setting up another barrier for the wolves." Jeanne waited as they came up to her. "Peter, try to hold the time spell a while longer. I know that what Elin's trying will work, but I don't want to have to put all our luck on it."

Peter reached into his mind and gathered the unraveling threads of the spell together. "How much longer?" he asked, feeling the fragility of the threads. "The other two spells never lasted more than a few minutes."

"You didn't know how to control magic before. Hold it as long as you can without tiring."

Leereho glanced sharply at the dark-haired girl. "It was through Elin's memory of lore that some of the spells lost under the curse were remembered."

"I'm not doubting Elin. His spell won't hold the winged hounds, though."

Hahle snorted disgustedly. "I knew it! I knew it would only be a matter of time before he tried to use that stuff he's been learning!"

Elin trotted up to them. "There, that's done. Up on my back now, Jeanne."

"Elin," Hahle said angrily, following his friend as Elin trotted off with his rider, "you can't be a wizard without hands!"

"Don't need hands for this spell. Just feet and a will to form the pattern." He glanced back at Jeanne. "It's not as good as a thrice circle, but they won't cross that line." Jeanne smiled at the self-satisfaction in the stallion's voice.

Hahle snorted. "Magic!"

Jeanne tickled a gray ear. "They can fly over it."

"So who's afraid of winged hounds?"

The company retraced their steps, hurrying back along the ridge until they came to a gentle, tree-covered slope. "Any goblins about?" Leereho whispered.

Jeanne shook her head, her expression puzzled as she slid off Elin's back. "I can't sense a thing. How large a range does that spell have, Peter?"

"Had," Peter corrected, feeling a fragile thread stretch thinly. "I can't hold the spell much longer."

Leereho nodded. "Even so, wait for my signal before following." He lightly sped up the slope, his yellow hair shining against the dark trees.

"Dwarfs and elves coming from your left, Renw."

The roan turned at the girl's warning and moved away from the slope, scuffing the few footprints visible in the snow. Elin and Hahle went to guard their back trail at a swing of the roan's head. "Jeanne..." She joined him as he moved in the direction she had indicated. "Have they recovered completely from the Change? No leftover loyalty to the witches?"

"So far as I can tell they're free of any witch taint."

Peter felt a spell-tie break within his mind. Something suddenly stirred in the bushes behind him, and he drew his sword, conscious as he turned that Jeanne was running towards him.

"Get away, Peter!" she yelled. "He's got a—"

Peter heard glass break at his feet and, with a blinding flash of violet light in his eyes, felt the world dissolve around him.

CHAPTER 15

BEFORE THE CRYSTAL THRONE

"Peter!" Jeanne stopped short and felt her heart catch and turn over at the sight of the ragged circle of bare ground. "No. Oh no." The tears filling her eyes were not entirely from the billows of choking smoke dispersing slowly in the still air. *Peter!*

The bushes to her right snickered. Jeanne turned, fighting the dizzying effects of the smoke with her powers, as a goblin emerged from hiding holding a short sword curved at the tip like a claw. Leering at his unarmed prey, the purple creature moved toward her.

Elin coughed within the smoke cloud. "Jeanne! Where are you?"

Jeanne stared blindly at the advancing goblin. In her mind she could see only Peter, a second before the globe caught him, and again in the depths of a dungeon as the Mirror had warned her. Her anger and grief grew as she sensed the twisted coil of cruelty and hatred that was the goblin's mind. She wanted to smash that tangled pattern, hurl it to the very edge of madness and beyond. She had no awareness of anything but the focus of her anger; yells and a horse's scream in the forest behind her meant nothing. Only a faint voice from her memory intruded on her anger, held her wrath from breaking, a tiny sorrowful voice whose words were drowned out by the snarling hate growing within her.

"Peter! Jeanne!" The black stallion reeled out of the thinning mists and lurched toward the goblin. Coughing, nearly blinded by the smoke, Hahle stumbled and crashed to the ground almost at the very feet of the goblin. The creature looked down at the struggling Windkin, savoring the moment. He raised his sword.

"No!" The last fragile restraint snapped. Forgetting all but the burning anger and grief within her, Jeanne struck, blasting the goblin's mind with her rage.

She staggered as the bolt connected, sharing the goblin's fear, feeling his pain within her own mind. *No! What am I doing?* a part of her mind wailed, striving against the anger ruling her. Jeanne ignored the voice. She wanted to hurt the goblin, to bring pain as it had done to Peter. If only it didn't *hurt* so much.

The glitter of the ring caught her attention. Instantly, the goblin appeared to change, to grow into a huge violet-scaled creature that staggered with the force of her anger and crashed to the ground.

Shocked, Jeanne stared at the creature. *I did that?* Suddenly she felt another's anger still battering at the dying creature, battling the aura of great evil that clung to the dissipating life. She turned to see a tall, dark-haired woman dressed in the green of new leaves near her. The woman swayed and fell to her knees. Jeanne saw the horror and pity reflected in the dark eyes, the lovely face etched with lines of agony, and felt the empathic linkage between the woman and the creature. *If it dies, she dies also*, Jeanne realized. *She doesn't have to kill. Why is she violating her own powers?*

The vision abruptly vanished, and Jeanne found herself once again facing the pain-racked goblin over the still body of the stallion. *No! What am I doing?*

She released the creature and it slumped to the ground, unconscious. *What have I done? What did I almost do?* She reached for Hahle, intending to cure him of the smoke-induced weakness and felt herself falling as her knees buckled beneath her. She felt snow under her hands, the warmth of Hahle's body somewhere ahead of her. She clung fiercely to the edge of consciousness, ignoring the pounding in her head, the numbness stealing through her body. *No wonder Sensitives aren't supposed to hurt people. I feel as if I hit myself harder than I did the goblin. But who was that other Sensitive? She felt...familiar somehow.*

She caught the faint pulse of the goblin's mind and winced. *Salanoa was right to worry. It would be all too easy to kill.* She clutched feebly at the snow, the icy touch against her fingers pulling her back to herself. *Why? How could I lose all control like that? I'm supposed to heal people, not kill them! To have taken a life—for what? Revenge? Revenge won't help Peter—I've got to!* She closed her eyes and told herself firmly that the ground was not moving. *Help me, ring!*

Snow creaked as Hahle tried to regain his feet. "Goblins!" he whispered. "Jeanne, can you hear me? Goblins!"

Jeanne raised her head and saw through the dark veil of her hair the bright splash of red-violet uniforms against the shadow-cloaked trees on the slope above them. Her eyes suddenly focused on a faint wall of rainbow light between herself and the stallion. She forced her protesting body to move, crawled to the struggling Hahle and flung herself across his back, holding him down. The magical shield retreated before her, stopping inches away from the fallen goblin as she thus forced the ring to protect Hahle as well as herself. "Stay down!" she whispered, searching for Elin's and Renw's minds behind her. "Let them think we're helpless!"

"Think?" Hahle sneezed weakly.

Where's Le? Jeanne wondered as she listened to the rattle of sliding pebbles and earth. She sensed the goblins' confusion when they glimpsed the two before them in the smoke-filled shadows. The rasp of swords drawn sounded harsh in the sudden stillness.

"For the Heartsharer!" someone suddenly yelled behind her.

The girl inwardly groaned as she sensed the once-Changed elves charging to meet the goblins. The lead goblin, determined not to lose any captives, threw a violet globe at the two in the same instant as another hurled a spear.

The globe and spear together struck the rainbow wall and together bounced back. Light exploded among the goblins, and a new swirl of smoke billowed up from where they had once stood.

"Oh no, not more!" Hahle sneezed helplessly. "Jeanne... Jeanne!"

She heard Hahle's call as if from a great distance. A roaring sound filled her ears as the world slowly rolled on end and over into darkness.

* * *

Bright light blazed about Peter. The whirling sensation of empty space ceased, and he could feel solid ground beneath his feet again. He smelled flames, felt their heat about him. Squinting against the light, he tried to force his mind and eyes to focus.

Judging from the faint echoes of his movements, he seemed to be standing in a vast room. Light coruscated off mirror-bright panels of crystal, danced and spun in the very air. He tried to shield his eyes from the glare and discovered lines of force linking his wrists with bright shackles of light.

"Mine!" a shrill voice screeched. Shadow spread like an ink stain through the light. "Take your filthy spell off him. You promised! You promised that the next prisoner would be mine!"

A tendril of fire halted the shadow's spread. "The Other said to wait for her arrival," chided an amused voice from the light about him.

Peter listened in fascination to the new voice, forgetting even the impulse to break free of his spell chains. He wasn't sure if he had heard that strange melody of tones with his ears or with his mind. Strength pulsed behind its words, the strength of a being secure in its own powers, unmindful of restraint. He shook off the thrall of that musical voice, sensing a trap behind its laughter. "Could someone dim the lights?" he asked, trying to sound brave but hearing the trembling in his voice.

A low chuckle of amusement rewarded him. "A bold creature," the rich voice laughed.

The bright glare dimmed. A circle of violet flame leaped about him, curling near then swaying away as if in a dance. Before him, three high-backed thrones stood on a crystal dais. One throne was draped with shadows and seemed filled with a deeper core of darkness. The shadows shifted as he watched. "Mine," a sullen voice sulked.

The second throne burned with violet flame, and from the foot of that throne fire streamed across the floor to feed his circular prison. Peter watched the flames cautiously, realizing that no breeze caused their dance. The musical laugh echoed about him.

The third throne, carved from a single massive crystal, was empty.

Peter felt his mouth dry with fear at the sight of his strange captors. This was far beyond special effects. He caught himself with an effort. *Don't believe in them. Don't believe in anything here.* The spell shackles abruptly dissolved, and he looked down in dismay. *Now I'm over-reacting. You fool, why don't you just wear a big sign? If they know that magic's no good around me, they might think it safer to kill me instead of only holding me captive.* He rubbed his freed wrists, feeling a brief burning tingle where the shackles had rested.

The flames leaped away from him. "Interesting," the flame witch commented humorously. "I did not sense power about you."

"You must know what it is you seek," a husky voice said.

Startled, Peter looked up and caught his breath at the lovely vision seated upon the crystal throne. Braided black hair was bound about her head like a crown, and her long black dress was richly embroidered with silver, belted with spun silver, the flowing sleeves sparkling with diamonds and moon crystals. Large violet eyes that held the promise of dreams dominated the delicate features of her face.

Peter hesitated, caught by those eyes. There were unseen depths waiting behind the dreams, depths that triggered his own inner alarms. *Oh no, I'm believing what I see again*, he groaned. *This is Vana the Immortal, not some fairy tale princess*! He remembered Jeanne's vision and decided not to disbelieve too strongly. He didn't want to see her true appearance just yet.

"Well, human," the husky voice purred, "you have been the most enjoyable opponent I have found in a long time."

Peter bowed, averting his eyes from her face, afraid of what he might see. "You honor me, Vana."

He sensed her sudden start. "Where did you hear that name?"

Before he could think of a safe answer, light suddenly exploded behind him. He turned, shielding his eyes from the glare, wondering with a sinking heart which of his friends had been caught as he had.

The light died, and Peter choked on a laugh at the ludicrous sight of a tumbled heap of goblins. They seemed to have suffered from the whirling trip worse than he had. Their movements were fumbling and confused, as if they still spun through space. One goblin attempted to regain its feet and crashed to the ground again in a tangle of bony limbs. Peter struggled to contain his laughter.

"What is the meaning of this?" Vana rose to her feet in one fluid motion and stood surveying the cluttered floor. "Did I not forbid the globes to be used for simple transport?" Her eyes caught and held those of a goblin who had a band of brown winding about both violet sleeves. "You were to have ridden the hounds back. Was that not my command?"

The goblin crawled unsteadily to the foot of the dais.

"Well?"

"W-wizard," he croaked, finally getting the word out past his fear. "She cast the globe back upon us, Mistress of Illusion."

The flame witch lifted her fiery head. "Shall I send them back?"

"And have her bounce them back yet again? No, she can do us no harm. Recall your hounds, Sender of Darkness, and lower the mists. We have more important matters than a mere wizard."

She reseated herself upon her throne and turned her gaze upon Peter. "My spies informed me that the Ring of Calada awakened when you entered the land, human. But I see it not on your hands. Where have you hidden it?"

"My goblins shall find it on him." The flame witch pulled the fire circle back into herself and nodded to the shaky goblins to approach

Peter.

"No." Vana raised one hand, and the goblins cringed. "No, the Eldest of Fools has not earned his keep today. Come forth, Eldest."

The Dark One snickered when no one answered Vana's summons. Vana glanced at a grayish shimmer to the back of the dais and her face hardened. "Come forth, Eldest!"

The shimmer moved forward, resolved itself into a gray-haired man cloaked in silver, holding a dull gray staff.

"Graylod!" Peter did not realize he had spoken aloud until he heard Vana's laughter.

"Ah, so you know my Gray Fool? Such a powerful wizard, but he seems to have misplaced his name."

"Graylod, can you hear me?" The wizard advanced to the edge of the dais, and Peter saw the emptiness in Graylod's eyes. *What am I doing? He's been Changed, he doesn't remember me.*

"Search him, Gray Fool. No, no, use your staff. The Ring reacts to physical danger. Do you wish to free him?"

The wizard lifted his staff, and a blue glow surrounded Peter. All three witches seemed surprised. "That is an odd color aura," the flame witch commented. "What type of human have we here?"

"Blue is the color of most human magicks." Vana frowned. "But that shade..."

The wizard's voice sounded distant and rusty as if he seldom spoke. "Blue...of faith...and belief."

"Faith!" Vana snarled. "That seldom did them any good, the stupid weaklings. I did not ask for a lecture. Where is the Ring, Gray Fool?"

"Not on this human." The flames danced with amusement. "The mere wizard must have it, Mighty One!"

The core of darkness shifted. "No wizard," the Dark One suddenly grumbled. "Two humans escaped me. The girl must have the ring."

"Girl?"

Peter felt a chill run down his spine as Vana straightened. "A human girl? Odd, I never sensed her presence." Vana spoke casually, as if she was totally disinterested in how many humans there were, but Peter, with a sudden flash of empathy, caught a cruel hunger from her that sickened him. He fought to control his stomach.

Vana moved sinuously down the steps of the dais, reminding Peter forcibly of some great jungle cat. The wizard lowered his staff and shuffled after her like a windup toy. "I think that I shall take personal charge of the hunt for this missing human." She caught sight of Peter's white face and gestured swiftly towards the shadow witch. The Dark One rocked back against her throne as if she had been slapped.

"Leave him alone," Vana purred.

"But I did nothing!"

"Leave him alone. I want him unharmed. I may need him for bargaining."

"It is my turn!" The Dark One flinched as Vana lifted a beringed hand and thoughtfully studied glittering gems. "You plan to bargain with the human girl?" the shadows asked sullenly. "Why?"

"A human with the Ring of Calada is a threat to us," Vana said slowly, as if explaining to a child. "The Ring does not always remain silent. Who knows what powers it may have taught her?"

She suddenly remembered Peter's presence and gestured to the goblins. "Bring him down to the dungeons. Gently, gently, my dears," she scolded as Peter struggled in their cruel grasp. "I don't want him damaged—yet."

* * *

The soft murmur of voices surrounded Jeanne, soothing the inner alarm that had awakened her. She drifted on the sound, idly trying to distinguish words amid the murmur.

"They can't understand us." That was... Renw?

"Where is Leereho? Never can find that elf when you need him."

"You had best hope he stays away, Hahle, or we'll be in worse trouble than we are right now." Renw again. She felt pleased with herself as she identified the voices. She knew where Leereho was. Her pleasure dwindled. The elf felt concerned, helpless, but she couldn't sense what disturbed him. Alarm jabbed again and she struggled to shake off her daze, wondering why her mind felt fuzzy at the edges.

"Never mind Leereho," Elin said worriedly. "We have to get Jeanne away before those goblins come back."

"Elin, by the Wind, if you two hadn't stopped to argue with these elves, we all would have been away from here by now."

"Heartsharer, can you hear me?"

Jeanne came fully awake at the unfamiliar voice. *What* had it called her?

"Heartsharer, we have rescued you from the Changed Fleogende. You are safe now."

"Are you sure the Fleet Ones are Changed, elf?" a deep voice grumbled. "I seem to recall that the Other sent us out to capture those with the Windlords. Would the Sensitive have broken our Change but not theirs?"

What is going on? Her awareness seemed crowded, and the scattered wisps of anger and fear made her head pound. She felt the chill wetness of snow against her cheek and realized that she was lying partially on her right side. The voices seemed to be coming from the direction her head faced, and the subtle aura of hound stirred slowly behind her. She cautiously opened her eyes.

An elf, with hair as pale as Leereho's, stood by her shoulder, glaring disdainfully at the black-bearded dwarf approaching them. Glancing past the elf's boots, she counted two more blond elves and three dwarfs. All had either swords drawn or axes raised, suspiciously watching the Windkin, who stamped in rage, trying to pass the armed guards. Hostility and frustration hung like a storm cloud over the deadlock. She closed her eyes, deciding to stay quiet and listen.

The elf near her dismissed the dwarf's question. "The Fleogende sought to stop us, not the goblins. How else do you explain a defenseless human girl so near the castle?"

Defenseless! Jeanne fought to keep her temper. *Who does he think freed him?*

Hahle snorted in similar disgust. "I'd like to see how frisky he would be after breathing all that poisoned air! Windspin! You'd think our own neighbors would learn to hear us!"

Renw sighed. "When have you ever seen a Highlander out of his hills?"

"But isn't Leereho…"

"Leereho's father's kin are Glen dwellers. Outcast, according to the Highlanders."

She felt Elin's surprise. "Renw, you can't be referring to that old quarrel the elves once had over teaching humans magic? Why, that was settled back when the People of the Wind were learning to talk!"

"Elves can be just as stubborn as any of the Folk. The Highlanders never gave up the quarrel, they just moved away from it. Haven't you wondered why the Highlanders refuse to have anything to do with the rest of the Folk?"

The dwarf harrumphed thoughtfully. Jeanne peeked cautiously and saw that the elf had turned away from her to face his shorter ally. "The Sensitive must have had some reason for coming this far into the Mist Lands. Perhaps she is the human the Wise spoke of, the one who will break the witches' curse."

The elf stared thoughtfully at his sword. "And if you are right, what then, dwarf? The only road to the castle is down in Silent Forest, aye, and spell-guarded. Do you think a human can prevail against the Three when elves cannot? Will you permit one who saved your life to go to certain doom, mountain dweller?" He studied the stallions. "I will not."

Jeanne reached out with her mind to turn the elf's anger and drew back in dismay when that power did not respond. The painful throbbing in her head abruptly increased. *Worse than the time Robin threw me into that fencepost*, she thought. *I'll have to try something else.*

She drew on the ring's energy as she gathered her thoughts, wove them into a tight strand, hoping all the while that she had not forgotten how to speak mind to mind. *Elin*, she called silently, casting the strand of the thought-call out from herself.

The gray and white stallion froze, then cautiously glanced in her direction. "I hear you, Jeanne," he said aloud.

Hahle peered worriedly at his friend. "Elin, I don't hear anything."

"Didn't the time you spent with us in the Glen teach you anything?"

Hahle made a sour face. "Magic, again?" He hesitated. "Is she all right?"

"None of us will be if we don't escape from these Highlanders," Renw said abruptly. "It won't be easy. The Highlanders are good trackers."

Hahle started at a distant screech. "How much longer will your...spell hold? I don't want to have to fight wolves as well as these Folk."

"Watch the Fleogende," the elf by Jeanne ordered. "You know their curse when the winged hounds are about."

Elin, did you hear that? She sensed a struggle in the distance, felt the sharp pang of shape-changing, and gave Elin no chance to reply. *Do you know any illusion spells? Could you hold the spell if I formed it?*

"Wh-what? Why illusions?" The screech came again, and Elin firmly shook his mane. "Jeanne, I don't want to leave you."

Lore-Master, you're the only wizard around. The Folk don't know about the Watch Way. They'd follow you and Hahle down into Silent Forest and never turn back. Renw and I will go on to the Watch Way. She paused, sensing the turmoil in his mind and the anger in the distant thoughts. *Elin, those hounds aren't going to wait.*

An angry screech came from overhead, and a hound glided swiftly over the treetops. The elves and dwarfs glanced skyward, and Jeanne took a deep breath and cast an illusion of invisibility over herself. She rolled over and began to crawl towards the bare patch on the mountain

171

slope, using illusion to mask the tracks she made in the snow.

She heard a shrill whinny of fear behind her. *Hahle should take up acting*, she thought with a smile. The cold and wet penetrated her clothes, chilled her hands, but she ignored that, focusing her thoughts on the illusion she needed next.

She turned in time to see the elf staring wide-eyed at the spot where she had been. "The Heartsharer is gone!"

As if his words had been the cue, a solid wave of mind-torturing sound washed over them. Hounds flowed overhead, forming a huge dark cloud as they escaped in flight over Elin's spell barrier. And while they flew they shrieked, a long loud continuous sound of anger.

The Fleet Ones reared wildly, scattering the Folk attempting to control them. *Don't desert me now*, Jeanne pleaded to her weakened powers. She concentrated and suddenly there was another Jeanne running across the snow. The girl weaved, dodging the reaching Folk, and caught Elin's saddle. The stallion plunged away as the illusion seemingly scrambled into place. Hahle, his scream of anger faint amid the hound's shrieks, wheeled, knocking a hindering elf aside, and followed the gray and white stallion into the shadows.

"Stop them!"

"After them!"

Jeanne dropped her invisibility as the oddly assorted chase vanished among the trees. She felt her throat tighten with tears.

A soft nose nuzzled her. "They'll be all right," Renw said gently. "Can you stand up and hold onto my saddle? I'll take it slow up the slope."

A lagging hound shrieked, struggling to catch up with the screaming flock. Jeanne glanced upwards after it as they climbed and noticed the mist slowly curling down from the sky.

She felt the stallion's worry. "Leereho's all right, Renw. He's waiting up ahead." She glanced down the mountain. "I hope Elin and Hahle—"

"That pair?" Renw interrupted. "You should have been around when the Dark One tried to ambush the Wise in Dewin Heights. Hahle and Elin were the first out, and Hahle was carrying old Nain, the fattest dwarf in the Two Kingdoms, at the time." He chuckled thoughtfully. "I'd worry more about the dead of the Last Kingdom. Can you imagine that herd charging through Silent Forest?"

"The dead's confusion will be a sight to see," Leereho said softly. The elf emerged from the shadows at the top of the slope and boosted

Jeanne onto Renw's back. He studied her worriedly. "I wish we could take the time to allow you to rest, Jeanne."

"I'll be all right. How soon should we reach the Watch Way?"

Leereho smiled up at her. "That all depends on whether my partner here can keep pace with me."

Renw pawed the ground, and Jeanne had the impression that this was an old game between the two. "Try and pass me," the roan challenged and plunged away into the descending mists.

* * *

"Well, one vision from the Mirror is no possibility," Peter mused aloud. "Here's the dungeon and here I am." He looked about the stone cell distastefully. It was a large room about twenty feet square, poorly lighted by the torchlight shining through the large barred opening set at eyelevel in the door. The stale air smelled musty, and moisture condensed on the stone walls, dripped slowly down dangling chains bolted into the stone. The cell was bare of furniture, with nothing to sit or sleep on but the ankle-deep straw, which covered the floor. Peter made a face, thinking of cockroaches and mice.

He glanced out through the bars and saw no sign of any trolls or goblins in the corridor. Turning away, he leaned heavily against the thick oaken door and experimentally flooded his cell with disbelief. Nothing changed. Sighing, he began to pace, kicking aside the damp straw.

"Now I know," he muttered softly, "that Jeanne saw at least one more future for me after the dungeon, and it frightened her. So I guess there's still a possibility that I might be Changed."

He glanced suspiciously at the deeper shadows in the back of the cell. Not long after the Mirror had predicted his capture, Peter had managed to pry the workings of the Change spell out of Leereho, and the information was not encouraging.

"Name spells vary with their purpose," Leereho had said. "A Changed slave must be able to move freely, to mingle unnoticed with the Folk, so physical means to torture the body and sway the mind are not used. The Change starts with fear and, when a weakness is uncovered, that too is used to gain control over the intended slave." The look on the elf's face had been painful to see, and Peter remembered that Jeanne had glanced anxiously at Leereho, frowning at Peter for upsetting the elf.

"So," Peter decided, glancing at a set of chains, "I keep disbelieving everything here. I definitely don't want my body wandering around to someone else's commands until Jeanne can free me."

He glanced once more through the barred opening. The corridor was still clear. He lifted up his shirt and, wincing, pulled at a strip of duct tape stuck to his skin. Since he had placed it there after the visit to the Mirror and Jeanne's vision of his capture, it didn't come off very easily. "I knew this would come in handy," he muttered, freeing his Scout knife from the tape. He opened a blade and started to work on the lock.

* * *

Jeanne forced her bleary eyes to focus on the tumbled rocks at her feet. The narrow trail had ended abruptly back in the mists, and she had continued to scramble on over the rough ground, orienting herself through her awareness of Peter. She stumbled slightly in the rocky clutter and caught herself before she could fall. Perhaps she should stop and rest awhile. She had been walking for hours now, and it would be difficult to sneak into the castle if she was too tired to cast any illusions.

Jeanne sighed tiredly. *Sneak into the castle, huh? Try not to get caught first*! According to her senses, trolls and goblins were out in force tonight, and she hoped her friends had managed to escape them. She felt a hound drift overhead and fed a little of her illusions into the ring's light so that the hound would not spot a rainbow glow on the mountainside.

She pulled the hood of her cloak up over her hair as a light snow drifted down, hiding the patches of ice and making the slippery rocks even more treacherous. She glanced out at the blackness on her right and wondered if beneath her was the Silent Forest or some unnamed crevice between the mountains. She shook her head wearily. Perhaps she really should stop and rest, just for a little while.

Her boot suddenly slipped on a patch of ice, and with a sick horror she felt herself falling sideways and out into empty space. For only a heartbeat or two she fell, the wind catching at her cloak. She crashed into an unyielding surface. Her mind seemed to explode with shock and pain, then went out.

* * *

Peter lunged to his feet, only half awake, and looked wildly about his darkened cell. "Jeanne!" He fumbled for his faint awareness of her, feeling again in his mind its sudden sharp snapping. "Jeanne! Come back! Je—"

His ears caught a faint rustling in one corner of the cell, and he turned warily towards it, coming fully awake as his senses warned him that danger watched there. The torch that had burned outside the door was gone and the cell was pitch black.

"Poor little human," a shrill voice crooned from the darkness. "All alone in the dark with no dwarfs and no squeakings to help." The Dark One cackled softly.

Peter felt some of his fear leave. The Dark One was powerful, but he had tricked her before and planned on trying again. He was glad that it had not been Vana watching there; he had more respect and fear for that witch.

He heard the rustlings coming closer. He edged away and felt damp stone press against his back. Following his first defensive plan, he slid left along the wall into the corner, building up his disbelief as he moved and preparing to project it into a protective shield before his corner of the cell. His Scout knife, hidden again under his shirt, pressed into his side.

"You dared entrap me with fire." The Dark One's whisper was meant to threaten, but Peter sensed the witch's unease. She seemed puzzled over his odd behavior and he wondered briefly what other prisoners had done when suddenly faced with a rustling in the darkness.

"Blinding me with light," the shrill voice continued, growing again in confidence as Peter stood still, "burning light."

"Did you mention light, my dear?" an amused voice inquired. Bright flames unexpectedly danced along the ceiling and the Dark One, only a few feet from Peter, cried out and bent into a hunched figure of shifting shadows.

"Aiee! I do not have my light shield!" the shadows wailed. From out of the gloom, a hand like the talons of a bird gestured at the fire. "Dim yourself, fool!"

"The more fool, you," the flames laughed. "I have warned you to either keep your shield about you or remember the spell a little quicker." The flames dwindled slightly and turned a dull red. "Is that better?"

The hunched figure slowly lifted its hidden head. "I will damp your laughter one day!" it snarled.

"And I will torment you with flames at the Other's command, once she discovers that you have been playing with her captive."

"Her captive!" the voice hissed. The shadow-hidden face turned toward Peter once again. "The next captive was promised to me!" Peter tried not to shudder as the claws reached for him.

"Must I blind you again?" the flames sighed.

The claws retreated. "He hurt me," the Dark One said sullenly.

"The Folk grow bolder, it seems. I wonder." The flames flowed across the ceiling, swirling and merging in strange patterns. "Do you remember what that wizard bleated before his name was removed?"

The hunched figure shrugged. "Something about banes, and the Change losing its power. What of it? Wizards always threaten with words."

"And too often their words hide an actual threat. What if the Folk have discovered a way to destroy us? Why not test their spell on our Changed slaves? Have any of your slaves returned? Mine have not. Even my most trusted goblins have vanished."

"So they died. As you will die, mouse!" The hidden face turned toward Peter again. "But first you shall plead for death. The Change takes time but I know best how to prolong it without damaging the specimen—days of excruciating agony, nights of unending torment."

Peter, listening to her voice, felt a stabbing sharpness in his chest. *There is no pain*, he told himself firmly. The ache vanished as he closed the chink in his defenses. *Pay attention to what you're doing*, he told himself, shutting out the Dark One's murmur. *She's only toying with you this time.*

"Enough," the flames sighed.

"It is not enough!" the Dark One shrieked. The figure rose as it turned, claws extended as if to rake the flames from the ceiling. "It is not enough!"

"And if the Other finds out?" The light flickered with laughter. "I daresay you will find her anger more than enough to blast you back into the Caverns of the Stone Demons without even your shroud to shield you from their searing gaze. You should remember who summoned us into this land. Or have you so soon forgotten the spell binding us to serve her? The Other has not. Oh, not that one."

The figure gathered darkness about it like a cloak. "Do not test *my* anger. Water will dampen your humor."

The flames laughed. The fire flared brightly to flood every corner of the stone cell with blinding light. The shadowy figure shrieked and abruptly vanished.

Peter shielded his eyes against the glare. Laughter swirled about him, and suddenly there was darkness outside his shielding hand. He peeked out cautiously.

The cell was empty. No faint fire. No moving shadows. Peter took a

THE CRYSTAL THRONE

deep breath and slowly relaxed. He cautiously sat down in the musty-smelling straw, feeling indeed like a very tiny mouse that two lions had bickered over and then ignored. He puzzled over the last words of the flame witch. Vana had summoned them? Hadn't they invaded this land with Vana and the other six?

He sneezed on the dust from the straw and wished for the warmth of his cloak as the damp rock pressed against his back. *Might as well wish for a hot meal and a comfortable bed for all the good wishing will do. Might as well wish that Jeanne and I were back home.* "Jeanne!" he whispered, suddenly remembering. He reached out carefully with his mind, seeking some sign of the girl.

A sudden fear touched him as no answer came to his silent call. "No. No, Vana couldn't have caught her." *Jeanne!* He tried to reason with his fear. Maybe she had put up her block for some reason. Maybe that was why she had suddenly seemed to vanish. He sent his mind out again.

* * *

Torchlight shone through the open doorway, blinding his dark-adapted eyes. Peter stirred, and realized from his stiffness that he had been sitting against the damp rock wall for hours.

A wooden tray was thrust inside and the massive door swung shut with a slam and a click from the lock. The silent jailer stomped off down the corridor. Investigating, Peter found a bowlful of a greasy lump that looked like meat in the near-darkness, a few stale slices of bread, an empty cup, and a sealed pitcher containing a clear liquid.

He sniffed and tasted the liquid suspiciously and found it was only water. The meat he rejected with a shudder. He choked down two slices of the dry bread and, although he was still hungry, put the rest aside for later. Somewhere he had read that starvation was an important part of brainwashing, and he wasn't sure how much longer they would feed him.

Time passed slowly in the dungeon. Peter occupied himself by alternately searching for Jeanne, trying to pick the lock of the cell door, and trying to devise a way to overcome his jailer without warning half the castle of his powers. The rusty chains resisted his attempts to pull them out of the walls and the wooden tray was too light to be of any use. He even went so far as to explore the floor and walls for hidden doorways.

Hours passed. The torch outside the door burned out, leaving him in blackness. After waiting anxiously for the Dark One to appear again,

Peter finally dozed off, planning to wake before his jailer returned with a new torch and tray. When his eyes again opened, however, a new tray of food rested in the pool of torchlight. He groaned in frustration, then hesitated, feeling a familiar touch stir against his mind.

"Jeanne!"

Reassurance touched him, and then an odd combination of curiosity and concern tapped lightly. He smiled as he realized that that was her way of asking how he was and wondered at the same time why his impression of her was so faint, as if she was far away or had her block partially up. Impatience slipped out before he could control it, and there was a ripple of amusement in answer. He tried to convey a warning for her to be careful, that Vana was seeking her, but the communication link faded away, and he was left again with only the touch of her presence against his mind.

* * *

Jeanne snapped the communication link before Peter could sense her inner agitation and kicked irritably at a loose pebble. It shot off the ledge that formed her prison and rattled downward into the chasm below.

She glanced briefly after it. "Of all the times to fall off a mountain," she muttered. She pushed her hair out of her face and stared sourly at the ring glittering on her finger. "Instead of giving me nightmares," she told the ring, "why don't you show me how to become a shape-changer? That's what I need now!"

She sensed the last of her aches dwindling and wondered again how badly she had been hurt in the fall. It seemed to her as if she had been unconscious for quite a while; the light snow had covered her in a thick blanket before stopping. "Must have been a very long time. Peter seemed awfully worried." She scowled and kicked at another pebble. "*He*'s worried! I'll never make it to the castle in time now!"

Unbidden, her mind pulled the last vision of the Mirror of Truth out of her memory: that of Peter wearing the violet uniform of the witches, with the trapped look of a Changed One in his eyes and a barrier of disbelief about his mind, set to keep her out. "I won't fail him again! I won't!" The echoes repeated her shout mockingly.

She shook off the memory and returned to the present. Her main problem was getting herself out of her latest predicament. She glared reproachfully at the smooth rock wall before her. She could see no convenient handholds to use in climbing up. The way down looked worse. She glanced into the mist-choked chasm and shivered. She had come so close to falling to the bottom of it.

She squared her shoulders. Never mind what could have been; right now, she had to get off this ledge. She attacked the wall, her fingers searching for tiny cracks she could use to climb out of her prison. On the fifth attempt, she managed to claw her way up a scant four feet before her tiny finger-and-toeholds crumbled away.

She landed on the ledge again, the impact knocking the wind out of her. She sat still a moment, studying the short distance she had climbed and trying hard not to cry. Glancing at her broken nails, she tore a strip of cloth from her already ripped sleeve and wrapped it around a bleeding finger, ignoring the fact that it was healing even as she watched.

Blinking back tears, she climbed to her feet, wiping her eyes on her dirty sleeve and smudging her face. She started again on the wall.

A faint sensation touched her mind. Jeanne quickly jumped back down to the ledge, preparing for an attack. She tilted her head, listening with her mind, and slowly smiled at the faint hint of smugness in the approaching thoughts. She absently rubbed a healing scratch on the back of one hand. *It feels so proud of itself for finding me. Too bad the capture is not going to go the way it plans.* Her eyes lost their focus as she reached out with her mind, sensing rather than seeing the long shadow drifting toward her from the snow-covered peak of the nearby Silver-Haired.

* * *

The lock suddenly clicked. Peter looked at his Scout knife, a slow grin spreading across his face. It finally worked!

His grin vanished as he heard the sound of his jailer's heavy feet approaching. He peeked through the bars and saw the faint gleam of torchlight bobbing closer. *He's back early!* He looked at the flickering torch outside his cell and thought quickly. This could be bad; it could mean that he was about to be Changed. He glanced at the distant light and decided his jailer was too far away to see him. Opening the cell door wide, he stepped into the passage and behind it. His plan was simple. Once his jailer saw the open door, he would naturally look inside. Then Peter would close it with him inside. He looked down at the Scout knife still in his hand and wondered how much of a threat that could be. The footsteps came closer. Peter tensed, readying his mind.

The sound of footsteps paused before the open cell door, but instead of an outcry, there was a soft thud inside the cell. Peter pushed the door closed and found himself confronting a small troll. "Good, you got the door open," it said. "I couldn't find the one with the key."

Peter blinked. "Jeanne?"

The illusion dropped away and Jeanne stood before him, her long hair tangled and her face streaked with dust. Her clothes were smeared with dirt and one sleeve was ripped. Peter opened the cell door and glanced at the goblin snoring inside the cell. He closed the door again, shaking his head, and looked again at his partner. "Am I glad to see you!" He closed his knife and hooked it on his belt. "Is that blood on your arm?"

"Hmm?" Jeanne was looking him over as closely as he was studying her, and he hastily brushed off some of the straw clinging to his clothes. She glanced almost indifferently at the brown stain he pointed out. "Could be. I fell a few times—Leereho's old Watch Way isn't all that smooth. Are you—"

Peter sniffed. A faint odor of musk clung to her clothes. "What is—"

Jeanne noticed his look and sniffed at the wrist of her sleeve. "Oh. The hound. I said Le's road wasn't very smooth. I had to ride a hound in."

"You what?"

Jeanne clapped her hands over her ears. "Don't rouse the entire castle. I don't sense any pain about you and your mind isn't trapped, so do we have to stand here and play twenty questions? Have you seen Graylod?"

Peter sighed and started down the corridor. "Quit acting like Salanoa. And why should I worry about rousing the castle? If I know you, probably half the guards are asleep already. Why did you ride a hound in? Couldn't you walk?"

"No. Have you seen Graylod?"

Peter glanced to where she walked beside him, moving as silently as his own shadow, and saw that she was not going to explain further. "Briefly, in the throne room," he said, answering her question. "He's casting spells for the witches now. Vana took his name from him."

"Oh no." Jeanne twisted the ring worriedly. "If she has his name, she probably has ours as well."

"I don't think so. She didn't call me by name, just 'human.' Anyway, now that you're here, Graylod will be free in no time."

"I hope so," Jeanne said tonelessly. "But since neither of us knows his true name, I don't know how we're going to break Vana's hold on him."

"What do you mean? Isn't he just Changed? You can break that." Peter stopped at the foot of a darkened staircase, wishing he had brought the torch with him. Rainbow light grew beside him, and, with the ring lighting their way, they started up the stairs.

"The Change, yes," Jeanne said, continuing the conversation. "That I can break. But the Change is only a minor name spell compared to being nameless." She snapped her fingers. "That's why I can't sense him anywhere! His name is gone!"

"Huh?"

"Vana took his name," Jeanne said. "I...can't explain exactly how this works, Peter, but without his name, Graylod...isn't. Just his body exists. His mind, his *self*, is held with his name."

Peter heard the chill in her voice and realized what she was leaving unsaid, that Vana would try to do the same to her.

Jeanne sensed his concern. She smiled weakly at him. "Well, even if Vana is the most powerful being around, most of her concentration should be focused on holding Graylod's name captive. All we need to do is distract her, disturb her concentration a little, and Graylod might be able to break free on his own."

"And then it would be the three of them against the three of us." Peter glanced at the cold stone about them. "Once we ever find him, that is."

"Now that I know to look for his body and not his mind, it shouldn't be too hard." She smiled at his expression. "Cheer up, Peter. All we have to do is fulfill the Glen's riddle." She recited, *"For the Heart-sharer before the crystal throne, must the lost name with fire be spoken. The doom of the false for the dead shall atone, and two curses of hate be broken."*

"Yeah. That's all we have to do," he said, adding a Hahle-like snort.

They crept cautiously up long flights of stairs and stole silently down the numerous corridors. Peter had not realized before how immense the castle actually was. And yet, for all its size, the stronghold seemed deserted. There was no outcry from the dungeons, no alarm at his escape, and Peter began to wonder if their invasion was even noticed. Then he saw that no guards stood where he had last remembered them and grew suspicious all over again. Where *was* everyone?

"Found him!" Jeanne took a step towards one of the many hallways intersecting theirs. "I found him, Peter! He's—oh!"

The girl faltered suddenly, caught at a wall for support. Peter felt shock swirling about her. "Jeanne, what is it?"

He reached for her, but stopped in surprise as his hand grew warmer the closer it came to her. The air about the girl seemed to waver, as if he was looking at her through a heat haze.

"Heat... Jeanne!" Peter wasted little time. He projected a barrier of disbelief about himself and the girl, reached through the haze and pulled her out of it. Holding tightly to her, he ran down the corridor she had chosen, forcing the strangely groggy Jeanne to keep pace with him.

A second later, he heard a slight "pop" behind them and turned to see a section of the floor and wall gone. "That flame witch certainly likes transporting tricks," he muttered. "Jeanne, are you all right? What happened?"

Jeanne held her head. "Wow, that elemental has a strong mind. I...think I must have bumped into its thoughts, or it bumped into me. Either way, that hurt. Thanks, Peter."

"'S'okay. Where are we—oh, I remember this corridor. Graylod's in the throne room?"

"Along with the Dark One and the fire elemental. I can't sense Vana around anywhere, though."

Peter mustered a faint grin. "I'll bet she's probably still out looking for you. At least we won't have to face them all at once."

Jeanne glanced nervously behind them. "The elemental just vanished. I can't sense it anywhere."

"Graylod's still in the throne room?"

At her nod, Peter took a deep breath and tried to adjust his nonexistent sword. He looked at the massive crystalline doors at the end of the corridor and back to his partner. "Shall we?"

Jeanne nodded and started forward. Peter forced himself to relax, to send the fear from his thoughts as each step carried them closer to the doors. *Don't believe*, he told himself. *Don't believe in anything here but Jeanne.*

They stopped before the doors and together reached for the heavy golden rings of the latch. The doors swung away from their hands, opening under another's power.

"Enter, my dears," a shrill voice crooned. "We have been expecting you."

CHAPTER 16

THE LOST NAME

Peter and Jeanne entered the crystal hall, and the great doors slowly swung shut behind them. Peter squinted against the dazzling glitter of light reflecting off the faceted mirrors of walls and floor and tried to see the dais at the far end of the room. Jeanne took a moment to glance curiously about her. "Looks as if we're inside a big diamond," she said softly.

Peter nodded, recalling the resemblance, but not willing to look and thus believe in his surroundings. *This isn't real*, he reminded himself.

Together they walked towards the dais, their distorted reflections in the crystal walls moving with them. Jeanne tried not to look at them, realizing that the reflections were intended to distract them, to draw their attention and make them easy to attack. *Wish I could just disbelieve, like Peter, and make them go away.*

They had covered half the distance to the great dais when the room slowly began to change about them. The dancing lights slowed, became subdued and dim. Shadows crept out of corners, flowed across the floor, swallowed the reflection in the crystals.

Jeanne felt a troubling before her and stopped. "I'd wondered why the Dark One said 'we.'"

Warned by the odd note in her voice, Peter looked ahead and stopped in his tracks.

A huge pool of darkness wound about the base of the dais. Ripples appeared on the side nearest them, and the pool slowly spread in their direction.

Jeanne backed a step. "It's alive!"

Peter, accustomed to darkness after his experiences in the dungeon, stood firm and formed a wall of disbelief about them. He glanced up at the top of the dais. Only one witch was present, its form all but hidden in the shadows about its core of deeper blue-violet darkness. The other two thrones were empty, but he could dimly perceive a grayish shimmer beside the crystal throne. "Graylod's up there. See if you can get any response from him," he whispered.

"I've *been* trying."

The huge pool of darkness rose from the floor and gathered itself into a vaguely man-shaped form, its head brushing against the distant ceiling. Peter felt a chill emanating from it as it swayed, reaching tentatively towards them.

Its groping hand encountered Peter's barrier and slid aside. The shadow-creature tried again and again to reach the humans, its movements growing frantic as each attempt failed.

"We shouldn't waste your powers on this thing," Jeanne finally whispered. She held up her fist, activating the ring's glow and forming a circle of light about them. The hesitant fingers of gloom retreated at the touch of rainbows.

The darkened figure on the throne hissed in anger. The giant shadow-creature cowered at the soft sound, but continued to withdraw from the painful light.

"You can't harm us," Jeanne said firmly. "But we can hurt you, if we wish. Let me help you. I can free you from the Other's will, if you promise to leave this land forever."

The Dark One hesitated, then cackled shrilly. "You...help me?"

"Are you crazy?" Peter whispered under the wild laughter. "That thing *likes* to hurt people!"

"I had to try."

He sighed. "I know."

The laughter stopped. "I am bound to no one's will," the Dark One snarled.

Jeanne touched again the fine net of control stretched about the Dark One's mind and said nothing. Vana was either an extremely powerful witch or the shadow witch a very weak one. She wondered if the fire elemental was also bound to Vana's will, since, in the stories that she had read, an elemental was powerful within the limits of its substance but not as powerful as a true witch. The ring sparkled as it held back the shadows, and the thought crept into Jeanne's mind that darkness was itself an element, like fire or air. *Not a shadow* witch, *then*, she decided, *but a shadow elemental.* Somehow, the idea did not surprise her; Vana had not appeared to be one who would be willing to share power.

She spared a moment to wonder from what source the thought had come, for she could sense no other minds besides Peter's and the Dark One's. *Graylod?* she tried, but no answer came to her silent call.

The shadow-creature slumped back into a pool of darkness, flowed and spread about their protecting circle of light. Atop the dais, the Dark One rose from its throne and sent the cloak of its shadow down to merge with that of the creature.

Peter caught his breath. "That thing is *part* of the Dark One!"

Jeanne tightened her grip on his hand and waited.

Half-seen things moved in the shadows about the circle of rainbows, the light reflecting off pale eyes that flickered in and out of visibility. Peter heard the click of claws against the crystal floor, furtive paddings that stopped on one side of the circle only to begin again on another side, and a heavy panting that seemed to move closer and closer...

"You cannot harm us," Jeanne repeated. "We do not fear you or your shadows."

A venomous hiss was the only answer. The sounds of creatures hidden within the surrounding darkness multiplied.

Jeanne released Peter's hand, took a step forward. "Get ready," she said, her eyes on the dark figure before the throne. Peter reinforced his barrier, tried not to listen to the movements about them.

Fire suddenly exploded in the midst of the darkness, encircling the humans in its searing light. The shadow-creatures drew back with moans and squeals of pain.

"You fool, you're protecting them from me!" the Dark One shrieked.

The flames gave a rippling laugh and flooded the great hall with a white light that flared the brighter reflecting off the crystal walls. Darkness crept hurriedly back to its throne.

The shadows snarled and a tall violet wall of darkness rose at the edge of the dais. The wall fell like a wave upon the fire beneath it, swallowing the light, the cold wind of its descent blowing Jeanne's cloak out behind her.

The flames gasped in dismay. Angrily the fire blazed brighter, forcing the hungry dark to retreat, but a quarter of the flame circle had been blotted out. In the sudden silence, scattered fires merged into a tall flame. "I have warned you," the elemental said with a light laugh, and launched itself directly at the shadow-hidden figure.

Fiery light dove into the heart of the dark. A terrible shriek echoed wildly in the hall, answered by chilling laughter.

"Stop!"

Light and dark surged apart, turned toward the shadows about the crystal throne.

"Witling! Miserable fool!" the voice raged. "The Folk gather on the very borders of the Mist Lands and you must drag me from my hunt to settle one of your petty arguments over an escaping prisoner? Imbeciles!"

Jeanne turned to Peter. "Vana?" she asked.

Peter nodded. "Vana."

The flames bowed gracefully, its laughter undiminished. "I had thought you wanted him alive. Also—"

"That was my command." Vana dismissed the light impatiently.

"You do not command me," the Dark One growled.

The gloom vanished from about the throne and before the carved crystal stood a tall beautiful woman dressed in the green of new leaves. Emeralds sparkled amid the masses of her fiery red hair, and an angry light glimmered in the large violet eyes. "You blind worm," she said in a cold, merciless voice. "Do you think because you are of the same substance as the Shadows that you hold Their power? Of course I command you. Did I not summon you, the both of you, here?"

The darkness swirled, rose to tower over the witch. "You do not command me!"

Vana eyed the muttering shadows with disdain. "I gave you such simple tasks, and yet you failed me. Your presence was to have befuddled those prying Wise Ones so that they would not know of me, but a human knows. You were sent to capture him at Gimstan Mountain. He escaped. You knew of the human girl, yet you did not tell me."

"She is—" the flames tried.

Vana waved the interruption aside, her attention on the turbulent shadows. Slowly, as if pronouncing a doom, she said, "You are a flawed tool. I need you no longer."

With a piercing shriek, the darkness fell upon the witch, burying her in blackness. From the depths of the writhing gloom, Vana's voice shouted one word in a harsh tongue. A light blazed in answer, shredding the violet shroud, and flung the tatters of the elemental's broken form to the flames for dispersal.

Jeanne cried out, struck to her knees by the force of the deathblow.

The light about the witch flickered and died as the woman turned at the faint cry. Surprise and amazement were evident on Vana's face as she stared silently at the girl, and Peter realized that she had not even known that Jeanne was there.

"I tried to tell you," the flames whispered apologetically.

"A Sensitive," Vana breathed. "Ah, that explains a great deal."

Peter stepped before the fallen girl to shield her as a strange light grew in the witch's violet eyes. Vana paid no attention to him but turned instead to the waiting flames. "Go and drive away those witlings that dare to call themselves 'wise.' Once I have finished here, you may name your reward for delivering this prize to me."

The bright fire hesitated. When it again spoke, the laughter was gone from its voice. "I desire my freedom, Master, but that reward is not mine to claim. These came freely into the net." In the middle of a bow, the elemental abruptly winked out.

Peter watched Vana suspiciously over his shoulder as he helped Jeanne to her feet, but the witch only studied them, puzzlement furrowing her brow.

"It happened so fast," Jeanne whispered numbly. "I couldn't block in time." Her breathing was ragged as she struggled to lock away the pain, forced herself to concentrate on her own body, to feel it whole and healthy, not scattered like the dark cloud. The effort robbed her of needed strength, she knew, and left her vulnerable to attack.

Peter knew that also. Half-supporting the girl, he looked up to meet the faintly amused eyes of the witch. "So only seven witches and warlocks fought the seven Wise Ones," he said, stalling for time. "Not nine, as you wanted everyone to believe. How did you survive?" He glanced at the grayish shimmer beside her. "Did you know Graylod's name even then?"

The violet eyes mocked him, seemingly seeing through his ploy. She gestured, and a thin spear of force shattered against the barrier of his disbelief. A finely sculptured eyebrow rose, and the witch thoughtfully settled back into her throne, studying the two before her. "You are more than you seem," she remarked. "But not enough."

A blast of wind struck Peter from behind, knocking him off balance. He slipped on the suddenly slick crystal, felt the wind pushing him—pushing him away from Jeanne.

"Pe—" Jeanne bit off the word, realizing with a sick horror that she had almost given his name away. She glanced up at Vana to see if the witch had heard, and abruptly felt her gaze caught by the amused violet eyes. They pulled at her, forcing her to look deeply into their depths. She felt herself teetering on the brink of an abyss and struggled to keep from falling. The ageless eyes compelled her to cease her struggles, to release her hold and drift without care, without thought. She felt a scream build up within her.

Then suddenly the compulsion ceased. Jeanne wrenched her eyes away, felt the witch's hungry eagerness slowly turn to puzzlement.

"I told you she wouldn't get you with me around," Peter said softly. He walked through the howling wind as if it did not exist and turned to stand by her side again. "Sorry it took me so long to get my barrier up."

Jeanne braced herself and looked up at Vana. The witch seemingly had recovered from her surprise and now toyed with a lock of red hair. "So you came here freely, did you?" Vana asked lightly. "Why so foolish, my dear? Do you have a death wish, perhaps? Not even a wizard would enter my gates uninvited."

"I…" Jeanne took a deep breath. "Actually, I didn't enter by the gate," she replied in the same light manner as the witch had used. Distrusting Vana's sudden willingness to talk, she tensed as the witch turned to Peter.

"Yes, I knew Gray Fool's name. I knew all their names. That is why I survived and those other fools perished. But I did not want Gray Fool here to die until I was quite finished with him, so I allowed him to live and bring hopelessness upon his people."

Jeanne sensed several lies and started to speak, then glanced at Peter and subsided, waiting.

Peter wondered why Jeanne kept warning him. For once, he was getting some answers. "But you still hid behind the Dark One and the Fire," he persisted.

The violet eyes studied him and dismissed him. She turned back to Jeanne. "But now you have come, my dear. And you have brought me the Ring. The powerful Ring of Calada. I no longer need to hide." Her eyes flicked greedily over the girl.

Jeanne hesitated, ignoring the clammy sensation of the witch's gaze. Although she could sense no treachery, she still had the distinct impression of a trap reset. The previous attack could have been only a test to discover the extent of their powers. She had best play the game and hope that words were not Vana's most powerful weapons.

Jeanne inclined her head gracefully and felt Peter's inward sigh as he recognized Salanoa's regal bow. In her teacher's best amused but superior manner the girl added, "Yes, Vana, *we* have come. Of our own free will. Are you sure you do not need to hide?" She displayed the ring. "Remember, this is the bane of name-thieves."

Vana stared at the glittering ring as if hypnotized, then visibly controlled herself. She smiled coolly. "So it is 'we,' then? Be wary of the help you accept, my dear. How do you think I was able to follow your exploits so easily, to know when best to drop hints to my creatures as to your whereabouts? My source was very close to you."

Jeanne glanced nervously at the ring and Vana laughed softly. "The traitor was not you, child. Indeed, had I realized that you even existed, that you accompanied our brave hero, I would have come to visit you myself instead of delegating his capture to my two very inept servants."

"What are you trying to say?" Peter demanded.

Jeanne gripped his arm, warned by the sudden anticipation in Vana's mind. "Don't listen to her! It's another trap!"

Vana's ageless eyes drew Peter's, compelled him to listen. "You are alien to this land, my fine lad. Your presence, like that of most humans, interrupts the flow of magic, creates a disturbance that those with the eyes to see can see. I knew, the very instant you stepped through the Last Door, that a human had entered. I knew where you were at any moment and could have captured you with ease at any time."

Peter felt as if she had struck him. He had betrayed them to the witch! He was the means by which they had been tracked across this land!

"Not your fault!" Jeanne whispered roughly, keeping her eyes on the witch. "Not your fault! Don't let her get to you! Don't believe!"

Peter wasn't listening. Again and again his mind went over how easily the hounds could find them, how the two patrols in the desert had almost trapped them, and how on the slopes of the Silver-Haired the soldiers had materialized about them. And he was to blame!

Jeanne felt the choking guilt rise within him and realized too late that that had been Vana's intention. The witch was adding to Peter's feelings of guilt, overwhelming him as his disbelief changed to belief. Hurriedly Jeanne threw up a block to protect him, but Peter had accepted the guilt as his own. His emotional presence suddenly vanished from her senses.

Jeanne turned and stared into Peter's unseeing eyes. There was no sign of life about him. He stood as still as if he had been time-trapped. "No," she said softly, her fear growing. "No!"

Vana laughed. "Humans," she said in disgust. "Tell them first a little truth and they will believe and be lost!"

The cruel laughter rang an inner alarm along Jeanne's nerves and she pulled away from Peter, on guard for another trick. "'Beware the voice of the Shadows,'" she said softly, quoting one of Elin's sayings. "'Its strongest weapons are half-truths and lies.'" Although she stood away from Peter, her mind still worried at the spell holding him like fingers upon ropes. She came up against a curious resistance, almost as if Peter himself had flung up a wall to shut her out.

She glanced askance at Vana, avoiding the witch's eyes. "I hadn't expected compassion from you. I thought that you would want him to watch our battle, not shield him from it. But don't think that you'll be able to disguise yourself as me—even if you wear my body—once you release him."

"Compassion, for such as him?" Vana broke into a derisive laugh. "Only his body is trapped. His mind is free to observe—and to fear. He will be easier to Change once he realizes that it is futile to try to fight me."

Jeanne tried not to show her relief. If Peter's mind was free, the witch couldn't hold him captive for long. She had to stall for time and hope that Peter would shake off Vana's trap of guilt.

Slowly, casually, she began to inch away from Peter, carefully closing the rainbow glow about herself so that Vana's attention would remain centered upon her, not Peter. "I'm flattered, Vana," she said lightly, her voice steadying as she concentrated on what she must do. "You could sense him halfway across this land, but not me. Not even when I stood in the same room with you." Cautiously she added doubt to the witch's mind, sliding it in so stealthily that she was sure the woman would not notice.

"Do not credit yourself with great powers," Vana said contemptuously. "You may be human, but you are also a Sensitive. As such, you blend with the land, not stand apart from it. Had I realized that I was looking for a Sensitive, I would have found you."

Abruptly she pointed, and a jagged bolt leaped from her fingertips to crack the crystal floor at Jeanne's feet. "Surrender, Sensitive. You know that I am the stronger. Give me your name now and make this easy and painless for both of us."

Jeanne glared at the witch, unable to hide her defiance, and the red-haired woman laughed again. "You will learn. Even the mighty Graylod has learned to obey me." Vana gestured, and the tall wizard by her side picked up the long staff of gray wood from its resting place against her throne. The staff shimmered coldly at his touch.

He descended the steps of the dais slowly, as if moving to the measured beat of a march, while Jeanne's thoughts fluttered frantically about his mind, seeking some chink in the armor of Vana's control.

Vana chuckled softly. "Do you hope to release the wizard as you did my Changed slaves, Sensitive? He cannot help you. He tried a little name spell when I first captured him, but mine proved the stronger. Poor Gray Fool. He did not realize that I had developed defenses against that particular spell."

Lies and half-truths, Jeanne thought. But which was the lie? What was the truth? Had they come all this way on a hopeless quest? *Graylod, can you hear me? Fight her. Please try to fight her.*

The gray-garbed wizard stopped before the girl and raised his staff. Jeanne looked up into Graylod's empty eyes and the fear almost broke from her tightly held control. She sensed the power gathering about the wizard, ready to strike her at the witch's command. The staff glittered like one of the silver trees in the Glen.

In her mind's eye, she suddenly saw the Glen shining faintly under a white moon. A younger Salanoa and a dark-haired woman stood arguing before the oldest of the silver trees, and Jeanne felt again Salanoa's sorrow.

Still caught in the vision, she spoke to the stranger. "Why does Salanoa pity you?"

The sudden shock in the witch's mind snapped Jeanne back to the present. "She dares?" Vana hissed. "She dares pity me? Me? Is that how my foolish student thanks me for tolerating her continued existence? With pity?" She rose in one fluid motion and spat a curse at the dark shrouded throne. The stone shivered briefly, then crumbled into dust.

Jeanne froze in horror. Her student? Salanoa had been Vana's student? "I learned my first spells from a Sensitive," Salanoa's voice whispered in her memory.

"Oh my gosh." The exclamation was a small whisper. Jeanne reached out and felt the elusive familiarity about Vana, the touch of a common bond between them. She remembered the ring's visions—the throne room she had seen in the desert, the woman battling the violet creature she had seen on the mountainside and the recent one of Salanoa and the dark-haired woman—and understood now the warning it had tried to convey.

A Sensitive. Vana the Immortal, the body-stealer, the bane of her own people, and—a Sensitive. But no ordinary one. Vana had been the Sensitive who had killed, for now the power to share emotions was crippled within her, had been replaced by the limitless strength of a witch. Jeanne cursed herself for a fool. The clues had always been before her and yet she had never seen, never guessed.

She glanced at Peter, still trapped within the spell, and wondered numbly if he had known. *What am I to do? I can't stop her. Can't even bluff my way out of this. She knows! She knows what I can and cannot do. I've lost before I've even begun.*

Vana muttered angrily to herself, not noticing the turmoil in Jeanne's mind. "Thus the Folk rewards their saviors. When I demanded that the powers I lost be returned, who but Salanoa, she who I had once foolishly trusted with my name, dared bar me from the magic of the Glen, naming me Vana, the False. The False! I, who was once known as..."

Jeanne waited, not daring to believe her ears, as the witch abruptly caught herself in mid-sentence. Vana had almost revealed her true name! *After a near-slip like that*, Jeanne thought gleefully, *I won't quit. Vana's going to defeat herself at this rate.* "Known as...?" she prodded softly.

The violet eyes glittered. "Clever, clever child!" Vana drew herself erect and studied the girl with a grudging respect. "Almost you trapped me. But I am the stronger, and I weary of your games. Graylod!"

The gray staff glittered. But before he could strike, Jeanne hurled all her frustration and fears full into the wizard's mind. She whirled and ran as he staggered from the blow, the staff falling from his nerveless fingers to ring against the crystal floor.

"Stop!"

Jeanne braked as a bolt shattered the floor before her. Abruptly she felt herself caught and held by an invisible force. She fought uselessly, unable to move even her arms from her sides.

The force turned her about until, still held within its grip, she faced the dais. A faint surprise and fear touched her when she noticed the huddled heap of gray upon the floor. *Must have hit him harder than I thought.* She probed the stunned mind and frowned as she sensed the net of control still in place.

A probe lightly touched the surface of her mind and she slapped it away, renewed her efforts to free herself from the power holding her captive.

"Do not struggle so! I have no desire to harm you and risk damaging my body-to-be."

Horror spread through the girl but so, after a moment's thought, did relief. There were, after all, only a limited number of ways Vana could control her without physical harm. And without the knowledge of her true name, Vana was restricted to the weaker spells that Jeanne also knew.

With that faint encouragement, she continued to work on Vana's emotions, supplementing doubt with other, conflicting feelings to further muddle the witch's thoughts. She wondered as she did so why the woman still had not noticed that her mind was being tampered with. *It's almost as if she* can't *tell. Has she forgotten that much of a Sensitive's ways*? Somehow, Jeanne doubted that.

Slowly, the green gown whispering at her movements, Vana regally descended the stairs and swept across the floor towards the imprisoned girl. The woman ignored the still statue that was Peter and walked past the fallen wizard without a downward glance.

Watching the green-garbed woman approach, and knowing what was hidden under the illusion of beauty, Jeanne felt the urge to do something, anything, to escape. Ruthlessly she pushed panic away, tried to seem the very picture of defiance despite her bedraggled appearance.

I ran in the right direction, she thought, studying the scene before her. *Now if I can keep Vana's back towards Peter and Graylod, they can free themselves without her noticing. C'mon, Peter, snap out of it*!

She gathered all of her powers back to herself, except for the link through which she fed doubt into Vana's thoughts, and reluctantly withdrew her contacts with Peter and Graylod. She could do nothing more to help them, and only a little to help herself. Considered realistically, her part in this quest was doomed. Even if she fought on a purely defensive level and did not waste energy trying to influence the former Sensitive, there was only a remote possibility that she could resist Vana for a while. Even then, she would have to rely heavily on the ring. Her own powers had been weakened too much by the backlash from the Dark One's death to last for long.

The gold band on her finger glowed green in warning as the witch neared her. Vana stopped a few feet away and studied her prisoner with a mocking smile. "Will you give me the Ring or must I take that from you as well?"

"Try and take it," Jeanne retorted angrily. She hoped the witch would try and be blasted by the ring as the goblin had.

Vana shrugged, the emeralds sparkling in her hair. "As you wish. There is but one safe way to take the Ring against its choice. And that is by the name of she who made it."

She raised her arms above her head, the long sleeves falling away from her pale skin. "Calada! By your name, I bind you! *Pine name Calade ic saelan pec!*"

Jeanne could not restrain a gasp as the rainbow light about her abruptly vanished. The ring was now cold dead metal about her finger, no longer responsive to her.

Vana did not move to take it from Jeanne's hand. She smiled patronizingly at her captive. "Now it is your power against mine, child. But I shall be merciful. I will not keep your name long, I need it only to exchange our bodies. Your spirit will go free after your death."

She reached out and placed her hands on either side of Jeanne's face. Jeanne tried to jerk out of her grasp, but the cool hands held her head as firmly as the witch's will held her body. She squeezed her eyes shut as her head was turned towards the witch.

"Open your eyes, Sensitive, and look at me. Give me your name."

"No! Leave me alone!" Without thinking, Jeanne blasted Vana's mind with fear and anger. The hands released her with a sharp cry, and Jeanne felt the witch's pain in her own mind.

Colored lights flashed and fused in her mind, and she would have fallen had it not been for her invisible prison. *Of all the stupid—* Judging from her giddiness, she had greatly reduced the amount of time left to her. *Peter, I need help!*

She opened her eyes and saw Vana a few feet away, cradling her aching head in her hands. The witch's eyes glittered angrily as she slowly lifted her head. "I...underestimated you, child. I shall not do so again."

Violet eyes held those of blue-gray, tugging at the mind behind Jeanne's inner defenses, drawing her from her locked fortress of self. Jeanne's scream died unvoiced.

"Give me your name." The relentless command pounded on her innermost door.

She was drowning in the violet eyes, losing all will to fight. Words struggled in her throat. Abruptly she was looking at her body through the witch's eyes, felt Vana frown, heard her say softly, "Humans have stronger wills than I remembered. But my full strength will break you, Sensitive." Then she was back in her own body, falling into darkness without end.

* * *

In the Gray Hills, a flame elemental led the armies of the Other against the advancing Wise Ones. Suddenly it sprang into the air and, with a wild cry of "Free! Free at last!" it leaped for the sun, leaving a trail of fire across the sky.

And in the front ranks of the Free Folk a brown-garbed wizard looked towards the hidden castle and fingered her pendant worriedly.

In the ranks of the suddenly leaderless army, the few remaining Changed Ones shivered as if a chill wind had brushed them. With a battle cry that sounded more like the rumble of falling rock, a released dwarf charged the line of trolls ahead of him, and the Battle of the Gray Hills began.

In a crystal hall, a semiconscious wizard stirred slightly, feebly sensing his enemy nearby but lacking the strength to do anything about it.

Standing near the wizard, a human boy held his head for a moment, shattering a field of paralysis without realizing that he did so.

Peter felt as if a great weight had been lifted from him. He couldn't remember exactly what had happened, only that it had been his fault somehow.

Shaking his head as if to jog loose a memory, he lowered his hands and looked about the darkened hall. For a moment, he thought he was alone, then he spotted movement not far from him and felt the cold grip of fear close about his heart.

"Lifetrust!" he yelled.

The use-name and title of the once most honored Sensitive in the Free Lands cast ripples into the stillness and, as intended, caught the attention of its owner. An ancient face slowly turned towards him, a face ravaged with time, stripped of all illusions by the need to concentrate its complete will upon its prey, who now slipped from the witch's hold to lie silent upon the floor.

Peter shuddered at the sight of the dreaming violet eyes set in the loathsome skull-like face. Steeling himself for what he had to do, he uttered one word more powerful than any of her spells. "Alitha."

The figure froze at the sound of that name, but Peter did not dare relax. The saying of her true name would not hold her long, he knew, only long enough for him to recite the name spell Salanoa had taught him. Hurriedly he reached into his memory for the spell to lock Vana powerless in her aged body. The figure stirred, and Peter, startled by her swift recovery, caught up and flung the first words that drifted to his grasp. "*E leocht urora maglod rwit!*"

He stood a moment in horror, suddenly realizing what he had said, waiting for the reaching flames of the warped spell to touch him, but no fire answered the summons. A faint shimmer of blue light crawled over the surface of the crystal floor, leaving broken, age-crumbled rock in its place.

The aged crone cackled softly at his horrified expression. From the depths of her sleeve a bony finger emerged to point directly at him, accompanied by mumbled words that grated harshly on his ears.

While she chanted, the witch did not appear to see a blue shimmer suddenly cease its aimless drifting and begin to flow swiftly towards her. The air about her crackled with growing magic and blue flames slowly began to rise from the floor, encircling the witch while it fed upon the magic, neutralizing it.

All of the blue light was about the witch by the time she finished her spell. Surprise and puzzlement flashed in the violet eyes as Vana saw that her spell had not worked, and Peter wondered at her confusion. Hadn't she heard what he had said?

Frowning uneasily, Vana noticed the flames playing gently about her. Moving her hands as if to brush the light away, she uttered one sharp word.

With a roar of sound, the blue flames flared upwards, engulfing the witch. The tall column of burning light screamed.

Peter closed his eyes in horror, clapped his hands over his ears to shut out the dreadful sound. He tried to concentrate, to will the flames out of existence, but still the screams echoed through the hall.

There is no fire, he thought firmly. *No blue light.* He held the thought, put the full force of his mind behind it. The screams died away.

He opened his eyes to darkness. The flame was gone and he could see nothing in the blackness, could hear nothing but his own breathing.

"Jeanne?" He suddenly realized that he could not sense the girl's presence at all. "Jeanne!" he yelled, moving cautiously in the direction he had last remembered seeing her.

Rock groaned in the darkness, and he stumbled and fell several times before he realized that the floor was moving beneath him. The castle seemed to be shaking itself apart. "Jeanne! Answer me! We've got to get out of here! Jeanne, where are you?"

The floor shook again and he heard the sound of shattering crystal, felt small pieces from the ceiling pelt him. "Jeanne!"

A light sprang into existence behind him, and Peter turned to see Graylod struggling to his feet, the top of his staff glowing with a pearly light. "Hurry," the wizard ordered, limping after him, "we haven't much time."

In the light, Peter could see a pile of dust in a fire-blackened circle on the floor. Beyond that was the motionless body of the girl. He ran towards her as the castle groaned again.

A huge slab of crystal fell from the ceiling to shatter the dais. Peter hurriedly bent over the girl, shielding her, and felt a few fist-sized fragments strike his back. He looked up at a faint sound and saw another slab cracking loose directly above them.

Graylod limped to his side and gripped Peter's shoulder for support. As the slab began to fall, the wizard raised his staff—and the hall vanished about them.

Grayness surrounded them. Peter shivered in the cold air, then disbelieved his surroundings. The mist and the chill retreated, and he could see trees about them, feel a faint troubling as if someone nearby watched him, hating him. "Silent Forest?" he asked the wizard, who was leaning on his staff as if only that would keep him on his feet.

Graylod nodded absently, staring expectantly into the mists. Peter began to wonder if the dead were gathering once again when suddenly a thunderous crash rumbled through the mists.

The echoes had barely died away when a warm wind suddenly rose, scattering the mists until the forest could be seen. Sunlight shone through the treetops, dappling the ground with warmth. The snow began to melt swiftly in the light, disappearing into deep rich earth. Peter looked into the once-threatening shadows and realized that he could no longer feel the troubling of the dead.

Graylod straightened as if a great weight had dropped from his shoulders and turned, his smiling eyes seemingly guessing Peter's questions. "The castle has fallen." The wizard stamped his staff on the ground then raised it high over his head and shouted, "The doom of the false for the dead has atoned, and two curses of hate are broken!"

Peter smiled at Graylod's jubilation. He was simply relieved that their quest was finally finished.

He looked down at Jeanne and felt the smile fade as fear touched his heart. "Graylod! I can't sense—She's not—Jeanne!"

CHAPTER 17

THE LAST DOOR

The wizard awkwardly knelt beside the silent girl. Across from him, Peter watched anxiously as Graylod felt for a pulse, then gently placed his hands on either side of Jeanne's face.

"Her body lives," he said, his attention still on the face between his hands, "but I cannot reach her mind. I only hope that Vana did not—"

He did not complete the sentence, but Peter could guess what the wizard left unsaid. "The ring isn't glowing," he said dully, feeling his throat tighten.

"Jeanne Tucker," the wizard intoned in a distant voice. "By your name I bid you come. Jeanne Tucker. Come!"

Peter looked away, stared sightlessly at the sunlit forest. His mind kept reaching for hers, but felt instead only emptiness. He rose to his feet and turned away, unable to watch the wizard any longer. He wished he could ignore the dull ache within himself that easily.

Finally, the wizard rose to his feet with a sigh. "I cannot reach her." He was silent a moment. "I do not understand. Even if Vana had removed her name, Jeanne still should have been able to respond to my calls."

"Can't you do anything?"

Graylod sighed and glanced back at the Gray Hills. "Even with my old memories, this matter is beyond my skills. But I know of one who helped in a similar situation. I hope my summons does not come at an inopportune moment in the battle."

Peter opened his mouth to speak, then noticed the staff shimmer in Graylod's hand, the distant look in the wizard's eyes, and decided to ask his questions later. He returned to Jeanne's side and tried once again to reach into the emptiness.

Presently he felt a tremor in the ground, as if pounding hooves were rapidly approaching. He peered around Graylod.

A familiar gray and white stallion could be seen among the trees, racing towards the wizard. His rider, clad in brown doublet and trousers, was equally familiar. Somehow, Peter was not surprised.

The stallion pulled up sharply before the wizard. "Graylod." Salanoa greeted the wizard worriedly, her long braid swinging as she slid off Elin's back. "We came as soon as I heard your call. What is—?"

The wizard moved away from Peter, and Salanoa paled. "Jeanne! No, the Green would not be so cruel as to repeat the past! To turn my own mistake back upon me!"

Graylod's eyebrows lifted. "Your mistake?" He shrugged. "I did not count it a mistake for you to save the life of a friend that long-ago day."

"Kelan did!" Salanoa retorted, fingering her pendant and glancing anxiously at Jeanne.

"Because Alitha had broken the laws of Green magic, and Kelan knew how dear the price of that misdeed would be. But not one of us—no, not even Kelan—suspected that she had not learned from her loss." He caught Salanoa's arm, turned her towards himself. "Listen to the truth, Salanoa, before you risk harming Jeanne with your self-anger."

Salanoa was silent. Her eyes met Graylod's, and Peter sensed that the two members of the Wise continued their talk in silence. His fingers searched Jeanne's wrist for her pulse, and he calmed at its steady beat.

The stallion shook himself and trotted to Peter's side. "Their thoughts go too swiftly for me to follow their conversation," he complained. He breathed gently on the girl's face. "Why did Graylod sound so worried? She lives."

Peter decided to start at the beginning and wearily explained what he remembered of their battle with Vana. "Graylod says that he...can't reach her mind," he finished haltingly, "but he also said that Vana couldn't have taken Jeanne's name from her. So I don't know what's wrong."

Elin nuzzled him. "Peter..."

"I can't sense her, Elin. No matter how hard I try. And Vana was standing so close to Jeanne. Too close. Jeanne wouldn't have been able to shut out Vana's death." He shook his head. "If Jeanne's hurt because of my doing, I—"

THE CRYSTAL THRONE

"Salanoa will know how to bring her back to us," Elin said worriedly.

"The lost name with fire," Salanoa said aloud in a dazed voice. "Who would have imagined it?"

"It's all my fault, Salanoa," Peter said miserably.

"Now don't you start that," Elin scolded.

Salanoa's green eyes looked quizzically at Peter. "Oh?"

"Graylod must have told you that I forgot the name spell."

He was surprised to see Salanoa suddenly smile at him. "Peter," she chided gently. "Don't you remember? The Glen said that the lost name must be spoken with fire. Graylod knew the same name spell that I taught you, and he used it when he was captured."

"Without the slightest effect on Vana," the gray wizard inserted.

"So you see, Peter, the spell you did use was the only one that could have stopped Vana. You saved Jeanne from a worse fate."

Peter frowned but the brown wizard did not wait for the rest of his arguments. Kneeling beside the girl, Salanoa placed one hand on Jeanne's forehead, grasping her pendant with the other. She waited a moment, marshaling her strength, and then the taut lines of her face relaxed, her breathing deepened and slowed.

The wizard remained in that position for several long moments while those about her watched and waited in silence, so as not to disturb her trance.

Salanoa stirred silently, and her eyes regained their focus. She glanced down at the unchanged face of the girl and took a deep, shuddering breath. "I thought I felt..." She closed her eyes briefly, wearily, then looked at Peter and the Windkin behind him.

"Peter, Elin, you two are closer to her than I. Help me, before she slips beyond our recall."

Salanoa fell back into her trance, and Peter tightened his grip on the girl's limp hand, concentrating on reaching the familiar pulse of her emotions. In his mind Salanoa seemed to be weaving the emotions of all three searchers—boy, stallion, and woman—into one sending of their friendship and love for the one they sought, lowering a lifeline into the cold empty depths of the void. Again and again they called, reaching for the lost mind to guide her back.

Suddenly Peter realized that the mindlink was gone and that only he still called. He returned to himself, saw the despair in Elin's eyes, the wondering hope in Salanoa's. He glanced at the ring, thought he saw a glint on it that was not from sunlight, then decided that he was only deceiving himself.

It was no use. She was gone, and it was all his fault. *His* fault, no matter what Salanoa might say. He would never forgive himself for—

"Not your fault!"

Hardly daring to believe his ears, Peter looked down in amazement and narrowly missed a swinging fist. Jeanne was struggling in his and Salanoa's grasp, her eyes as wide and unfocused as if she was trapped in a nightmare.

"Not your fault!" she yelled. "Vana's trying to trap you, Peter! Don't believe her! It's not your fault!"

"Jeanne!" Peter caught her arms, forced her to look at him.

Slowly the wild light in her eyes died. "Peter! I thought..."

Abruptly she flung her arms around his neck. "Oh, Peter, you did it! You beat Vana!"

"I did it, all right. I almost got you killed, too." Peter tried to loosen her stranglehold on his neck, then peered through the dark cloud of her hair. "Hey, are you crying?"

"I couldn't escape her," Jeanne mumbled into his shoulder. "No place I could run to in my mind without her right behind. She broke all my mind snares with a thought. I withdrew into the emptiness, the way Salanoa showed me, and still she followed me. I went so far that I couldn't see the way back, and still she came. And then I felt her d-die."

She shivered uncontrollably, and Peter suddenly shared her terrible, frightening feelings of utter hopelessness, of being trapped with no escape and a dreadful, relentless force closing in. He felt, too, a brief moment of Vana's death, and hurriedly retreated, remembering all too well his own encounter with the burning blue flames.

"You're back," he said gruffly. "You're all right now."

Elin nuzzled her, adding his own form of comfort to Peter's, and Jeanne slowly calmed. She released Peter and looked up at the two above them. "Elin," she said, stroking the soft nose. "Salanoa. Peter." She named them, then took a deep breath and released it. "Thank you. I don't know what I would have done—how I can ever—"

She shook her head and started again. "Just when I began to give up hope of ever finding my way back, I heard your voices calling." She glanced at them again, and her eyes grew puzzled. "But I thought I heard someone else calling with you. A strange voice, but one that I remember from somewhere."

She climbed to her feet and leaned against Elin for support as she looked about slowly. "Is this Silent Forest?"

"It was." Graylod smiled. "Now we shall have to find a new name for it."

"Graylod. I'm sorry that I had to hit you."

"I'm glad that you were able to stop me. I did not wish to harm you."

"Sit down and rest a minute before you keel over again," Peter scolded. "You must be tired, the ring isn't glowing."

Jeanne glanced down at the gold band and he caught an instant of sadness and a sudden surprise. "It was you?" she whispered. "All along?" She looked up at Peter. "I know," she said softly. "But it won't ever work for me again."

A sudden silence followed her words. Salanoa sighed gently. "Oh, Jeanne, I'm so sorry."

Jeanne bit her lip and nodded. She slowly removed the ring from her finger and stared at it, blinking back tears.

"Sorry about what?" Peter asked, uneasy at their reactions. "Why won't it work, Jeanne? Did Vana do something to it?"

"She did, but that spell broke when she died. It's the ring's doing, Peter, its decision. It's chosen someone else."

"Wh-what? Why, Jeanne? How could it..."

"I don't know. I don't even know why it chose me in the first place." She closed her hand about the ring, then opened her fist to stare at it again. "I...kinda expected that something like this would happen. After all, the curse is broken and now we'll be going home. The ring has to stay here, with all the other magic. But I wish, somehow, that I..." She brushed at her eyes. "But I can't."

"Do you know where its choice is, Jeanne?" Graylod asked gently. "Will the ring allow you to present it?"

She nodded. "It will. It's chosen you, Elin."

"M-me?" The Fleet One stared blankly at the glittering ring in the girl's out-stretched hand. "No, Jeanne. Not me. The Ring of Calada has never chosen a nonhuman before. Never. Not even an elf."

"Well, it's about time it did." She glanced at the stallion and a rueful grin crossed her face as she looked down at the ring. "There must be some way you can wear this."

"There is." Salanoa yanked the cord from her long braid. "Use this until we can find something more suitable."

Jeanne threaded the ring on the brown cord and tied it about the silky neck. The ring fell against the gray and white hide and instantly the rainbow glow reappeared.

Jeanne studied her handiwork, reached out to lift his mane out from under the cord. "There. The cord's not too tight, is it, Elin?"

Elin nudged her worriedly. "Jeanne, I..."

"Hey, don't apologize!" Torn between laughter and tears, Jeanne hugged the stallion, burying her face in his long mane for a few moments. When she finally released him and stood back, the tears were gone and Elin could see her pride in his good fortune shining in her eyes. "You'll be the best wizard ever, Elin. I just know it!"

* * *

When they left the Glen on the final leg of their journey westward, the elves at the Watch Tower had warned them that a few witch hounds had escaped the Battle of the Gray Hills and now prowled the Great Woods in wolf-shape. But the possibility of attack did not perturb the six walking under the moonlight-dappled leaves. An elf led the company, his blond hair shining white under the stars. From time to time, the words of a song, barely discernible over the cricking of insects and the stirring of leaves in the breeze, drifted back to his companions.

Behind the elf paced a gray and white stallion, his eyes studying the forest about them as if seeing it for the first time. Occasionally he dropped his head to lightly touch a glittering ring on a fine gold chain about his neck.

"Just look at him!" Hahle muttered to Peter. "I hate to think of what our people will say. A wizard! It was bad enough when he was studying to be a Lore-Master, but magic? It's indecent!"

"It is not," Peter disagreed. He adjusted the pack containing his Earth clothes more comfortably on his back and gave up his attempts to catch a few words of Leereho's song. "I don't see what you're so upset about. The Windrunner seemed quite pleased with him."

"The Windrunner is used to magic, even if he is the only member of the Wise without it. It's the common herd's reaction that's bothering me. They'll either cast him out entirely or make a laughingstock out of him. A wizard without hands!" He shook his mane worriedly. "I dread returning to Windgard."

"So who cares what other people think? He's your friend, that's all that matters, right?" He peered askance at the stallion. "What's gotten into you lately, Hahle? Magic has saved you quite a few times."

Hahle's ears flicked back in embarrassment. "Never mind that," he said angrily. "I'm just worried about Elin."

Peter shrugged, thinking that Hahle had a strange way of showing his concern. He had wondered why the two Windkin hadn't spoken to each other since Hahle rejoined them in the Gray Hills, but it seemed as if now was not the time to ask. He tried to think of a safer subject. "Will they be able to change Windgard back the way it was?"

"In a few years, we hope. But I don't know what will be done with all that sand. The Wise think that they'll be able to recover most of Windgard, and maybe even the Wasted Land as well. The elves have volunteered to provide trees and help with the forests—they can make plants grow quickly when there's need."

"I know," Peter agreed, remembering the Glen's swift recovery.

Hahle sighed unhappily. "But we'll have to leave Windgard until the Wise have finished with it. Sounds like we won't even be able to stay by the oases. Graylod mentioned something about a flood before he and the Windrunner dashed off for the Council, but I wasn't able to corner him again before we left."

The black mane rippled as he shook his head. "It wouldn't be the first time that the People of the Wind are homeless wanderers. Won't be the last time, either." He snorted. "Perhaps we can even try living in the Gray Hills, now that the goblins and trolls have been chased back to the Shadow Land."

Feeling an instant's brush of a bittersweet sorrow, Peter looked back to where Jeanne and Salanoa walked and caught the girl's eye. She smiled apologetically at him, but Peter felt her block snap into place. Somehow, that did not reassure him. The nagging feeling that she was planning something surfaced once again, as it had so often during their journey back across the Free Lands, but he knew that his suspicions were justified. Jeanne had been withdrawn and silent at odd moments, and several times, he had caught her looking at the land about them with a strange longing in her eyes.

He watched her for a few more seconds, Hahle's problem temporarily forgotten. *She wants to stay here*, he told himself. *I can feel it.* He looked at the darkened trees and felt a similar longing stir within him. *I can't blame her. Earth is going to be quite boring after this.* With an effort, he shook off his bleak mood and wondered again what Jeanne was planning. Since the ring had left her, he knew that she would return with him. But there was always another question she could ask.

Jeanne was already asking it. "Salanoa, can I ever come back?"

The wizard looked at her sadly. "After all the sorrow this land has caused you, do you really wish to return to it?"

"Yes...and no." She looked down at the ground, unconsciously rubbing her ring finger. "I love Earth—my family is there and my friends and everything I always thought important. But," she looked up to meet the knowing eyes, "I feel as if I belong here."

"Magic is no game, Jeanne."

"Don't you think I know that?"

This time it was Salanoa who looked away. "I am sorry for that, Jeanne. If the matter had not been so desperate, we never would have used you and Peter in such a way. But we were desperate and you two were our only hope."

"I know that, Salanoa. I didn't mean to sound as if I was blaming you or anyone else. I just wanted you to realize that I do know something of both the good and the bad in magic. Remember, I was almost a part of Vana for a while. I guess I did think of magic as a game before that happened. I don't now."

Jeanne scowled and adjusted her pack, searching for the right words. "It isn't as if I can't go back to using only a tiny part of my powers—that's not the reason I want to stay, Salanoa. I think I can go back to the way I was before, although I know I'll feel crippled for the rest of my life."

Salanoa nodded sadly. "'You know the words of the spell, but the power no longer answers.' Alitha described it that way to me once, before she turned to evil." She sighed. "This land has traps even for the wary, Jeanne. Magic is a dangerous path to follow; and, if you return, you would find yourself in that danger again."

"Earth isn't all that safe, either. And you yourself taught me that I can't deny what I am. It's funny, but, ever since I got here, I've been trying to go home. And now that I've finally got my wish, I don't want to leave here. *This* is home, now."

"But your family, young one. What about them? Could you leave them? And Peter. He might not wish to leave Earth. Could you leave then, knowing that he would stay behind?"

Jeanne bit her lip and glanced ahead to where Peter talked with Hahle. "I...don't know, Salanoa."

"You are young yet, which is all the more reason for you to wait before deciding one way or another. Wait a few years, sample what your world has to offer before you cut yourself off from it. The Last Door is not for idle use. Only in times of crisis will it swing freely between worlds. At all other times, those who come willingly into this land must stay here forever. If you came back, there would be no return for you."

Jeanne turned, hearing a familiar laughter on the wind. Distant dots of light danced in the shadows far behind them, and she could almost imagine the fairies at their play. Her eyes still on the bobbing lights, she said, "You still haven't answered my question, Salanoa. *Can* I come back? You see, I've read fantasy, and I know that it's not too easy to find the Land of Faerie once you leave it."

Salanoa laughed. "My suspicious little sister. You have learned well from Peter to see what would remain hidden. Truthfully, then, the Watcher decides who enters its Door. But do not despair. I believe that, if you truly wish to re-enter the Free Lands, you will be able to convince it to let you pass."

Jeanne studied the wizard, realizing that she held something back. "Elin once said that the Wise delight to speak in riddles. You're no exception, Salanoa."

"Ah, but a good magician never reveals all. You will decipher this riddle, in time." She glanced ahead. "I see Leereho has found a place to stop for the night. Go join the others, Jeanne. I must find a quiet spot to mindspeak Jonhree."

Jeanne obeyed, feeling slightly awed at a mind that could reach across the distance separating them from the Glen. She looked uneasily at those gathering about the small fire Leereho had lit and decided that she didn't want to talk to anyone just yet, especially Elin and Peter. They were too liable to guess her plans for the future and she was reluctant to spoil her last night by arguing with them. Perhaps she should take a short walk to settle her thoughts.

She put her pack down and slipped into the shadows, smiling as she sensed a familiar mind drawing near. With luck, no one would notice her absence until she had returned.

Peter stood at the edge of the firelight and looked through the thinning stands of trees to the wide plains beyond. Elin had left the group to graze on the long grass, and his white patches shone under the moon. Behind the boy, Leereho hummed an odd tune as he heated *serwasn* over the tiny fire. The quick step of hooves suddenly sounded nearby.

"There you are!" Renw trotted into the light. "Do you realize that I had to ask two fairies and a unicorn before I could find you? Who are you hiding from, Leereho?"

"You saw a unicorn? There's a unicorn around?" Peter turned and looked through the trees again, trying to catch a glimpse of the creature.

Renw shook his mane. "No. They're rather shy beings. The small creatures carried the news of this herd to him."

The roan chuckled suddenly. "Ho, Hahle! No wonder you wouldn't tell me how you got your battle wound! You should know better than to try sneaking up on a dwarf. Good thing it was only your tail, dwarfs usually don't miss that badly."

Peter leaned back against a tree and gave his complete attention to the stallions. Hahle hadn't told him the story, either.

"Good?" Hahle stared sadly back at his ragged tail, one side now four inches shorter than the other. "I doubt you'd be so pleased if it had happened to *your* tail. And I didn't sneak up on him. He just popped up out of the mists with his axe swinging."

"Uh huh. That wasn't what I heard. Did you actually yell a bloodwind call and charge that poor sentry?"

Hahle hung his head. "He *did* look like a troll in the mists. How were we to know that the Folk had moved into the Gray Hills?" Renw laughed, and the black stallion glared crossly at him. "Who told you?"

"Not Elin. I couldn't get two words out of him the entire time that we were in Windgard. One of the fairies told me."

"Oh no," Hahle groaned. "That story will be all over Windgard by the time I get back."

"So? Everyone will say that it sounds like something you'd do." He dropped his voice and nodded towards Elin, out on the plains. "And, seeing as how he saved you from worse hurt with that spell of his, I don't think that it will be that horrible a tale. Might do him some good, if you know what I mean."

Peter followed Renw's glance. A dark-haired girl had joined the gray and white stallion, standing by his shoulder while he grazed. Peter wondered what the two were discussing.

"I don't know, Renw," Hahle said worriedly. "You know how some of the herd feel about magic."

"Hahle, if you're any indication of how 'some of the herd' feel about magic," Peter said in disgust, "Elin shouldn't return to Windgard."

"Why, I—"

Renw swung his head to eye both Peter and Hahle. "What do you mean, Peter?"

Peter turned and directed his comments to the flustered black stallion. "For one, Hahle, you haven't spoken to Elin once since you came back."

"Yes, I have!"

"All right. So you said 'Good morning' occasionally. The rest of the time you act as if he isn't there. He's still Elin, still the same Fleet One who was once your friend. Why are you hurting him like that?"

"He can do magic!"

"Big deal. Practically everyone in this land has some type of magic, from the trees to you Fleet Ones."

Renw started a step. "Us?"

"No creature can run as fast as you Fleet Ones. None. It's absolutely impossible, and yet you do it. That's magic."

Hahle looked as if his world was turning upside down. Peter could sympathize with him. He had felt much the same once. But the same instinct that had once prompted him to befriend Jeanne had awakened. He was not going to stand back and let Elin be hurt as Jeanne had been.

Leereho caught the boy's eye, slid the pot of *serwasn* away from the fire, and slipped into the shadows, taking an oddly silent Renw with him. The roan's voice trailed wistfully out of the night. "Can we truly do magic, Leereho?"

Hahle started at the faint question. "Magic ruined our land," he said as unemotionally as if reciting an ancient truth. "It has brought us nothing but suffering."

"Nothing, huh?" Peter snorted. "And what do you call it when it helps you? The Wise are going to use magic to recover Windgard, but you have nothing against that, do you?"

Hahle shook his head bewilderedly. "It's not the same."

"Not the same? Magic is magic. It can be used for good or evil, but it's still magic. Why are you only punishing Elin? Le uses magic, do you hate him? How about Jeanne? You even helped with her training in magic. Do you hate me for using magic to break the curse?"

"You're a human!"

"So what? What does being a human have to do with magic? The humans here didn't like magic, either, and look where it got them."

The stallion lapsed into a stubborn silence, and Peter decided to try another tack. He shook his head tiredly. "You know what I think, Hahle? I think you're jealous."

"Jealous! Why, I—"

"Yes, jealous. It was all right when Elin just told stories, that didn't threaten you. But when he started to use what he had learned, when he started casting spells—"

THE CRYSTAL THRONE

"No! You don't—You have hands. The People of the Wind don't. That's why you humans imprisoned us, long ago, because you had hands and we do not. Well, we don't need hands, and we don't need anything that hands can do. We don't need magic."

Peter stared wordlessly at the black stallion, suddenly realizing the reason behind the stubborn pride and undercurrent of bitterness in his voice. He remembered Elin's protest, back in Silent Forest, when Jeanne had accused him of denying his destiny, and the last pieces of the puzzle fell into place. No wonder Hahle had sounded as if a wizard without hands was the ultimate paradox!

"Hahle, I—"

The stallion turned to leave. "Keep your pity to yourself!" he snapped.

"Hahle, you absurd Windlord!" Hahle turned and glared angrily at him. "Pity you?" Peter shook his head, choosing his words carefully. "Vana was certainly a powerful witch if she could make Fleet Ones believe her lies even now. Hahle, anybody pitying a Fleet One is either jealous or stupid. That is as senseless as pitying a unicorn!"

Hahle blinked. "Unicorns can do magic."

"Right, and they don't have hands. You don't need hands, either, Hahle! But if you think it takes magic, instead of bravery and wisdom—which you Fleet Ones definitely have—to win people's respect, well, you now have Elin, the wizard without hands."

"I...never thought of it that way." He nuzzled Peter. "Thank you. I have to—I must talk with Elin." The stallion whirled and vanished into the night.

"Well said, Peter."

Peter turned and saw Salanoa watching him, her green eyes oddly intent. He sighed and set the pot of *serwasn* back on the fire. "I'm glad you think so. Halfway through that speech, I was sure that I was losing him."

The brown-haired wizard smiled. "Do you still doubt yourself, Peter? I tell you truly, Hahle would not have believed those same words had they come from anyone but you. You have the seeing eye, and the curiosity of a wizard."

"Thanks, I think."

She glanced out at the plains, where three Windkin, an elf, and a human girl seemed to be playing a wild game of tag. "I wonder if we shall ever know the full extent of the harm Vana caused us."

"Salanoa, is Jeanne coming back to the Free Lands?"

The green eyes smiled kindly at him. "I cannot see the future, Peter. But I extend the same invitation to you as to her. If, when you are older, you truly wish to leave your land forever, you shall find that the Door will open for you."

Peter remained silent, not knowing how to answer her. Salanoa smiled again, fingering her pendant, then she turned to view the five playing under the star-filled sky. "We shall have a long walk tomorrow," she mused, "but by dusk you two will be home."

* * *

In the morning, Peter and Jeanne donned their Earth clothing, packing away the garments the elves had given them. Jeanne scowled suddenly and stuffed her jacket back in the pack. "I'm going to wear my cloak," she said, turning a rebellious look on Peter.

Peter shrugged. "Did I say anything?" He looked down at his blue jeans. "I feel lopsided without that sword."

The company walked across the grassland at a steady pace, finally coming within sight of the solitary tree by mid-afternoon. Salanoa stood silently atop a small hill, her fingers smoothing the brown stone of her pendant as she studied their back trail. Jeanne could feel the wizard's mind reaching out, seeking an awaited contact.

"Look!" Renw shouted. "Someone's coming up behind us!"

The rest turned and saw a small cloud of dust moving swiftly across the plain towards them. Leereho reached for the bow on his back, then his arm fell. "It's the Windrunner!" he exclaimed. "And he brings the Elder!"

"Show-off," Renw grunted. "Him and his elfin eyesight."

"Go on ahead," Salanoa said absently, her thoughts already with the Elder. "I will wait here for them."

"Race! Race!" The three stallions tore across the long grass, manes streaming and tails flying in the wind.

"I wonder what brings them here," Peter said as the remaining three walked on. "Hope they haven't changed their minds about letting us go home."

"Don't be silly. I'm glad they came." Jeanne glanced ahead. The three Windkin had circled about the large tree and were heading back at a breakneck speed. "I didn't get a chance to even say goodbye before we left."

The elf was silent beside them, but Jeanne could sense what his silence hid. "I'll miss you, Le," she said softly.

"And I the two of you. I wish our lands had not separated."

The three stallions thundered past them with a rush of wind, joyous whinnies trailing behind.

Peter stopped and looked back. The night-black stallion pulled up sharply before the brown-garbed wizard, the Elder sliding off the broad back to greet her. The three wildly racing stallions wheeled about the three Wise, flattening the grasses in their passage. Only two Windkin raced away; Elin dropped back to walk with the Windrunner, leaving the wizard and the elf to continue on at their own pace.

Jeanne sighed. "I dread having to go back and face Amy Evans."

"What, after standing up to Vana?" Peter laughed. "Coward. I'll be there to protect you."

"I don't need protection!"

"Hah!"

* * *

The gnarled tree brooded silently before them. Branches swayed on the light breeze, and the rustling of the leaves resembled murmuring voices. Recalling his last encounter with the Watcher, Peter literally had to force himself to stand with the others, within reach of the long branches. Jeanne had changed her cloak for her red wool jacket and stood beside Peter, facing the three Wise.

"We could not reward you as you deserved and as we wished," the Elder said slowly, "not only because you did not wish a reward but also because the Watcher forbids the passage of objects from world to world. Over one element only has the Last Door no command, and that is the substance of the Doors, even of those Doors closed and sealed long ago. The First Door stood within the Glen of Ancient Voices, and by the Voices' will these were fashioned for you."

Salanoa presented her gift to Jeanne first, and Jeanne stared in astonishment. "A ring," she said slowly. "A silver ring!"

"Peter."

Peter looked away from the ring glittering on Jeanne's finger and bemusedly took the object that the Elder held out to him. It was a wide circular band of a strange, silvery shining substance. "It looks like metal, but it feels a little like wood," he said slowly, running his fingers over the band, which to his eyes resembled a large bracelet.

"It's a wristguard, Peter," Leereho remarked with pleasure. "A bowguard. Or swordguard, depending upon which wrist you wear it."

"Swordguard! It isn't...magic, is it?" Peter asked hesitantly, looking up at the Elder. Hahle snorted amusedly behind him.

The Elder laughed. "No. These but serve as keys to the Door from your land. The Glen itself formed these for you, to permit your return to this land, should you wish it."

"Should I wish it!" Jeanne flung herself at the surprised Elder and from him to Salanoa. "You and your riddles, Salanoa! When I think of—"

She sobered suddenly, her eyes on her clothes. "But I haven't been thinking. Of all the stupid, thoughtless—" She looked up at Salanoa, her eyes stricken. "Salanoa, we've been gone from home for so long! Our parents—"

"Will never suspect anything amiss," the wizard finished kindly. "The Last Door is a time portal as well. You shall return but an instant after you left."

Branches swayed over their heads, and the murmur of the leaves increased. The Elder seemed to listen—either to the leaves or some unheard voice, Peter wasn't sure—and then he nodded. "The time to depart is now. The portal will remain open but a few moments."

Peter and Jeanne hurriedly took leave of their friends, their farewells nonetheless heartfelt for their haste.

The Elder waited for them. "Peter, since you were the last through you must be the first to enter. Then you, Jeanne. Go now, and may the Green go with you."

* * *

The first thing Jeanne noticed when she stepped through was the sheer volume of sound pounding against her ears. Wild screams, both human and equine, echoed through the once quiet woods.

Then the frightened horse rearing a few feet before her caught her attention. The mare's sharp squeals of fear sliced through the terrified human screams ringing somewhere off to the right. Jeanne had only a moment in which to spot Jody, still screaming, backing wide-eyed towards the trail when she sensed that the Appaloosa had bolted.

"Robin!" Without stopping to think, Jeanne sent her mind out after the mare, willing the skittish creature to calm. The mare stopped.

"Peter! I... I did it! I stopped Robin!"

"Right. Now could you do something about Jody?" Peter edged closer to his twin, who stared at him as if he had turned into a monster before her very eyes. "Jody! Quit screaming, willya?"

A thought slipped smoothly into Jeanne's mind. Deftly it touched certain connections within her being and then left, taking with it...

"My memory!" Peter held his hands to his head, then lowered them, staring at the silvery guard about his wrist as if in reassurance. "No.

No, I haven't forgotten anything." He glanced at Jeanne. "Did you just have the impression that—"

Jeanne nodded numbly, not daring either to put what she had felt into words. Her senses tensed. "It wasn't aimed at us. Look at Jody. Catch her, Peter!"

Jody clutched wildly at the bush beside her and pulled herself back to her feet. "Peter! You...she...no, it couldn't have been!"

Peter glanced back at Jeanne and winced as she relayed the bewilderment in his twin's mind. How much did Jody remember? A scowl deepened his features as he realized what *he* remembered. "You've got some explaining to do," he growled.

From the expression on Jody's face, she had also remembered what he was referring to. She backed away, dropping her betraying jacket. "Now, Peter," she said hastily, "it was only a joke. Jean wasn't hurt—see for yourself!—and I didn't mean—"

"If I ever catch you I'll show you just how funny I think your little joke was!"

Jody screamed and ran down the trail as if a ghost pursued her.

"She's heading the wrong way."

"Good," Peter grunted. "I hope she gets good and lost. She'll wish she had, once Dad hears of this."

"It was only a prank."

"Only!" He glared at her, but Jeanne, stroking the quieting mare, met his angry gaze calmly. "That little prank could have gotten you killed if the Watcher hadn't interfered. By the way, what do you suppose that tree was up to, taking Jody's memory the way it did?"

Jeanne shrugged. "Could have been protecting either us or itself. Probably both. It would be in its own interest not to have many people know what it is."

"So why the haunted tree routine? Oh, windspin! We've got to write an essay on that foolishness, too!"

The tree creaked softly and Peter froze. "What's it up to? Can you tell?"

Jeanne smiled. "Feels like it's falling asleep. Odd, but it feels different on this side than it did on the other. Its mind doesn't seem to be in just this tree. I get the impression of hundreds—all at great distances apart, too."

"Graylod did say that the Watcher searches all human lands."

"That must be how." She glanced up through the treetops. "It's getting late, and I've got to get Robin home." She bowed slightly to the tree. "Thank you, Watcher. I won't say goodbye—you'll see me again."

"But not without me. Promise, Jeanne?"

"Only if you promise not to stop me."

"By the Blessed Winds."

She studied him. "You've been hanging around the Fleet Ones too long." She led Robin back to the main trail. "It's going to take me forever to get re-accustomed to Earth horses now. Hey, I've got an idea for the essay. Do you want the Old Ones of the Great Woods or the trees of Darkling Valley?"

"Definitely Silent Forest. Miss Long wouldn't believe it if I suddenly said that trees move."

Their laughter drifted through the forest, back to a gnarled old tree with claw-like branches. It creaked again, settling down contentedly for another long nap.

KATHRYN SULLIVAN

Kathryn Sullivan has been writing science fiction and fantasy since she was 14 years old. The world set up in *The Crystal Throne* has been developing since then, although some of the short stories have escaped into fan zines, print zines and ezines. *The Crystal Throne* won the EPPIE Award in 2002 for Best Fantasy Book!

Kathryn's stories have appeared in *Professor Bernice Summerfield and the Dead Men Diaries*, *Twilight Times*, *Anotherealm*, *Shadow Keep Zine*, *Fury*, and *Minnesota Fantasy Review*.

Kathryn is Distance Learning Librarian at Winona State University in Winona, MN, and coordinator of the library's webpages. She's owned by two confused birds—one small jenday convinced that he's a large guard dog and one large cockatoo convinced that she's a small bird.

The list of her stories is at...
http://kathrynsullivan.com

AMBER QUILL PRESS, LLC
THE GOLD STANDARD IN PUBLISHING

QUALITY BOOKS
IN BOTH PRINT AND ELECTRONIC FORMATS

ACTION/ADVENTURE	SUSPENSE/THRILLER
SCIENCE FICTION	ROMANCE
MAINSTREAM	MYSTERY
PARANORMAL	FANTASY
HISTORICAL	HORROR
YOUNG ADULT	WESTERN

AMBER QUILL PRESS, LLC
http://www.amberquill.com